Cast Iron
Alibi

Books by Victoria Hamilton

A Gentlewoman's Guide to Murder

Vintage Kitchen Mysteries

A Deadly Grind
Bowled Over
Freezer I'll Shoot
No Mallets Intended
White Colander Crime
Leave It to Cleaver
No Grater Danger
Breaking the Mould
Cast Iron Alibi

Merry Muffin Mysteries

Bran New Death
Muffin But Murder
Death of an English Muffin
Much Ado About Muffin
Muffin to Fear
Muffin But Trouble

Lady Anne Addison Mysteries

Lady Anne and the Howl in the Dark
Revenge of the Barbary Ghost
Curse of the Gypsy

Cast Iron Alibi

Victoria Hamilton

BEYOND THE PAGE
PUBLISHING

Beyond the Page Books
are published by
Beyond the Page Publishing
www.beyondthepagepub.com

Copyright © 2019 by Donna Lea Simpson.
Cover design and illustration by Dar Albert, Wicked Smart Designs.

ISBN: 978-1-950461-26-4

In Sue Grafton's memory, I'd like to dedicate this book to Kinsey Millhone, who knows that peanut butter goes with everything.

Cast of Characters

in the Vintage Kitchen Mystery Series:

Jaymie Leighton Müller: wife, stepmom, and collector of all things vintage kitchen-y!

Jakob Müller: her husband, dad to Jocie, Christmas tree farmer and junk store owner.

Jocie Müller: *little* little person (as she says!) and happy daughter to Jakob and Jaymie.

Becca Brevard: Jaymie's bossy older sister and co-owner of Queensville Fine Antiques.

Georgina Brevard: Becca's sister-in-law and manager of Queensville Fine Antiques.

Valetta Nibley: pharmacist and lifelong friend to Jaymie and Becca.

Brock Nibley: Valetta's older brother and Queensville's best real estate agent.

Heidi Lockland: Jaymie's friend.

Bernie Jenkins: Heidi's best friend, Jaymie's good friend, and local police officer for the Queensville Township Police Department.

Mrs. Martha Stubbs: Jaymie's elderly friend and confidante.

Johnny Stanko: Queensvillian and Jaymie's friend.

Detective Angela Vestry: Queensville Police Department's first female detective.

Officer Ng: Queensville police constable living on Heartbreak Island.

Hoppy: Jaymie's Yorkie-Poo.

Chief Horace Ledbetter: former Queensville police chief and friend of Jaymie's.

Mamie Ledbetter: Chief Ledbetter's wife.

Sammy Dobrinskie: Heartbreak Island resident, landscape student, and friend of Jaymie's.

Ruby and Garnet Redmond: Heartbreak Islanders and co-owners of the Ice House restaurant and the cottage on the road behind the Leighton cottage.

Tansy and Sherm Woodrow: co-owners of Tansy's Tarts, the Heartbreak Island tart shop.

Cast of Characters

in *Cast Iron Alibi:*

Mario Horvat: local handyman.
Kory Jamison: Mario's assistant, boarder, and friend.
Hallie Granger: Mario's live-in pregnant teen girlfriend.
Ellen Granger: Hallie's mom.
Melody Heath: Jaymie's romance author college friend.
Andrew Conners: Melody's husband.
Rachel Kimball: Jaymie's study-buddy college friend.
Brandi Xylander: Jaymie's party-girl college friend.
Terry Xylander: Brandi's ex-husband.
Courtney: Brandi's party friend and Jaymie's unexpected houseguest.
Gabriela Offerman: Jaymie's serious college friend.
Logan Offerman: Gabriela's husband.
Fenix Offerman: Gabriela's daughter.
Tiffany Offerman: Logan's sister.
Ashlee: Sammy Dobrinskie's current girlfriend.

✄ One ✄

"TO THE RIGHT . . . no, wait, that's your left . . . to the left! *Sorry!*" Jaymie sang out, waving to her husband, Jakob, as he backed the funky vintage trailer she had renovated along the lane and over the top of the hill. On the other side was a slope descending to a deep grove that was the lawn behind the Leighton family cottage, Rose Tree Cottage, on River Road.

Fortunately Jakob was adept at backing up a heavy trailer with his pickup, since he often had to deliver things from his shop, The Junk Stops Here. He smiled, waved, checked the side mirrors and continued, disappearing over the top of the hill as he descended the grassy slope toward the patio stone platform they had laid for the trailer. They had removed trees to access the ravine through the Redmonds' property on the next road back from the river a couple of years before when they put in a new leaching bed and septic system. That had left them enough room for the patio, where the trailer would sit for at least the next few weeks.

"Can I get in the truck with Daddy?" Jocie, Jaymie's step-daughter, asked, twisting and looking up at her stepmom. Jocie, though almost ten, was the height of an average four-year-old; she had achondroplasia dwarfism, a genetic condition that would keep her smaller than others her whole life. Her blonde hair was done up in pigtails, and she wore a turquoise and white shorts and T-shirt set. She was cute as a button, but inclined to get her own way.

"Not now, Jocie," Jaymie said. It was tough looking into the big brown eyes of a child she adored and saying no, but she was practicing.

"Aw! Why not?" Jocie pouted, pushing her bottom lip out.

"Daddy asked you if you wanted to ride with him and you said no, you'd stay with me," Jaymie said, steeling herself for a fight while tucking Jocie in close to her body. "You had that chance before he started, but not now while he's in the middle of it."

"Okay." Unexpectedly, Jocie gave up and stopped pouting. Maybe consistent firmness was working! Or more likely, Jocie had other options. "Can I take Hoppy for a walk?"

Jaymie smiled down at her and her little tripod Yorkie-Poo, who yipped and strained at the leash. "Okay, but don't go onto the wharf while the ferry is there and don't go along the docks, please." And that was another motherhood skill she was practicing: letting go. She had become overprotective at one point, and Jakob had to gently tell her that they needed to give Jocie all the freedom any nine-year-old deserved. The island was safe; they had to let her explore. Being small for her age didn't mean Jocie felt or thought any differently than her average-size friends. "I'm trusting you with Hoppy, sweetie, so watch over him. Keep the leash short."

Jaymie watched Jocie walk away, down the lane and to the dirt road, staying close to the row of pines that lined it. Determined to not be a helicopter parent like the ones she had read articles about, the ones who hovered and worried constantly, she turned back and eyed the family vacation home. Rose Tree Cottage was a sweet blue and white cottage on the American side of Heartbreak Island, a roughly heart-shaped island in the middle of the St. Clair River near Lake St. Clair. It had been in the Leighton family for generations, and for most of the summer it was rented out by visitors to Queensville, Michigan, or Johnsonville, Ontario, on the other side of the river.

Right now it was vacant, but in two days Jaymie and her friends from college days would hold a reunion of sorts, a revival of their former habit of camping together for a week each summer. That had started while they were all students at the University of Western Ontario in London, Ontario, and shared a rental house, and had continued in the years since they graduated. They had not managed it for the last three summers, though, for various reasons: jobs, baby births, illness, weddings, travel plans.

It had almost not happened again! Brandi, the friend who made the arrangements, had called two weeks ago and said that the campground had canceled their reservation because of plumbing problems that forced them to close. What could they do? Brandi asked. When Jaymie suggested finding another campsite, Brandi said she had already called all of them and there was nowhere that could accommodate them.

Jaymie strode over the hill and down the slope. She stood out of the way in the shade of a pine, wiping sweat from her brow as she watched her husband adroitly back up the trailer. This was a day she had looked forward to for a long time, but it was hard to muster the energy for enthusiasm. August in Michigan could be brutally hot and they were in the middle of a sweltering heat wave, moisture shimmering in the air even as the grass yellowed and bushes became dusty and desiccated. They needed rain.

Now would come the tricky part, Jaymie thought; Jakob lined the trailer up with the patio stone platform at the bottom of the ravine, where it was overlooked both by the Leightons' cottage and the Redmonds' cottage on the hill on the other side. At least Jakob had help. Sammy Dobrinskie, their landscaper, now finished with his second year at college, had done the prep work on the trailer pad and (having lots of experience himself with backing up boat trailers into water and work trailers into tight spots) was guiding Jakob. They maneuvered back and forth, working together to get the position perfect.

The trailer had been Jaymie's spring and summer project. It was an adorable vintage Shasta trailer, in a pretty retro turquoise, white and silver, with the absolute coolest silver wings at the top, like a trailer version of Mercury's winged hat! The interior had been in rough shape, but Jaymie had fixed and cleaned and rebuilt. Jakob taught her how to use a circular saw and a jigsaw, and she had replaced the subfloor herself, then installed funky black and white tiles from a box of peel-and-stick tiles left over from someone's kitchen project and dropped off at The Junk Stops Here. She had painted the interior then decorated, furnishing it with vintage linens and kitchen stuff: melamine dishes, a funky chrome sixties perco-lator, and a chrome breadbox, among other items. She was proud of the result. Only the small fridge and stove were new.

Sammy, now taller, more muscular and more confident than he had been two summers ago, beckoned with one hand as Jakob backed the trailer onto the pad and stopped, finally in the perfect spot. Her husband got out of the truck and with their young friend began the complicated procedure of unhooking the directional and brake lights and the tow hitch.

Jaymie's mind returned to her university reunion and how they had solved their dilemma. As they chatted about the campsite cancellation Brandi had asked, by any chance was Jaymie's family cottage available? Fortunately, it was; they had had a cancellation at the last minute, something she had already shared on their booking app. The Leightons had planned to use the cancellation time to have some work done—there were always issues with rental properties—but that could be put off until September so the "girls" could use it for their reunion. Jaymie told Brandi she hadn't suggested it because she wasn't sure anyone else would agree.

They had *always* camped in Canada, and Jaymie, at least, had been looking forward to camping again. But staying at the family cottage was simpler for her—no travel, and no toting of camp stove, tent, tent flies, sleeping bag, pillow, cooking pots and dishes—and the others didn't mind. For the second-to-last week of August, plus or minus a few days, they were going to have a grand time. Jaymie was over the moon with excitement and had planned some activities she hoped her friends would enjoy.

But first, she thought, watching Jakob mop his red face with a hankie, she had to face the inevitable, saying goodbye to her family. Jakob and Jocie were going to Poland for ten days to visit Jocie's mother's family. Inga, Jocie's birth mom, had moved back there when Jocie was a toddler and had tragically died not long after. Inga's parents, Jocie's maternal grandparents, had not seen their granddaughter since she was a few months old. They were older and not well, nor were they prosperous, so they couldn't travel, though they had exchanged gifts and pictures over the years. There were aunts and uncles, cousins, and a great-grandparent or two. Jakob was determined that his daughter have the benefit of her whole family, so the trip to Poland had been planned for the end of August.

Jakob had asked if Jaymie wanted to go, but she felt that this first time, when Inga's parents were eager to get to know their granddaughter, it should be with Jakob alone. She was the second wife, their daughter's replacement, in a way, and she didn't want to create any awkwardness.

Jaymie strolled across the lawn and sat down at the wrought iron table in the shade while the fellows worked. Two years ago the Leighton family had taken advantage of a plumbing problem at the cottage that required a lot of digging—for the new septic system and leaching bed—to redesign the land attached to their cottage. It was now a lovely grotto, a refreshingly shady spot with a flagstone patio, retaining wall, a firepit area and lush gardens. Ferns grew in abundance, and each year they planted colorful coleus and New

Guinea impatiens to add color. Birdbaths and feeders attracted robins, blue jays, cardinals, orioles and rose-breasted grosbeaks . . . a rainbow of birds to enjoy. She was proud of the work they had done on the landscaping and the cottage, and looked forward to showing it off. She hoped her friends would enjoy it.

"Jaymie, come here," Jakob said, beckoning to her. His cheeks were flushed with the heat, but he had a smile on his bearded face. "I want you to see how to do this."

She jumped up and joined Sammy and her husband as they used the stabilizing jacks, which were new — the original ones that came with the trailer were rusted out — to support and level the trailer. He showed her how, and she did two herself, red-faced with the effort in the humidity but determined to understand every aspect of trailer maintenance. Everything else, from how to look after the composting toilet to how to change the propane tank she understood from working on the little trailer all spring and summer.

She stood back after they were done and admired her fourteen-foot trailer, proud of her handiwork. Inside was even better; she had sewn funky starburst turquoise fabric into curtains for the window, and had gotten Jakob to make starburst-patterned countertops out of vintage materials rescued from home renos. She had redone the upholstery for the dining table benches in a tropical surfing print. It was bright and kooky and adorable!

The trailer might become an additional space for cottage renters who needed room for more guests. Or maybe not; she hadn't completely decided yet. Mostly, she had bought it for a song and enjoyed fixing it up. By the time Jocie brought Hoppy back from their walk, both the little dog and little girl weary, they were done, the trailer stabilized and ready for inhabitants.

"Thank you, Sammy, for your help," she said to the young man.

He ducked his head in reply, then said, dusting his hands along his grass-stained cargo shorts, "I'd better get going. I have a job to get to!"

• • •

IT HAD BEEN A LONG DAY. Jaymie and Jakob sat snuggled together on the sofa in the great room of their log cabin with the TV on a nature show, while Hoppy snored in his basket by the fireplace.

"Are you sure you want to take Jocie and me to the airport tomorrow? It's a long drive; Dad would do it," Jakob murmured.

She relished the feel of her husband's arms around her. Jaymie had been afraid Jocie would be too keyed up to sleep, but after such a long day she and her kitten, Lilibet, had fallen asleep almost immediately. "That would be too hard on your dad. I'm not a big fan of traveling down I-94, but I'll feel better putting you two on that plane myself." She looked up into his brown eyes and smiled, teary-eyed. She stroked his beard and thumbed his lips. "I'm going to miss you both!" she whispered, not trusting her full voice.

"Are you kidding? You and your friends can have a proper girls' holiday while we're gone. I want you to *enjoy* yourself." He kissed her exuberantly. "Now, tell me again, who all is coming?"

She knew he was trying to distract her from her sadness, but she appreciated the gesture. "Okay. You already know Melody Heath."

"That's your gloomy romance author friend, the one I first met at our wedding."

"Right. She didn't stay long. Her husband drove her down and was waiting for her at a bar in Wolverhampton. She said he wasn't one for weddings and had bowed out, though we invited him, too." She sniffed in disgust. Andrew, Melody's husband, had picked her up at the wedding venue, the historic home outside of Queensville, to take her home before Jaymie had had a chance to visit with Mel, as she called her friend. "I don't like him much. We visited her when we paused in Consolation on the drive up to the UP," Jaymie said, of the small Michigan town were Melody lived.

The autumn before they were taking a mini holiday up to the Upper Peninsula of Michigan, to see the fall colors, and had stopped to have coffee with Jaymie's university friend. Melody was a few years older than Jaymie. She had started at Western, as the Canadian university was known, at the same time despite that, having suffered a few years of uncertainty. They were in many of the same classes, had similar interests, and had become close, remaining so as Melody's romance fiction writing career took off.

"Her husband *is* a bit of an odd duck," Jakob said, yawning.

"I don't know what she sees in him." Andrew was quiet and stuffy. To Jaymie he seemed standoffish, not even warming up to Jakob. Every guy loved her husband; he was one of those men who everyone takes to. But Andrew . . . not so much. Something in the man's pale eyes was . . . off. Melody had confessed to Jaymie that she married him in a fit of loneliness. "I love Mel. I hope it all goes okay. She's looking forward to getting away from Andrew, I think."

"She doesn't drive, though, right?"

"No. Rachel is going to pick her up."

"And Rachel is—"

"Rachel Kimball. She moved into the house during my second year there. Wait . . . I have a photo album somewhere." She jumped up, retrieved it from a shelf by the fireplace, and opened it, then plopped down next to Jakob, putting her feet up on the coffee table and propping the album on her legs. "Here," she said, pointing to a pretty African-American girl with short natural hair. "That's Rachel. She couldn't come to our wedding, which is why you never met her. We got along famously. She went for her BA, but then continued on and got a master's degree in Project Management. She's project manager at an insurance company in Flint, now."

"Why did she go to school in Canada?"

"Western has a good business school and she won a scholarship. She was a good study buddy . . . totally focused. I had a tendency to wander off and make brownies or cook a meal, or read a romance novel, and she'd haul me back to cram. She's the reason I ended up on the honor roll my last year."

Jaymie flipped a page and chuckled. "And *that* is crazy Brandi," she said, pointing to a friend. In the photo Brandi stood on the roof of her car in the middle of a wild dance, bottle of tequila in one hand, maracas in the other. "Brandi Xylander, now, since her marriage. That was during homecoming week, which is why her face is painted purple and she's wearing a purple T-shirt." Purple and white were Western colors.

"What about this one, then?" he said, pointing to the next picture of Brandi wearing a green minidress, green plastic beads and a tall hat that said *Kiss me I'm Irish*. This time she was holding a yard of green ale in one hand and a stuffed shamrock in the other.

"That's on St. Paddy's Day, which is a big event for university students. Or at least the ones who drink. It was my one and only St. Paddy's Day party. We were at a student bar downtown, which is why she has the yard of ale, and why it's green. That girl was a party *animal!*" Jaymie sighed. "As much as I love her, she can be a handful. She behaved at our wedding, but that was a few hours. Brandi has a temper, hair trigger, and she'll lash out."

"That's not good. She's not violent, is she?"

"No, of course not! She's . . . temperamental. Changeable. She *can* be moody at times. I don't know . . . maybe she's changed some in the last few years. I haven't seen her much. She made up for her bad qualities, but you didn't want to be in her way when she was on a tear."

"She sounds a little difficult to deal with."

Jaymie shrugged. She didn't want to run her friends down. "She has a good heart, though. Anybody needs anything, she's there." She chuckled. "Sometimes she's more generous with other people's money and time than with her own, but . . ." She shrugged.

"Who is the one scowling beside her?"

"That's Gabriela. She's not scowling!"

He squinted and stared. "Looks like a scowl to me."

"That's how she always looks. That's Gabriela Smith, now Offerman. She has one of those faces . . . always looks faintly annoyed." Jaymie examined her friend. She was plump in school and had gained weight since. Marriage and a kid, she joked online; it'll do you in every time.

"Gabriela . . . so, Gabby for short?" Jakob asked.

"*Never* Gabby! Not unless you want a death stare and to be hated for all time."

"No sense of humor."

"Everyone has flaws; that's one of hers. She could be sneaky at times—things like eating someone's snack food and denying it—but she was afraid of us not liking her. I felt sorry for her. We had a running joke about her frown. She *is* nice. Quiet. A bit of an oddball. If you caught her in a lie, she would get all red in the face. She lied for the weirdest reasons, too; she borrowed Rachel's sweater once and it got torn. She claimed she saw a rat in the closet, and that's how the sweater was damaged." Jaymie shook her head. "There was no rat, but she kept it up for weeks, always screaming and saying she saw the rat."

"That couldn't have been easy to live with."

"There was no harm in her," Jaymie said softly. "She *could* be fun. She was our resident gamer, always playing Xbox. It's funny . . . she did *not* understand appliances, but she was good with electronics. She was the first one to have a cell phone when they were still a luxury to most of us."

"I have a vague memory of her with her husband and a child at our wedding?"

"She's married to Logan and they have a little girl, three and a half years old now. I think they're trying for a second. I went to her wedding six or seven years ago, and to her baby shower. They moved to a town in Ohio a few years ago to be close to his family. Her and Brandi live in the same town, so they'll be driving in together. It's a miracle we dragged her away from home; she's close to her husband." She twisted and kissed Jakob on the nose. "Kinda like me." She frowned and regarded him, head to one side. "You know, you *should* remember some of these people, at least the ones who came to our wedding."

"That day is a blur. I remember *nothing* from our wedding but your face and your lovely dress."

"Good answer." She kissed him again.

"That's it?"

"That's the crew." She counted off on her fingers . . . "Me, Melody, Brandi, Rachel, and Gabriela. Five of us for at least a week, maybe ten days. We'll see. There used to be a couple more, but they've drifted off and we lost touch. This is the core group. We're going to go up to Canada to the beach. We used to go to Grand Bend almost every weekend in summer," Jaymie said, of the Lake Huron beachside resort town. "It's close to London, kind of a wild beach town, lots of bars and partiers. I imagine we'll go shopping, do lunch, hang out on the beach. Another night we're going to do a dinner cruise on the St. Clair." Jaymie sighed and closed the photo album. "School, and hanging out all the time and partying . . . it seems so long ago now. I hope we all get along."

"Why wouldn't you? You've been together plenty of times since. You camped together every summer for a decade after school, right?"

"Yes, but . . . there will inevitably be tensions. Rachel is the cool one, the easygoing one. I've got no worries there. Other than that . . ." She shrugged. "Brandi and Gabriela never got along. There were fights. They have an intense relationship, either best of friends or mortal enemies. Someone was always stealing someone else's clothes . . . or boyfriend. But maybe it's different now, since they live in the same town and see each other so much more and have kids."

"How does your writer friend fit into all of this?"

"Mel got along. Kind of. She would make fun of Brandi, though. She's kind of high-strung."

"Melody?"

"No, oh no, *Brandi*. She was always a handful, life of the party, as I said. But she's a mom now. She has a twelve-year-old girl from her first marriage, and a four-year-old little boy from her marriage to Terry, her current husband. Or ex . . . I know they've been having some problems. Last time I talked to her they were in the process of splitting up. I think she's looking after another child, too, some relative of Terry's, or hers. So . . . I don't know."

"This is supposed to be a time for you all to forget being wives and moms and be those crazy university students again," Jakob said, stroking her hair.

"I guess," Jaymie said. Did she *want* to forget being a wife and mom? Did she really miss the old days? Sometimes, when life was tiring and complicated she daydreamed about it—the freedom of no one depending on her—but she had a sneaking suspicion "back then" wasn't any simpler than now. "Let's go to bed. I want to make the most of tonight."

⌘ Two ⌘

MORNING DAWNED HUMID, with clusters of dark clouds piling up on the horizon, distant thunder rumbling as they packed the car and drove to the airport. It had not been an easy parting. At the last minute Jocie had been whiny and upset, clinging with sobs to Jaymie. Close to tears during their goodbyes, Jaymie worried it was her own sorrow communicating itself to their sensitive daughter. She took a deep breath and calmed herself, then had a talk with Jocie, kissed Jakob goodbye, and saw them through security before letting her tears flow.

The weather held until then, but to make her misery complete a deafening thunderclap roared and rain poured as she ran across the parking lot to her SUV. She sat for a while in the car, letting the defogger clear the windows and the air-conditioning kick in, then she drove north along I-94. It was hard to tell sometimes if the mistiness was rain or her tears. She played an audiobook of Melody's latest romance to try to ease her melancholy, but it was a long, dreary, teary drive home from the airport.

Her composure returned as she entered their log cabin. Lilibet, Jocie's cat, was staying with Jakob's brother, Helmut, his girlfriend Sonya, and their kids, Jocie's cousins, for the duration. Jaymie washed and dried the breakfast dishes, folded and put away the laundry, then locked up the cabin and took Hoppy with her in her roomy white Ford Explorer. She was going to stay in Queensville for the night, before her friends arrived on the island the next day.

The Queensville house, a big yellow-brick Queen Anne she co-owned with her sister, Becca, was cheery and comfortable even in the rain, but as much as she wanted to, she couldn't linger. She told Hoppy to stay and headed right back out to go over to Valetta Nibley's place. Her best friend was on vacation too and had home projects planned. Today she had handymen scheduled to give her an estimate on expanding her "catio," the outdoor cat enclosure that gave Denver—once Jaymie's cat but now Valetta's—room to roam outside in safety.

Valetta's home was a cottage close to her work as pharmacist, her pharmacy counter stationed within the Queensville Emporium, a store on the main street of town that sold a little of everything. It was so close she could walk to work and home for lunch. Jaymie pulled up behind a battered pickup truck in the drive, eyed the pouring rain, and decided she'd better make a dash for it up to the covered porch.

Valetta, barefoot and in a T-shirt that read *That's MISS Crazy Cat Lady to you!*, answered the door, her face red and her expression annoyed. "Thank goodness you're here," she said, standing back to let Jaymie in. "A friendly *female* face. I'm going mad listening to those baboons." She pushed her thick glasses up on her nose and slammed the door, the glass window rattling. "I'm fed up and ready to tell them to go stick it."

"What's going on?"

Valetta looked down the dim hall toward the kitchen, from which boisterous voices could be heard. "These two handymen that Brock suggested, Mario Horvat and Kory-with-a-K, they're both—"

"Val! Val, *come here*," Brock bellowed. "The guys have a question."

Valetta rolled her eyes. "Follow," she said to Jaymie. "I'm coming!" she yelled.

Jaymie trailed her friend through the living room to the kitchen, where Val's older brother, Brock, stood with two fellows in stained khaki cargo shorts, work boots and torn, stained T-shirts. The older of the two, a guy with coarse tanned features, a high forehead that climbed into wild graying sandy hair, sweat beading his furrowed brow, gave Jaymie a thorough perusal that made her feel uncomfortable. She pulled her sleeveless tee away from her body and shifted.

"What's up?" Val asked.

Brock, a neat enough man with slicked-back dark hair and a wide-mouthed, loose-lipped face, smiled and said hi to Jaymie, then turned to his younger sister. "These guys need to know dimensions. Like, what are you thinking?"

Valetta took in a long breath and let it out slowly. "Okay, once more: I *gave* you a drawing, and there are dimensions *on* it. Can't you read numbers and English?"

Jaymie's brows climbed her forehead. Normally unflappable, Val was unusually irritable today. There must have been quite a lot of idiocy preceding this. She followed the group back through the living room and into the spare room. Mario opened the window as

Denver, huddling in glowering fury in his bedroom, hissed and scooted out of the way of the handyman's clumsy boots.

He pointed through the window to the small catio Valetta already had. "Now, see, here you've got your thingamajig attached to your window frame, but in the drawing you did, you don't *say* that." Mario looked up at Val. He waved the drawing in his hand. "You don't indicate that *any*where."

Val again took in a deep lungful of air and let it out slowly, rounding her mouth and releasing a long yoga breath. It would take either medication or many cups of tea to recover from this. She jabbed her glasses up on the bridge of her nose. "Because, as *indicated*," she said, snatching the drawing out of his hand and pointing to a spot on it, "I am proposing a whole new entry and exit method for Denver. I want the catio to be attached to the siding instead of the window frame, and a platform attached to the window frame instead, kind of a launching pad for the dude. The catio is going to be a lot bigger. In fact, it will reach right down to the ground, where I would like a cement pad poured *first*." She handed the drawing to Jaymie. "Tell me if this is clear," she asked her friend, still glaring at Mario.

Jaymie perused it. The drawing was amateur, of course, but perfectly laid out with dimensions clearly marked. Valetta wanted a cat patio that would have, as its base on the ground, a cement pad, which she was going to line with outdoor carpeting. The dimensions were printed in neat block letters and numbers, with materials noted. Two-by-fours framed a large enclosure, six feet wide by four feet deep by seven feet tall. She had listed proposed materials along the side: wire mesh made up the enclosure walls and was stapled to the two-by-fours, and a rippled opaque polycarbonate roof covered the enclosure to keep out rain; the ripples were to channel rainwater away and must be pointed down. She wanted it affixed to the side wall of the back portion of the house, which had clapboard siding. The polycarbonate roof would be sealed to that siding with silicone or something like that, to prevent leakage.

"This is *perfectly* clear," Jaymie said, handing it back.

Val handed it over to the handyman. "I want an eight-by-five-foot cement pad poured first, with drainage channels so water won't gather, and then the new catio built and installed. So . . . can you or can you *not* do it? I need to know soon, and I want an estimate of materials and labor."

Kory-with-a-K, a younger whiskerless fellow with light brown long hair tied back in a ponytail, snickered. Mario whirled, glared at him, then looked back to Val. His cell phone pinged repeatedly, and his hand strayed to his shorts pocket, but he didn't look at it. "Now, Ms. Nibley, I'm sure we can handle all your needs. This is the kind of thing I specialize in, you know, room for your . . . pussycat." Kory stifled another chuckle. Brock shot a dirty look at him, eyes squinted. "Now, I just need to look outside," Mario continued with a gentle, mansplaining tone. "To see if there's room for what all you've got planned. We can't know that until we take accurate measurements, you see, because we need to be so far from your neighbor's house, and we need room to get in there with a wheelbarrow."

"There is *room!*" Val said emphatically, vibrating with anger. Her fingers moved convulsively, like she wanted to tear her hair out, or claw at someone's face. "My neighbor's house is eleven feet away from mine, plenty enough room to get a wheelbarrow in or one of those small portable cement mixer thingamajigs, the ones on two wheels. For an eight-by-five cement pad four inches deep you need thirty-six fifty-pound bags of concrete mix. A portable cement mixer is an absolute necessity. I measured the area myself, and I have my neighbor's permission to build it, as long as you don't tromp on her hostas," she said, glaring down at Mario's big boots.

"Calm down, now, no need to get hysterical. I want to check and make sure, miss," the handyman said, his hands splayed out in a soothing gesture guaranteed to irritate any intelligent female. He then gestured to Kory. "We need *accurate* measurements, you see. Come on outside with me," he said to his buddy, taking out his measuring tape. "Come on, Brock; I need your opinion."

"You need *his* opinion?" Val screeched. "He's never done a home project in his life!"

The two guys went ahead, but Brock stayed back for a moment. "Come on, sis, let them do their thing," he said, one hand on her shoulder. "They may be a little rough around the edges, but these are good guys. Mario needs the work. He's got a house out on Heartbreak Island . . . kind of a wreck I sold him to fix up. He's been watching these house flipping shows and thinks he can make a million." He chuckled. "Nobody else wanted that shack."

Jaymie stifled a sigh. That was Brock taking advantage of a dimwit, it seemed to her. But then, she had never liked her best friend's brother, and it didn't seem likely she would any time soon.

"Kory lives with them, pays room and board," Brock explained. "It helps them make the mortgage; Mario's girlfriend . . . fiancée, whatever you want to call her . . . Hallie, is real pregnant, ready to pop any day. And Kory . . . he got out of jail a coupla months ago after a coupla months in, and he's having trouble finding work." He perhaps realized these were not reassuring reasons his sister should hire them and put his palms together in a prayerful plea. "Val, I *promise* they'll do a good job. I'll guarantee their work myself."

"*You'll* guarantee their work? Have you had them do work on your house? You need the roof redone and the ceiling in the back entrance fixed."

"I . . . I've got someone else already to work on it."

"How reassuring," Val said, her voice dripping with sarcasm. "Nice that you're trying to pawn them off on me, but you won't let them work on your own house."

Jaymie touched her arm. "Don't worry about it," she said softly to her friend. "You know you're not going to hire them. As much as you want to tear them a new one, let them do what they want to do and go away." Louder she said, "Do you have something to drink, Val? I'm dying of thirst."

Brock followed the other men outside, and Val led the way into the kitchen and got out a pitcher of iced tea. She grumbled for a moment, but then asked how Jaymie was doing with her husband and daughter gone.

"I'm okay, I guess. I miss them already," she said, sitting down at the vintage dinette table and propping her chin on her hand. "But the gang is coming tomorrow, so I've got that to look forward to." She reiterated who all was coming, and told her friend about the trailer and how it looked in its new spot.

Ten minutes later Val looked up at the kitchen clock, a vintage cutie of a black cat with a swinging tail for a pendulum, eyes that went back and forth ticking off the seconds, and a belly filled with a white-faced clock. Valetta and Jaymie shared a love of thrift stores and vintage tchotchkes. "What the heck are they doing out there? Let's go out and see." She led the way out the back door. They could hear the men's voices. "Hush, wait a sec," Val said, holding up one hand.

Jaymie stopped. The rain had dwindled to nothing, leaving the air more muggy, like breathing through a wet cloth. She brushed the rain off a patio chair and sat down, sipping her iced tea and holding her thick ponytail off her sweating neck. The men's voices became clearer, as if they had moved. Brock was complaining about Val, and they all laughed over her sketch.

But it seemed that the conversation swiftly moved on to women, as they lounged and talked. The sweet drift of pot smoke came around the corner, Val wrinkling her nose. Brock protested, but Mario fluffed him off.

"Come on, man, it's a little weed to take the edge off. I have an old injury that gives me pain and this helps. I can't do it at home. Hallie says I can't smoke anything around her now and even after the baby is born." He sounded disgusted.

"Can't blame her," Brock mumbled.

"Women, can't live with them, can't knock them around," Mario said and laughed. The other two didn't laugh. "Guys, it was a joke. No one can take a friggin' joke anymore. Damn PC world."

"What's a joke is how many women you've got hanging on online," Kory said.

"Online? You're doing online dating?" Brock said. "But you've got a girlfriend at home."

"It's harmless," Mario said. "A little fun. Hallie's been busting my nads lately and don't want to do anything. You know what I mean? No loving at all. Total witch mode. A little online flirting makes it all better, you know?"

Jaymie and Valetta exchanged eyebrow-raised looks.

"So it's just flirting?" Brock asked.

"Mebbe a little more than flirting. Hey, what the old lady don't know can't hurt her, right?"

Valetta and Jaymie exchanged incredulous looks.

"I guess online you can be anyone you want, right?" Brock said.

"Yeah, he can be a stud. You can be as jacked as you want online," Kory said snidely.

"Shut up, jerk," Mario said. "You're jealous of the action I get. Women are looking for it big-time."

"Yeah, well, they can't see you online, can they?" Kory shot back.

Jaymie smiled. Kory had seemed quiet, but maybe that was just around women.

"You're a jealous toad, Kory. Online is where it starts," Mario said. "Flatter 'em enough and they'll do anything. I got this one chick, she's a fiery redhead . . . I call her Big Red. We've hooked up a coupla times in real life. They call that IRL, you know that? In Real Life. Like, hot motel fun. I got another woman coming on strong . . . might have to make a date with her *soon*. You should see the pics she sends me! Whoo-*wee*! Hot stuff. And then there is this other gal who is coming from out of state for a little Mario action. With all this going on, I might have to tell Hallie to take a hike. Big Red could move right into the house."

"That's disgusting," Jaymie whispered to Val.

"You can't do that to Hallie!" Kory objected.

"I can do anything I want," Mario said. "She can go live with her mother."

"But she's carrying your child," Brock said, his tone shocked.

"Is she?" Mario grunted. "Is she *really*? How do I know that for sure?"

There was deadly silence for a moment. Jaymie, shocked, shook her head.

"I've had enough," Val said. Raising her voice, she continued, "If you guys are done bragging and lying you can finish up and leave. I've got things to do."

Mario and Kory came back in and clumped through the house, heading to the front door. "I'll get you an estimate once I go to the lumber supply and figure out supplies and time," Mario said.

"Don't bother," Val said coldly. "I'll find someone else."

Mario whirled and glared, swearing gruffly. "You mean I was wasting my time and you already decided?"

"It sounds like you're *good* at wasting time," Val snapped. The two exited and she slammed the door after them, then turned to glare at her brother.

Brock shuffled his feet. He looked embarrassed, knowing they'd been overheard, but all he said was, "Come on, Val, boys will be boys, you know? A little locker room talk."

"Then you all can leave it in the locker room."

"I know it was not meant for a lady's ears, but—"

"That was meant for no one's ears, Brock," Jaymie said. "And you know it. Even Kory seemed ashamed of Mario. He's a cheat, and if he'll cheat on his woman, he'll cheat on the job. Besides, who wants a guy like that working on their house?"

"I get it. I do, Val; I understand. I gotta go. I have a house showing in an hour." He paused and turned. "I went to school with Mario. I feel kind of sorry for him. You know?"

"But not sorry enough that you'll have him work on your own home."

Brock nodded. "Point taken. I have to go, sis. Talk to you later."

Val sighed when he was gone. Jaymie gave her a look, but she shrugged. "What can I do? He's my brother."

℘ Three ℘

THE COTTAGE WAS CLEAN, organized and ready. Jaymie sat on the front porch with Hoppy, looking through the pines at the silvery river slipping past, awaiting her friends. From a damp start the day had dried out. It was hot but comfortable. Inhaling deeply, she could smell the damp sand, the fishy scent of the river, and woodsmoke from somewhere. And someone was grilling hamburgers; the aroma wafted through the trees, maybe even from the Ice House restaurant, not too far away.

She was nervous, and she wasn't sure why. There were and always had been tensions among her friends, tensions she had glossed over while planning this vacation. Wasn't that a fact of life in any group of individuals? It certainly was in the parent group she belonged to at Jocie's school. She and her friends had kept the timing loose, agreeing to at least a week together, maybe ten days. That had seemed a good idea at the time, but maybe it would have been better if they had nailed it down more precisely. Jakob and Jocie would be gone ten days, and it would be nice to have a day or two to get the cottage back into shape before they came home. Once her family was complete again, she knew she'd want to spend all her time with them both before school started back after Labor Day.

She looked at the time on her cell phone. Brandi had texted that they were almost there and the ferry was scheduled to arrive soon. "C'mon, Hoppy, let's go meet the girls." She snapped his leash on and followed the road down along the row of pines to where it opened out, overlooking the marina and ferry dock. She shaded her eyes and saw that the ferry was arriving, so she sped up her pace. Hoppy danced in his wobbly tripod manner and yipped as seagulls, following the ferry, circled and lit on a bench by the dock.

The ferry lowered the ramp that allowed cars to drive onto the island. The other ramp extended to the wharf for walking passengers. Jaymie kept watch and there . . . *there* was Brandi! Her friend was unmistakable: tall, lean, with spiral curled stiff hair that was emblazoned with mahogany and maroon tints that the sun burnished to a bright magenta. She was five seven—five nine in platform sandals—and wearing the shortest shorts anyone could wear, little more than a bathing suit bottom. She stalked along the dock tugging a wheeled suitcase with one hand, holding a floppy sunhat in the other, and with a huge hobo sack purse slung over one arm. Other arrivers trailed, but Jaymie didn't see anyone else she knew. Gabriela, who was driving with her, must be coming over on the next ferry for some reason.

"Over here!" Jaymie said, waving. Her hazel eyes concealed by huge designer sunglasses, Brandi waved her sunhat back. Jaymie trotted to her and flung herself at her friend; the two women hugged, laughing. When she released her she noticed another woman standing close by, similar suitcase to Brandi's standing on its wheels, similar sunhat in hand, similar sunglasses on.

"Jaymie, this is Court—Courtney—my best friend in the world." She tugged the woman close and slung her arm over her shoulders.

Brandi clearly intended Courtney to stay with them, but . . . she was a *stranger*. "I've never . . . you didn't . . . hello, Courtney," Jaymie said, dismayed and trying to hide it. She offered a hand and the woman took it, squeezed, then released it. Jaymie turned back to her friend. "Where's Gabriela? I thought she was coming with you?"

Courtney crouched and played with Hoppy, cooing over him and tickling his tummy. Brandi whipped off her sunglasses and rolled her eyes. "Oh, she did, all right, but she forgot half her stuff at home. I let her use the car. She went into town to get sunblock and other stuff at that cute little store you always talk about, the Emporium. She'll park in the long-term parking lot up there and come out on the next ferry." Jaymie had asked them all to leave their cars in the parking lot, as island residents were discouraged from bringing vehicles over. It was largely unnecessary except for folks with limited mobility, who were issued a parking pass for anywhere on the island.

"Let's go to the cottage and get you both settled, then I'll come back and meet her here."

"Lead on, MacDuff; didn't our English prof say that?"

"No, he said it was a misquote from *Macbeth*, that it's supposed to be '*Lay on, MacDuff*,'" Jaymie said. "And it means kind of the opposite, instead of leading the way it is an invitation to fight harder. Come on, Hoppy, no barking at seagulls."

Brandi snorted. "Aren't you a font of information."

Fount, Jaymie thought but did not say. When Courtney lagged behind a bit, taking pictures with her cell phone of the line of pines along the road and the cottages beyond, Jaymie muttered, glancing at her friend, "Brandi, you didn't tell me you were bringing someone else. This was supposed to be a gathering of college friends!"

"What, I can't bring a friend on *my* vacation?" Brandi said loudly.

"Shh, Bran!" Jaymie yelped, glancing back at Courtney, who was rapidly gaining on them.

"Cripes, I didn't think I had to ask to bring along a friend, *Mom*," Brandi said, still loudly, with an exaggerated sigh.

"It's okay! It's all right, of *course*!" Jaymie said hastily. "Room enough for everyone!" she added, trying to make her tone happy and welcoming. She didn't want the other woman to feel like an intruder. As usual, Brandi got her way by making it awkward if she didn't.

At the cottage Jaymie showed them around and helped them choose a room. There were two bedrooms, the sunny yellow one with two double beds, and a pale-blue-painted bedroom with a double bed and a set of bunk beds. She then showed them the bathroom—no shower stall, just a claw-foot tub with a shower over the top, a stand-alone pedestal sink, and the toilet—and supplied towels. Standing and chatting as she watched Brandi and Courtney unpack, stowing their clothes in the big chest of drawers and spreading their toiletries on the dresser top, Jaymie glanced down at her cell phone.

"Eek . . . the time! The next ferry is due! I'll go meet Gabriela while you two get settled," she said and escaped with Hoppy.

Despite saying the ferry was due, Jaymie was going to be early, but she needed a few moments alone. She sat on the top of the park bench listening to the cicadas buzz, watching the water slip past, and gazing across the river at the Queensville wharf, where the ferry was loading. She let her gaze rise above it, along the walkway that topped a long riverside park where annual Fourth of July celebrations were held, so folks on both sides of the river could watch fireworks erupt from a barge stationed in the middle of the river. Nearby was a row of ramshackle buildings, among them a marina shop and a bait shop; there was still much discussion about the fate of those structures. The owner, Miss Perry, was in no hurry to change the status quo. The shops had always been there, and likely always would be.

She felt a thread of unease that she hadn't acknowledged fully until now. Her nervousness about this vacation had been a frisson creeping down her spine; now it was, for some reason, blooming. It had been a few years since the group of university friends had managed their annual vacation. Maybe they had all changed too much to spend so much time together. Maybe they should have made it a weekend instead of a week or more. She rolled her shoulders, willing the anxiety away.

It was loneliness, she diagnosed. She missed Jakob and Jocie so much it hurt. She had cried herself to sleep the night before. Jakob had only had time enough to send her a text when they arrived, and a couple of photos of them and Jocie's mother's family. They were busy, and Jaymie was pleased that it looked like they were having fun. The primary reason for the trip was so Jocie could get to know her mother's family, but it wouldn't be a vacation without things to do. They were going with Jocie's Polish cousins to visit Malbork Castle, the Auschwitz-Birkenau Memorial and Museum (if it was appropriate for Jocie's age; that had not been settled yet), and a nature preserve in the mountains. They'd daytrip to Warsaw and Gdansk, but there were days set aside for visiting, relaxing, picnicking and shopping, too. Jaymie hoped they had fun, and couldn't wait for them to come home.

But her mind returned to her own vacation. Why did Brandi find it necessary to bring along someone no one knew? She didn't want to be mean, but Jaymie had been imagining a celebration of their long friendships, slipping into the easy rhythms they had experienced when they were all twenty-year-old (or in the case of Melody Heath, mid-twenties) college kids away from home, eating ramen, drinking cheap beer, and staying up all night studying, playing board games and laughing together.

But Brandi wasn't her only friend. She was closer with the others. The sun was high in the sky, and Jaymie took a deep breath, determinedly making herself cheer up. Maybe Courtney would blend in. Maybe she was an awesome person who would be the highlight of the vacation.

She dialed Valetta as she climbed down from the bench to let Hoppy sniff a clump of weeds and wobble as he lifted his leg to piddle.

"Hey, Jaymie . . . what's up?"

"Nothing much; waiting for more of my friends to arrive on the ferry." She swept her bangs out of her eyes, the wind tossing them right back in. "Just checking to make sure we're still on for the dinner cruise . . . and maybe Grand Bend, too, tomorrow? Bernie and Heidi are coming," she said, of two Queensville friends. Heidi, an heiress originally from New York but with strong ancestral ties to their town, and Bernie, who had moved to Queensville when she took a position as an officer with the police department, were best friends and had become close with Jaymie, too. She had felt a little guilty inviting them, given that it was supposed to be just the school friends, but it wasn't as if they were staying with them, as Courtney would be. Or at least that's how she justified it to herself, she realized with a wince. Maybe she had been hypocritical to object to Brandi's friend, she thought, resolving to get to know the woman.

Valetta agreed to both proposals. "Hey, instead of taking separate cars, I know a guy who will loan me his nine-passenger van. We could all cross into Canada together! I'll drive."

"That sounds like a good plan, Val."

"Okay. Done." Val chattered on about her desperate search for a Jane-of-all-trades who would be easier to work with than the Neanderthal twins, as she called them, Mario and his buddy Kory-with-a-K. Jaymie commiserated, and made suggestions, the easy back-and-forth flow of conversation soothing.

As she said farewell, she realized that maybe she was trying to hold on to — or recreate — something that didn't exist in her *old* friendships. When they had all lived together, with the daily tug and push of interaction, there had been many similar moments of easy conversation, quick affection, camaraderie simply expressed. But she, too, had moved on to new friendships, as Brandi had, and if that was going to make things awkward, it would be a long vacation.

At least there would be Rachel and Melody, the two that she was closest to. And all of them arrived together on the ferry this time, Rachel, Melody, *and* Gabriela, loaded down with luggage and bags, a camera, a purse, and more. After they all hugged Jaymie, Gabriela, the back of her long streaked brown hair twisted and fixed in place with a dollar store hair clip, spent the first bit of their walk to the cottage complaining about Brandi bringing Courtney.

"So you know her?" Jaymie asked, taking her friend's Queensville Emporium bags loaded with sunscreen, snacks, and various other items unneeded and unwanted.

"Of *course*. How could I avoid it?" Gabriela griped. She swept her long bangs out of her eyes, tucking the loose hair behind her ears. "Brandi doesn't go anywhere without her now!"

Melody slipped up beside Gabriela and took her camera bag from her, hoisting her own duffle high on her shoulder. As usual Melody, in cut-off jean shorts and a T-shirt, short curly brown hair and bright inquisitive blue gaze darting everywhere, taking it all in, had packed light, knowing that beyond bathing suits, shorts and sleeveless tees, all anyone needed was a nice sundress for the dinner cruise and any other possible occasion. She and Jaymie had talked at length, and Jaymie assured her that there was plenty of shampoo, conditioner, towels, toothpaste, soap, and moisturizer on hand in the cottage; no need to bring them.

Rachel hid a smile but met Melody and Jaymie's glance as Gabriela droned on. Her own springy natural hair was bleached in part and tipped in blue. Her round face was lit with a ready, toothy smile and bronzy cheek color, the only makeup she habitually wore besides a peach lip gloss on her cupid bow lips, above her pointed chin. She was wearing a sundress, a brilliant crimson and sunset abstract pattern that was set off beautifully by her dark skin, and fringed suede sandals on her feet. Round red-framed sunglasses perched on her nose.

"So, what's Courtney like?" Jaymie asked, once Gabriela had finally slowed.

She shrugged and adjusted her shorts around her plump middle. "Okay, I guess," she said as they approached the cottage along River Road.

"This is so *cute!*" Rachel said with a gasp as they stopped in front of Rose Tree Cottage.

Jaymie looked up at it with pride. It *was* cute, a blue clapboard and white trimmed cottage on a slight rise, with a wide covered porch along the front, surrounded on three sides with groves of pines and poplars. There was another porch on the back, above a sloping grassy lawn and steps that led down into the grove, where the flagstone patio and the firepit made a relaxing shady vacation hideaway. "Wait 'til I show you my summer project!" she said.

An hour later they were all sitting together in the shaded rockery, as she called the little valley between her cottage and the Redmonds'. Over the past year or so she and Becca and their mother, in her rare visits, had transformed the slopes surrounding the terraced patio into rock gardens with perennial alyssum, stonecrop and other sedums, and some hostas and annual coleus. The hill leading up to the Redmonds' cottage was thickly treed, a canopy of greenery shading the grove, with pine needle mulch making the slope slippery.

They quaffed iced tea—or in Brandi's case, iced tea with a hit of bourbon from a bottle she kept in her purse—and sat on the comfy lounge chairs the Leightons had furnished their patio with for the use of renters. Gabriela munched on corn chips, but everyone else was saving their appetites for dinner. They had gotten past the initial catching up, but it was too early to head to the Ice House, the restaurant on the island owned by the Redmonds. Hoppy had taken to Rachel, and was curled up in her lap as she stroked his ears.

Pink was shouting, from Rachel's cell phone through the Bluetooth speakers wired into the patio sound system, about getting the party started. Gabriela, between snacks, was playing some game on her cell phone, and Melody watched them all with the focused, darting interest of an anthropologist in a new community. A little older than the rest of them, and an introvert who did not shine at parties, she had always been the observer of their group, more so now as a full-time professional author of a couple dozen contemporary and historical romances.

There was a lull, a bit of an awkward silence. Cicadas buzzed loudly in the trees overhead, and squirrels rustled in the pine needles on the slope. A blue jay scolded, flitting from one branch to another and squawking loudly; they were sitting too close to the feeder full of peanuts that he preferred over the more standard birdseed mix. A chipmunk chipped his own alarm, upset by Hoppy's presence, though the little dog was quiet, for once. Gabriela looked up from her phone and glanced around. "This is nice, Jaymie," she said. "I've been needing a vacay. My new job is hectic!"

"Yeah, congratulations on that," Rachel said. "You sounded

excited when you got it. I don't think I understood what exactly you're doing, though?"

"My first job was as a quality control associate at a grocery store, but now I'm district manager of quality control, food handling and safety staff. I have to go to different grocery stores and stay on top of them about food safety and employee safety, make sure everything is up to code . . . you know, temps in freezers and fridges, meat storage and handling, that kind of thing. It's for a big chain. I have to travel a lot, sometimes overnight, all over Michigan and Ohio. Company car, though! And good benefits."

"I'm proud of you," Jaymie said.

"It's good for our bottom line. When we just had Logan's wages, we were living hand to mouth. But . . ." She sighed. "Don't get me wrong; I'm sure I'll have fun this week, but I can't help but wonder, should I have come away on vacation? I miss my hubby and baby so much!" Her eyes teared. "Fenix and Logan are my *world*! I expected Lo to message me before now, but I haven't heard a peep from him!"

"For cripes' sake," Brandi groaned. "You just left home this morning! There hasn't been time for your bed to get cold yet."

"No, I get it, Gabriela!" Jaymie exclaimed hastily, butting in to forestall Brandi, who always said whatever she thought, kind or not. "I miss Jakob and Jocie."

"But it's different. Jocie's not your *real* child," Gabriela said.

There was deafening shocked silence. Brandi snickered. "There you go," she said, raising her glass in a woozy salute. "And yet *I'm* the clueless rude one?"

Jaymie bit back her first response out of a desire to keep the peace, though it hurt to stay silent. Gabriela's comment was all too common. Folks often remarked, as an aside, when stating how moms and kids had a special bond, that Jocie was not her *real* daughter. "I love and miss her," Jaymie said softly. "And Jakob, too."

"You've only been married a year or so . . . just wait," Brandi said. She stood, swaying and clutching the back of a chair to steady herself. "All right, ladies, we are here to have fun, to cut loose, not mope around looking like sad sacks!"

Gabriela, her cheeks aflame, said, "Better a sad sack than a drunk who doesn't give a darn about her husband and kids."

"*Ex*-husband-to-be," Brandi said. "And yeah, I intend to have fun, get thoroughly wasted and find some guys to have fun with!"

"Just a normal Wednesday then?" Gabriela shot back.

There was snickering from Courtney. It was kind of funny, and unexpected coming from the usually mild Gabriela. But Jaymie didn't laugh, exchanging alarmed glances with Rachel and Melody. Brandi sat back down, her drink spilling.

"So, Courtney, how did you and Brandi meet?" Jaymie asked, determined to befriend the quiet woman. *And* change the subject away from the tension between Gabriela and Brandi.

"Don't answer that!" Brandi laughed, exchanging an arch look with her bestie. She took a long hit of what was left of her booze-soaked iced tea.

Courtney puffed on her Capri Magenta cigarette, then butted it out on a flagstone. "I hauled her ass home from a bar," she said with a sly smile. "Some guy had dumped her and left her to her own devices. She was sitting on the curb crying."

Brandi giggled, snorting. "Court said, 'Do you need a lift?' and I said, "Yeah, do you think you can carry me though?'"

Gabriela sniffed in disgust, but the others chuckled politely.

"When was that?" Jaymie asked.

"Last year," Courtney said.

"And we've been inseparable ever since," Brandi said, slinging her arm over Courtney's shoulders and pulling her close, giving her a wet kiss on the cheek.

"Someone has to head off the herd of guys and take your butt home when you've had too much and are getting in trouble!" Courtney gave her a kiss back, with a fond look in her eyes.

"Oh, look, Gabriela," Melody said with deadpan delivery. "Courtney is doing *your* old job."

An interruption was needed to ward off the acrimony that seemed to bubble under the surface of interactions between Brandi and Gabriela. Jaymie suggested they walk to Tansy's Tarts and buy the next day's breakfast—they were all on vacation, so pecan butter tarts for breakfast seemed reasonable, though Jaymie *did* have something else planned—and then after they picked up the tarts they'd head directly to the Ice House for dinner. Gabriela kept checking her phone as they walked and seemed more and more worried. When

Jaymie sidled up next to her and asked if anything was wrong, Gabriela said it was odd that Logan hadn't texted. She texted him to ask what was up. He had not responded. She was worried.

He was busy, Jaymie reassured her. She led the way, up the sloping sand and gravel lane to the road along the water channel that bisected Heartbreak Island into the U.S. and Canadian sides in a fairly even manner. The border was mostly on the honor system; if you were going to enter the Canadian side you were supposed to do so at one of the proper crossing points, several bridges across the narrow man-made channel. In the past folks had slipped back and forth through residents' backyards and hopped the channel, but most now used the border crossing points. If you had a Nexus pass it took seconds.

"I'll tell you the story of Heartbreak Island at the fire one night," she promised.

Tansy Woodrow's shop, Tansy's Tarts, was a bakeshop on the American side of the island. Tansy made the most exquisite tarts and pies for miles. Her specialty was butter tarts, the recipe a well-guarded secret that had been handed down from her Canadian grandmother. When you bit into a Tansy Woodrow butter tart, the filling gushed like liquid heaven, sweet and buttery, golden perfection crusted with buttery flaky delectability. There weren't any like them in the rest of the United States and she was not sharing the recipe.

The shop took up much of the main floor of a white two-story frame structure with a big pink-and-white-striped awning over the front window and door with Tansy's shop name in script; beyond the shop was the bakery at the back. Tansy and her hubby, Sherm, lived in the upstairs apartment and had a deck out back from which they could see over the narrow canal to the Canadian side of the island. Jaymie belatedly realized her impulsive suggestion to head to the bakery now was probably not the best plan. At this point in the day their stock would be depleted, but she'd go again the next morning if there wasn't much to be had.

They entered, the chimes over the door jingling merrily. Jaymie looked at the nearly empty glass case—the shop was lined with antique bakery cases, white porcelain and chrome, with huge glass expanses and wire shelves—and said, "I think we're too late." She approached the order desk, where a young girl with a distended pregnant belly sat on a stool looking tired. "Hi. Is this all that's left?" she said, indicating the few tarts remaining.

"Whatdya expect?" the girl said. "It's almost closing."

The girl was unfamiliar to her, perhaps a new summer hire; Jaymie didn't often get the butter tarts, as she was trying to stay away from too many sweets. She glanced at her name tag. "Hi, Hallie . . . uh, yes, I should have realized that."

"*'I should have realized that,'*" the girl said with a grimace, mimicking Jaymie's tone, or what she approximated as Jaymie's polite tone. She rubbed her belly.

"No need to get frickin' rude, little girl!" Brandi said.

"Brandi, it's okay," Jaymie said, putting one hand on her friend's arm.

"It's *not* okay!" Gabriela said, slipping her phone in her plaid cotton shorts pocket. She tugged her bright pink T-shirt down over her hips. "Brandi's right; she's a server here. She should be respectful of a customer."

Hallie . . . Jaymie remembered where she had heard the name before. *This must be Mario's girlfriend.* She couldn't be more than twenty, and he was in his fifties. *And* he was a creep. *And* he was cheating on her with anyone who would stay still long enough. Jaymie held up one hand to her friends. "It's okay, hush, everyone. Hallie, we'll take what you've got here." As the girl boxed the tarts that were left, Jaymie said gently, "I've met your, uh . . . I've met Mario. And Kory. They were at my friend Valetta's house, measuring to do some work."

The girl paused and turned. Wearily she said, slapping the lid shut on the cardboard box, "I don't give a crap what they were doing with your friend. I don't care if they were boning. That'll be ten dollars."

As they left the tart shop Brandi ducked back in, the door chimes jingling merrily, and made a rude gesture to Hallie, along with a loud raspberry.

"Brandi!" Jaymie gasped. "I have to live here, you know!"

But her friend merely laughed and sprinted ahead, whirling, hands in the air. "C'mon, Jaymie, don't be a spoilsport. We're young, we're free! Let's *live!*"

She skipped ahead, her drunken stupor worn off, it appeared, Courtney racing to catch up and Gabriela sighing but following quickly on their heels. Jaymie, Melody and Rachel were left behind, strolling the sandy dirt road as the sun began to descend over the line of trees that rimmed the U.S. side of the island.

"I didn't think being young and free meant being rude," Jaymie muttered.

"*So* embarrassing," Rachel moaned.

"Really, you two . . . what did you expect?" Melody said. "It's as if you've never met Brandi before."

"What do you mean?" Jaymie asked.

"She was always like this—impulsive and careless—you've forgotten. Or blocked it out. Don't you remember nagging her to do chores, like put out the garbage? She'd forget to lock the door after her, and we were robbed twice because of it. She ate our food and used our toiletries and never replaced them. She had—has, apparently—the attention span of a two-year-old and her manners are worse. Don't you remember her sneaking those two dudes into the house and keeping them in her room for a week? And how they scared the crap out of us by coming down for breakfast one morning?"

"I remember!" Rachel cried. "I was in my PJs and those two guys, neither speaking English—I think they were Colombian exchange students—crept into the dining room when I was having coffee. Gabriela makes me laugh every time she tells the story . . . her aggrieved expression is the funniest part. I almost called the cops on them. Brandi wasn't even there. She had gone out the night before and went home with some new dude and didn't come back. The guys got scared and hungry and came down, finally."

Jaymie laughed. It was funny now, but it wasn't then. "If Gabriela hadn't spoken Spanish we would never have figured out who they were and why they were in our house!"

✒ Four ✒

DINNER AT THE ICE HOUSE was, as usual, wonderful, though the owners were not there. The Redmonds, who had been on a month-long sailing adventure of the Great Lakes, were set to return any day. Good staff made the luxury of a vacation possible; the restaurant was efficiently run, the manager stern, competent and yet well-liked.

The restaurant, named after the ice harvesting storage facility it had once been, was right on the river. It had a long narrow outdoor patio that lined the whole front, overlooking the St. Clair and facing Queensville, with benches for those who wanted to sit and sip a glass of wine while they watched boats slip past. There was a larger patio at the back, where umbrella-shaded tables were popular for the après boating crowd. In late August the patio was the popular place to watch the sun go down.

But it was a hot evening, and the inside was dim, air-conditioned and comfortable. They took one of the larger tables, sitting near the big antique freezers that lined the back; they were no longer freezers, now acting as storage for barware and linens. Her friends asked what was good, and Jaymie said everything. She ordered the local perch and fries, Rachel had fish tacos, and the rest had the Ice House signature burger. Beer, iced tea, wine . . . soon their table was cluttered with drinks and plates and there was relative quiet as they ate.

Jaymie worried about how the time was going to pass, but as the mood mellowed, good food and drinks working their magic, she felt more optimistic. Her friends were tired, and it was always difficult to please a whole crowd. They'd work it out. It usually, if memory served her, took a few days for the group to find the rhythm of their past camping adventures, but by the end of it they'd be hugging and crying and not wanting to let go of each other.

The dinner crowd drifted away and the evening crowd, sunburned, waterlogged and ready to party, wandered in. Jaymie had plans for the evening and didn't want it to be too dark when they got back to the cottage. She suggested they leave, but Brandi and Courtney wanted to stick around for a couple of drinks. A local rock band set up on the corner stage, tuning instruments and checking mics, and soon oldies, done with tolerable talent but loud, filled the bar part of the restaurant. Brandi and her friend moved them to a table closer to the band, and Brandi flirted with the lead vocalist, a local who worked at the hospital in Wolverhampton during the week and played with his band on weekends. She took her drink and stood by the stage, chatting with him between songs as the singer's wife glared at the oblivious Brandi from her table by the stage.

It reminded Jaymie of being back at school. She had forgotten how Brandi would abandon her friends to chat with guys. She didn't mean anything by it, she was gregarious and she liked men. When they were on one of their camping trips she would stroll around the campground and stop to talk to people—men—often while their wives and girlfriends glowered. Occasionally she'd disappear for a night. She always said that vacation was a time to cut loose, and she lived up to that motto.

Courtney watched her closely. Jaymie was glad, now, that Courtney had come along because otherwise it would be up to one of them to get Brandi out of the fixes she always ended up in, with two guys fighting, or a guy getting handsy. Not that her behavior deserved such treatment, but it happened and it was uncomfortable. It had been a few years and Jaymie had forgotten about the bad moments Brandi had brought them. She hoped she wouldn't be forcibly reminded tonight.

The door from outside opened, letting golden sunset light stream in. Mario, Kory and Hallie entered, taking stools along the bar.

"You know, I feel bad about what happened earlier," Jaymie said to Melody, pointing over to Hallie. "The poor girl is clearly due any day. She's tired and Brandi was rude to her."

"She was rude first," Melody pointed out, having to raise her voice over the music.

"She's right, Jaymie," Rachel yelled, a finger in one ear. "The girl was rude first. Brandi was rude too, but by now it's probably forgotten."

"Do you think so?" Jaymie fretted.

"Why do you feel the need to make nice with *everybody*, regardless of how *they* behave?" Melody asked.

Was that true? She twisted her mouth and thought about it. "I don't like conflict, I guess."

"I remember," Melody said with a laugh, exchanging a bemused look with Rachel. "You were the peacemaker, the one who always stepped in between Gabriela and Brandi, who did Brandi's chores in secret so no one would rag on her, who slipped her a ten when she was broke so she wouldn't ask the other girls for money and start an argument."

Jaymie glanced at her in surprise. "You knew all that?"

"Sure."

"Jaymie, I hate to break it to you, but we all knew you did it," Rachel said, leaning in so she could be heard over the band. The bass guitarist was having a good time with the bass line in "Smoke on the Water."

"Why didn't you say so then?"

"Why would I?" Melody replied. "It was your business."

Brandi whooped to the song and shook her fist in the air, spilling her drink and laughing. Mario, at the bar, slid his glance past his pregnant girlfriend toward Brandi and her short shorts, and he watched her with an appreciative smile as Hallie and Kory chatted over drinks. The smile gave Jaymie the creeps, knowing what she knew and having heard what she heard. He must have a thing for redheads, given what he had said; Brandi's wild mane of magenta curls bounced as she jumped and gyrated. Courtney seemed to have a sixth sense for Brandi's male admirers; she caught sight of Mario and gave him a dirty look.

"Wow, if looks could kill," Jaymie said to Melody and Rachel during a pause in the music. She told them what she had seen.

"Courtney seems possessive of Brandi," Rachel commented. She pursed her lips and stared. "She's still staring. It's as if she's waiting for that dude to do or say something out of line."

Gabriela returned to the table from the bathroom, leaned in and said, "You have no idea! Haven't you seen Courtney's posts online? She takes a million pictures of Brandi, and you should see them out; she's *always* watching over Brandi."

"I'm not friends with Courtney online," Jaymie said as Melody and Rachel nodded in agreement. "I didn't know she existed until today." Jaymie didn't want to be a spoilsport, but she did have plans for their first night together and they didn't include sitting in a bar watching Brandi get drunk. She explained her plight and said, glancing around the table at her friends, "What do we do?"

Gabriela said, "Let me handle it." She went to Courtney and sat down next to her, then talked. The woman nodded and grimaced and nodded again. Gabriela came back to their table and opened her purse, putting her phone, sunglasses, and keys inside. "Let's get going, then, shall we?" she said to the others.

"Leave without Brandi?" Jaymie was worried. She watched Brandi, still flirting with the lead vocalist, and saw Mario getting up and heading toward the bathroom, veering away from that path as Hallie leaned in to talk to Kory. Instead of the bathroom he wove through the tables toward Brandi.

"I babysit her enough at home, I don't want to have to do it on vacation," Gabriela said resentfully. "When do *I* get a break?"

"What do you mean?"

"Brandi, she always needs a ride to work, or a babysitter, or somewhere to stay when her and Terry are fighting—which has been most of the time lately—or a reference for a job when she loses the one she has because she's always late! If Courtney's not around then it's me, always me!"

"I didn't know, Gabriela," Jaymie said, putting her hand on her friend's shoulder. The woman looked close to tears.

"I came away to have a good time, and now Brandi is ruining it. Yet again! And Logan hasn't bothered to text me today. At *all*!" she said, gulping back a sob.

That was the heart of her emotional response, Jaymie thought . . . she was worried that her husband hadn't responded to her multiple texts.

Rachel leaned in and gave her a hug. "I'm sorry. That sucks."

The band launched into a loud intro, a clash of drums and cymbals and loud guitar squealing, then into music.

"Logan is probably busy with your little girl, right? Dads lose track of time," Jaymie said in as soothing a tone as she could manage shouting over "Born to Be Wild," the band's sixties rock selection. They were apparently determined to do every song with the amp turned up to maximum.

Jaymie glanced over; Courtney was heading off Mario. She said something to him, and then turned to Brandi. Mario stood staring at them for a moment, then wandered off toward the bathroom. Courtney said something to Brandi, leaned in and apparently repeated it, and then motioned toward the rest of their group. Brandi waved at them, and smiled and nodded. And headed toward them, putting her drink down.

"So, what are we waiting for?" Brandi said, picking up her straw handbag. "Let's go back to the cottage and get our camp on!"

Jaymie sent Courtney a thank-you look and mouthed it to her. The woman nodded with a tight smile, more like a grimace, and a shrug. Jaymie picked up her cell phone as it buzzed, the screen lighting up. Who could be calling her? A photo flashed on the screen of the lower part of a male anatomy with the abs and exaggeratedly etched lower stomach muscles displayed. There was a message attached from someone with the screen name 1BuffDude, saying *Tell me ware 2 meat U 4 funn.* What the . . . ? Eyes wide in shock, she examined the phone and realized it was similar but it *wasn't* hers, it was Brandi's! She laughed and handed it back to Brandi. "A message for you, my friend," she said with an embarrassed laugh. So that's how she met guys?

They emerged from the restaurant to the sunset's lovely golden glow over the town of Queensville on the far banks of the river. As the door closed behind them, the noise of the band dulled, and Jaymie took a deep breath, looking across the river to the setting sun. Maybe now her vacation could begin. "Let's go," she said. "Back to the cottage!"

ɮ Five ɮ

THEY STARTED BACK TO THE COTTAGE with one brief pause when Gabriela ducked back into the restaurant, saying she had dropped her cell phone, typically scatterbrained for her. Then they walked back to the cottage in the cool of the evening, cicadas still chirring, a nighthawk squawking and the occasional soft splash of a fish in the river. Laughter and voices echoed in the evening, but otherwise as they got farther away from the restaurant the night became peaceful. Once home, Jaymie let Hoppy out. He wobbled to his favorite spot for a piddle and then joined them as they drew chairs close around the firepit. Rachel, ever helpful, carried wood to pile nearby so they wouldn't have to wander into the dark to get it later.

Jaymie smiled up at her friend as she knelt by the firepit, a shallow depression rimmed by stones gathered over the years from the riverside. "There's a laundry basket over there near the wood-pile," she said. "You can put wood in that to bring over." She stacked kindling in a crisscross pattern, then created a tripod of longer pieces over the top. She then tossed in balls of newsprint and dryer lint she kept in a bag in the cottage.

"What the heck are you doing?" Rachel asked.

"Using dryer lint! It helps the paper catch fire." Jaymie touched the barbecue lighter to the dryer lint and it flared up, the tiny dancing flame catching on the paper, then the kindling and finally the bigger pieces of wood. "This is why you *never* let dryer lint build up in your dryer vents!" She sat back on her haunches watching; the next few minutes were critical to make sure she had created a fire that would continue.

"You can hear fall in the air," Melody said as she set one of the chairs closer to the fire.

"What do you mean, *hear* fall?" Jaymie asked.

"Sounds; I associate sounds and smells with different times of year. Don't you?"

"I guess I do," Jaymie said. She stopped and listened. "The wind in the poplars . . . that's summer."

"And the *smell* of poplars when it rains . . . they have their own scent, kind of nutty, aromatic . . . it's a pleasant scent. But that faint rustle of the leaves . . . it means they're drying out; it's almost fall."

Jaymie smiled. "That's why I like your books. The sights and sounds and scents help locate the story in time and place. Like in a historical, when you describe the pop and crackle of coal in a fireplace, the oddly clean smell of horse dung and the dust created by sweepers cleaning it up, or the sound of a carriage driving over straw put down to dampen sound, past a house where there has been a death. I can imagine it clearly."

"How do you write the ones set in England?" Rachel asked, leaning her cheek in her hand and watching the author. "Do you go over and do research?"

Melody laughed. "You know me better than that, Rach. Remember when you wanted me to go to Jamaica with you, and I said I had wisdom teeth surgery that week?"

She nodded, then sat upright, her eyes wide. "You *lied!*" she yelped.

"I did. I've never gotten wisdom teeth." Her expression was one of chagrin, but she shrugged. "Sorry . . . really, I *am*. I feel like such a schlub sometimes. I'm no traveler. My idea of a big trip is going to the grocery store. This . . ." she went on, waving her hand around, "was a huge undertaking. I almost bailed." She glanced over at Jaymie. "Sorry, kiddo, but . . ." She shrugged.

"It's okay, Mel. Tell me the truth if you don't want to do something," Rachel said.

Jaymie said, "We don't want you to do anything you don't want to do, you know."

"I promise, I will. I told myself I'd tell you the truth and try not to fib anymore. I'll make a resolution: tell no lies, except in print."

Gabriela shivered. "Fall *is* coming. It's getting chilly at night." She pulled on a cream cardigan. "Brrr!"

Jaymie laughed and took the chair beside her. "Only *you* could find it cold near a roaring fire!" She glanced at her friend in the firelight and pulled a long red thread from the cream wool, tossing it in the fire, where it blackened and shriveled. "Come on," she said, putting her arm around her friend's shoulders. "Get closer and you'll soon be warm enough!"

Brandi broke out a bottle of tequila for those so inclined, just her and Courtney. Melody and Jaymie chose tea, while Gabriela drank nothing and Rachel stuck with water. They chatted for a while, reminiscing about school, living in Canada, and past camping trips. Courtney was quiet. Jaymie tried to draw her out, but she smiled and stayed silent.

"She doesn't talk much," Brandi said. "That's why she's the perfect friend for me."

"What about the friend who has put up with your crap for fifteen years?" Gabriela groused. "She's no longer the perfect friend?"

"Brandi didn't mean it like that," Jaymie said. "Come on, Gabriela . . . she was joking."

"No, let her talk!" Brandi said, glaring at her across the firepit with a flare of anger. "Miss Perfect needs to vent or she'll be a witch all vacation long. All she did on the way here was whine and moan."

Courtney hid a smile.

"I was surprised that you hauled Courtney along when she wasn't invited," Gabriela said, her cheeks red and her lip trembling.

Courtney's smile died.

"That wasn't necessary," Melody said.

Gabriela retreated into a sulk, crossing her arms over her chest and grumbling, "Just because you're the oldest, Mel, doesn't mean you're the boss. We aren't teenagers anymore."

There was a five-minute stretch of silence.

"Jaymie, didn't you say there was some dessert you wanted to make?" Rachel said with a smile, her face glowing in the firelight.

"Yes!" Jaymie said, thankful for the reminder. They needed something to break the tense silence. She jumped up and retreated to the trailer, coming back out with the tools and foodstuffs. "Pie irons . . . remember me doing those around the campfire once when we camped?"

"It was five years ago, not a million," Brandi said.

"I've never heard of such a thing," Courtney said. "What's a pie iron?"

"There you go," Melody said with a smile. "Someone who's never heard of pie irons. Have at it, Jaymie!"

Jaymie stuck her tongue out at her friend and knelt down by the small table she had moved close to the firepit. She described making the (to her) delectable treat of pie iron pies. "Pie irons are these," she said, picking up the long-handled hinged devices with two bread-slice-shaped indented sides. She had two in aluminum and one in cast iron, and she was anxious to see which worked best. It might become a "Vintage Eats" column—her food column in the *Wolverhampton Weekly Howler* newspaper—in the near future, so she'd be taking photographs.

"Bread first; white bread, no substitutes—this is never going to be a health-conscious dish—and buttered on the outsides. Spray the pie iron with cooking spray," she said, as the hiss of the spray echoed in the quiet woods around them. "Then one slice of bread, butter side against the iron . . . fill the center with pie filling." She opened a can of cherry pie filling and spooned some on the bread. "Then the other slice on top of it, butter facing up, and clamp the pie iron shut," she said, closing the device and engaging the clamp that held the other long handle firm. "There will be some extra bread . . . let that burn off." She picked up her camera and took a few shots of her concoction.

Rachel reached out. "I'll toast," she said, "while you make another."

"Thanks, Rach!" she said with a grateful look. She could always count on Rachel to step in and help, even when she wasn't feeling her best. Her friend seemed a little off; not depressed exactly, just quiet and more withdrawn than was normal. If there was something wrong, she would suffer in silence, though. Unlike other people—Jaymie glanced at Gabriela and Brandi, pointedly ignoring each other for the moment—she was not about to inflict her personal drama on the others. She'd have to check in with her friend tomorrow, though, when she could grab a moment alone. She put together a blueberry-filling pie iron pie and clamped it shut.

"Can I try?" Courtney asked, reaching out one hand.

"Of course! Watch Rachel, and turn it after about five minutes or so to get the other side toasted."

Melody watched her and smiled. "You're in your element, aren't you?" she murmured to Jaymie.

"I love camping," she said, glancing at the author, then returning to her task, making the next pie. "You know how much I did it as a kid with Dad and Becca."

"But more than that. You like showing people how to do things. You always have."

"Really?" Jaymie paused, head cocked to one side. She thought back to cooking demonstrations she had held back in the day in their rented house, where she was always showing someone the best way to cook scrambled eggs (to not torture them on high heat, but gently, slowly, let them set) or how to use the slow cooker. "I guess that's true." She handed Melody her camera. "Can you take some pics of the pie irons on the fire while I go on with this?"

"Sure. I take a lot of photos for inspiration." She took some pictures of the pie irons on the fire from different angles, then returned to her chair by Jaymie's food prep table. "You know, you should do vlogs, besides your written blog. Or a food podcast!"

"I never considered that." Her long-term goal was to publish a recipe book, but it was taking longer than expected. The one editor she had spoken to said that she needed more exposure, and to gain a following, so she had been working at it with the food column and blog. "Though I have been teaching Jocie a lot of crafts and projects lately. And I did a food demonstration for her class at school!" Maybe that was good practice, though she hadn't done it for that reason.

Melody watched her for a minute, biting her lip.

"What's on your mind?" Jaymie said, glancing up at her friend. It was unlike Melody to stay quiet about anything with her.

"I hope you don't believe that Jocie . . . that is . . . no matter what *anyone* else says," Melody said with a grimace toward Gabriela. "Jocie is your daughter. I've never seen you so happy. And at your wedding Jocie glowed with joy. You are truly her mother, in every sense of the word. You're not replacing her birth mom, but you *are* her mother."

Jaymie smiled and teared up, sniffing. "Thanks, Mel! I know that, but I appreciate you saying it." She cleared her throat and made the third pie iron, back to cherry.

"I think mine's done," Rachel said. She brought over the pie iron and opened it up, letting the pie, steaming hot, slide onto the melamine plate Jaymie held out. She had a sifter ready and dusted the pie with icing sugar, then cut it into wedges and took some photos. The red filling oozed out onto the plate. "I've got paper napkins and plates ready, Rach, if you don't mind doing the honors."

They all ate the pies and were polite about it, though they were scalding hot and a couple were burnt. Lips and tongues were burned and then cooled with iced tea, lemonade and beer. The women, more relaxed now, were yawning and stretching, long silences punctuating conversation that turned to life and love, kids and dating.

"You were going out with that hunky detective guy a few years ago," Brandi said with a glance at Jaymie. "We saw photos of him in your local paper. Lord, why didn't you grab *him* and marry him? I would have. You'd never see me outside of my bedroom after that."

There was polite if nervous laughter. Jaymie thought back to her most recent dating life. She had gone out with a few guys, but Joel was her first serious boyfriend; he moved into the Queensville home with her. It broke her heart when he cheated on her, then ditched her. After that came Daniel, the multimillionaire (probably billionaire by now) who wanted to move too quickly to marriage; she knew all along that it wasn't right with him. Then there was what Brandi referred to, her kinda-sorta flirtation with Zack, a detective. He was hunky, and dream-worthy, and . . . not right for her. They had nothing in common other than the way he showed up in her daydreams as the handsome duke from one of Melody Heath's historical romances.

"You have to find the right guy . . . the right guy for *you*, I mean. Not for the world, not for your friends or family . . . for *you*," Jaymie said. "Jakob is my guy."

Melody sighed. "I wish I'd waited for Mr. Right instead of Mr. Right-for-the-moment."

Jaymie watched her face, the flickering flames shadowing patterns over her cheeks. Melody was not beautiful, like Rachel was, or striking, like Brandi. However, when you looked into her eyes you could sometimes see a whole other level to her, a world behind them.

Did she know her friend as deeply as she thought she did? They talked on the phone occasionally, but Mel asked more questions than she answered. Older than the rest of them by several years, Melody had moved in with them midterm, responding to an ad on a billboard at the university, after a boyfriend she had been living with moved on and she couldn't afford the rent on their apartment anymore. She had been a good roommate, quiet and introverted, seeming to get lost in the bigger personalities of Gabriela, Brandi and the few others who moved in and out with them over the three years. Jaymie and her (and Rachel) got along better than the others, bonding over their love of history and books. "I'm sorry things are bad for you," she said simply.

Melody shrugged and shook her head. "Nothing I can't handle. Anyway, how about the rest of you. Rachel, you were dating someone, weren't you?"

"A nice guy at work, but it fizzled into nothing." She moved restlessly. "Everything kind of seems off to me right now. Mom and Dad have moved back to Jamaica. I visit when I can, but it doesn't feel like home to me, though I got a cute tattoo of a doctorbird . . . it's a swallowtail hummingbird from Jamaica!" She showed them the tattoo in the semi-light of the fire, on her upper thigh.

"Hey, tattoos! I've got a few," Brandi said. "My ankle bracelet is the latest"—she displayed the woven tattoo around her ankle—"and some more I can't show you."

Gabriela smiled. "I got a tattoo; one for my baby Fenix, right over my heart."

"I've never gotten one," Jaymie said.

"Me neither, though I've thought of getting a quill and scroll tattoo on my wrist," Melody said. "That would be cool."

"Anyway, work is okay, I guess. Good money," Rachel continued. "I hate my apartment. My cat died last year and I miss him, but I don't know if I should adopt another. No guy sparks me . . . you know?" she said. "Not like the way Jakob did for you." She rolled her eyes. "I'm whining, I know. Nothing is actually wrong, but nothing is right, either, you know?"

Jaymie nodded. "I get you, Rach. I've been there." So *that* was what was behind her friend's vague sense of unhappiness; it was life angst, the feeling of not being sure of what you're doing or how you're going. "For a long time I kept moving forward, lots of small jobs, but nothing I was crazy about. Then Joel dumped me. To make myself feel better I jumped into Grandma Leighton's old cookbooks and collecting old kitchen stuff, and . . . then I met Jakob—"

"And dead bodies piled up in Queensville," Melody muttered with a side-glance and smile.

" — and voilà!" Jaymie finished, with a laugh and look at Melody. "Happy as a clam now. *Despite* the dead bodies. You have to figure out what you need to make you happy and grab it with both hands." She looked over to Gabriela. "At least *you're* happy, right, hon? You've got it all."

She looked up with a smile. "I am. Logan is wonderful — "

"He's a bore," Brandi said.

"And I love being a mom," Gabriela said, making a face at Brandi. "In fact, it's hard being away from them."

"Men are effing users and creeps," Brandi said with a belligerent tone. She shot an odd look at Gabriela, maybe waiting for her to disagree, as Courtney nodded in agreement. "In fact, guys are such users, why shouldn't women play their own game back at them?"

There was silence for a moment, then Melody said in a mild tone, "You mean women should be users and creeps too?"

"Why not?" Brandi, her sharp bone structure and high cheekbones cast in sharp relief by the firelight, looked around the circle.

"You should know. You use guys and discard them like dirty socks," Gabriela said harshly. "Look at what you did to poor Terry."

"Poor Terry?" Brandi said. "What do *you* know about poor Terry?" She leveled a steady look at their friend, then looked away. "He had his chance and he blew it," she muttered, tears clogging her voice. "Marriage is dull anyway."

"But you're dating a lot?" Jaymie said, thinking of the sexy pic and text she had seen on her friend's phone. "All my other girlfriends say it's hard to meet guys. How do you do it?"

"Hah! She's the queen of online dating," Gabriela said, confirming Jaymie's guess. "She meets guys on dating apps and all kinds of social media."

"Dating apps, gaming apps, cheating apps . . . and why not? I'm hot, young, free and single, ready to mingle."

"And you have three kids at home!" Gabriela said.

"Who have everything they need or want!" Brandi yelled back at her. "You have to get down off your high horse. We're not all Miss Perfect Suzy Homemaker, not even Jaymie! *You* sure aren't, no matter how much you pretend."

Jaymie sighed and looked up the dark hill behind their property.

She was glad the Redmonds weren't home, but if Brandi got too loud, the cottagers on either side of her might complain. She heard plenty when the Leightons had renters who had loud parties and she didn't want to be accused of having one herself. Time to change the subject. "Anyway, so . . . we'll drive up to Canada tomorrow, right? And hit the Bend?"

"Woo-hoo!" Brandi said, punching the air with one fist. "Damn straight."

"What's the Bend?" Courtney asked.

"Grand Bend. It's a resort town on the Canadian side of Lake Huron. It's our old hangout when we all went to Western U. I hope you don't mind, guys," she said to the others, "but I've invited a few of my Queensville friends to join us. Just for the day, though. You met them at the wedding: Bernie and Heidi, and my best Queensville friend, Valetta."

"The more the merrier," Rachel said with a smile, touching Jaymie's arm.

"*Much* merrier, I hope," Melody said. "Can't get much unmerrier, can we?"

☙ Six ☙

AFTER PUTTING OUT THE FIRE and tidying up the grove, Jaymie scrubbed the pie irons clean, hung them out to dry on a nail on a pine tree near the edge of her property, and followed her friends into the cottage. And so, to bed. There was a traffic jam in the one bathroom, making for laughing remarks about how while camping, at least, there was one large public washroom they could all fit into.

Jaymie, Melody and Rachel were in one room, while Brandi, Courtney and Gabriela had taken the room with the two double beds. They were about to settle down for the night when Brandi, who had not yet changed into night attire, decided she wanted to take the pullout sofa bed in the living room. She liked to sprawl, to "starfish," as she called it. She dumped her pillow and pajamas on the pullout and said, with studied nonchalance, "I'm going for a walk now that it's cooler. I'll be back. Leave the door unlatched, will you, Jaymie?"

"Sure." Jaymie watched her stroll out the front door, lips pursed, thinking how odd it was for her lazy friend to take to walking in the middle of the night. *Oh well,* she thought, *none of my business.*

It was unexpectedly odd sleeping in a room with her old bunkies; at least back when they shared a house most of them had their own rooms, except for a couple who cut costs by sharing. What she discovered, as she tried to sleep, was that Rachel chuckled while snoozing, and Melody—in the top bunk—turned over and over and over either in her sleep or trying to sleep. Jaymie, who had taken the bottom bunk, was repeatedly shaken out of her doze by the shuddering of the bed frame. *Note to self,* she thought: see what she could do about tightening up the bunk bed frame for future guests.

But finally she slept. Some time later, with the cottage silent, Hoppy jumped up on Jaymie—she had taken the bottom bunk knowing that would happen—and licked her face, whining. "Hoppy, come on," she whispered, not wanting to wake up Rachel and Melody. "Not now." But the little dog had to piddle; he danced around beside the bed, humming an insistent whimper. He wasn't used to so many strangers, staying up late, and staying out at the cottage without family. She rolled out of bed and stole through the dark to the living room, hoping she didn't wake up Brandi. But as she tiptoed past the pullout, it looked odd . . . she crept close. It was exactly the same as she had left it, hours before. No Brandi.

Maybe she was outside on the deck.

But no, no Brandi there, either, nor anywhere else that Jaymie could see. Hoppy skittered off to piddle as she stood on the back deck watching the moon up in the sky. It was a lovely night. That same nighthawk circled and cried, and something small rustled in the bushes. She hoped Hoppy wouldn't go after it; God forbid it was a skunk. Crickets silenced as Hoppy nosed into the clumps of grass, but the peeper frogs kept up their incessant chirp. "Hoppy!" she whispered, sleepily wrapping her arms around herself. "Come on, sweetie, bedtime." Her little dog came back and she returned to bed, with Hoppy curled up at her feet, falling asleep with a doggie sigh of contentment.

Where would Brandi have gone, Jaymie wondered, on her walk? Even walking a circuit of the whole American side of the island wouldn't have taken so long. Brandi, like the circling bird, always was a nighthawk. Uneasy, she got back up and crept into the other bedroom. She approached Courtney and touched her shoulder. "Court," she whispered, hoping she didn't awaken Gabriela. "Courtney, Brandi's not in her bed. She wasn't too drunk, was she? Should I be worried?"

Courtney propped herself up on one elbow, blinking and rubbing her eyes. The tanned oval of her face was barely visible in the nightlight that illuminated the bathroom. "Don't worry about her, Jaymie," she whispered, knuckling her eyes. "She didn't want to make a fuss, but she was going to go to some bar on the mainland and check it out. She . . . she does bar reviews online and said she was going to do it."

"Oh. Okay. She could have told me. She does know that the ferry stops at eleven, right? How is she planning to get back here?"

Courtney shrugged and laid back down.

"I'm not her jailer," Jaymie muttered and headed back to bed.

• • •

THE NEXT MORNING DAWNED LOVELY, hot, a real August stunner, with cicadas buzzing at seven. Jaymie was first up. At some point in the night Brandi did come home and was sleeping, sprawled out, wearing a T-shirt and underwear. But they couldn't spend all day sleeping. "Who wants aebleskivers?" Jaymie said, loudly banging around in the kitchen.

"Whatchamacallits?" Rachel said, joining her and yawning.

"There's coffee there, Rach, in the pot," Jaymie said, pointing to the drip coffee maker. "Gabriela, can you or someone make sure Brandi is up? And Courtney?"

Brandi grumbled, but did haul herself out of the pullout. Mugs in hand, all were perched at the counter and table as Jaymie described aebleskivers. "They're like Danish donuts, kinda sorta, or little round pancakes, and they're made in this pan," she said, holding up a cast iron pan that had seven round indentations. She whipped up the batter and tried her hand at them on the stove. As each one fried golden she turned it over with tongs — it was said that the Danes used knitting needles to turn them — and finished them off, popping them onto small plates for her guests to try; each person got a couple. They were good, served with jam and syrup.

"Now . . . let's get moving!" Jaymie said, scrubbing the pan with plain hot water, then wiping it out with a clean cloth. "We're going to go to *Canada*!" She set the cast iron pan outside on the deck to dry completely, and hurried her friends along.

As she packed a beach bag with her favorite towel, a birthday gift from Valetta with a depiction of Hoppy on it, she shared the mirror for a moment with Brandi, who was carefully lining her eyes with black liquid liner. "I don't know how you do that," Jaymie said, grabbing her UV protector lip balm and tossing it into her bag.

"Practice."

"Say, Bran, what time did you get in last night?"

"About two," she said. "Why?"

"Oh, I got up to let Hoppy out to piddle, but when I saw you were still gone, I was worried. I asked Courtney, and she told me you had gone to a bar on the mainland." She watched her friend's face in the mirror. "How did you get back to the island?"

"By ferry, of course," Brandi said.

Jaymie didn't say anything about her friend's lie, but when she turned it was to catch Courtney trying to get Brandi's attention, her cheeks red. When Jaymie saw her, she turned away swiftly. Her feelings were a little hurt, but she was not going to dwell on it. Whatever Brandi had done, wherever she had gone—on the island, most likely, or she would have known the ferry did not run late at night—it was her own business.

"We'd better get a move on," Jaymie said as she checked her phone. Val had texted to say she and the others were on their way. Jaymie made sure she had taken care of everything. She got down on the floor and cuddled her little dog. "I have to go away all day, sweetie," she murmured, nuzzling the pooch. She had considered taking Hoppy to Canada with them, but Grand Bend beach was not open to dogs other than early morning and late evening; it wouldn't be fair to any of them to restrict their day. She put down multiple pee pads, made sure the air conditioner was on and working, and left enough food, water, treats and toys so that he would be all right for the ten hours or so they would be gone.

"Let's go so I can lock up!"

They walked down to the ferry dock, arriving as it pulled up. Valetta had, as she suggested, borrowed a passenger van from a friend. She brought it over on the ferry, accompanied by Heidi and Bernie. "Come on, folks," she said, motioning to them all. "We have to load up and get this van back on the ferry to ride over to Johnsonville, where we begin our journey into Canada!"

Jaymie reintroduced Val, Bernie and Heidi to her university pals, and to Courtney. After some questioning looks and snide remarks from Brandi toward a sweetly oblivious Heidi, who wore an itty-bitty bikini top and short shorts, they all piled into the van with beach bags, coolers, suntan lotion, a change of clothes (for after swimming, if anyone did so), and much more. They pulled back onto the ferry, were taken to the Canadian side of the river and disembarked at the Johnsonville CBSA, Canadian Border Services, then went through customs, where they declared that the intention of their visit was to get thoroughly burned and water-drenched by dinner. Brandi added *"to get wasted"* and flirted with the Canadian border guard; he stoically nodded, and they were off. From there it was north to Sarnia, then east on the 402 to Strathroy, then north again on Highway 81 all the way into Grand Bend.

It was a longish drive, and she worried that no one was as excited as she was. But Melody, at least, was happily in her element;

she sat in the back row of three seats between Bernie and Heidi, grilling them on their lives. Jaymie heard bits and pieces of conversation float forward . . . *What kind of gun training did you take?* to Bernie, and *Your family bought real estate in the early nineteen-hundreds in New York City? How much land? Where?* of Heidi.

Brandi groused, "Don't you ever stop working, Mel?" she shot over her shoulder, but the writer ignored her. "Mel . . . hey, *Mel!*" Brandi said. "Did you know your weirdo husband friended me on social media?"

There was silence for a long minute, nothing but the sound of the highway asphalt under the van and the growl of the tires on rumble strips as they approached a crossroads, then Mel, her voice filled with tension, asked, "You didn't accept his friend request, did you?"

Brandi chuckled. "Of *course* I did." She threw a mischievous grin over her shoulder and winked. "Don't I always say, the more the merrier?"

There were a few moments of silence after that, though Mel may have grumbled under her breath that even *she* hadn't accepted her husband's friend request. Brandi leaned her head against the window wearily, staring down at her phone and flipping through messages.

Rachel, always reliable, was the one who seemed wholly on Jaymie's wavelength. She reached over, clutched Jaymie's arm and bounced in her seat. "I'm excited to see the Bend after all these years!"

They shared a look; Jaymie knew then that at least Rachel, and *maybe* Melody, were happy to see their old stomping grounds. Gabriela and Brandi, ahead of them, were silent, but it appeared that Valetta, in the driver's seat, and Courtney, in the passenger's seat, were chatting amiably enough.

"What do you want to do first?" Rachel asked of them all, twisting in her seat, trying to get the conversation started. "Shop? Beach? Lunch? All three?"

"I want a drink," Brandi said, yawning. She pocketed her cell phone, leaned on the armrest and appeared to doze through much of the drive, after grumbling about being woken up at the crack of dawn.

It was on the tip of Jaymie's tongue to say that if Brandi hadn't been out most of the night she wouldn't be so tired. She had thought the point of the vacation was to spend time together, to relive their youth and refresh their old bonds. But to be fair — and she did *try* to be fair — just because that was her idea didn't mean they all felt the same. Her friend was a free woman, and this was her vacation. She could do whatever she wanted. Jaymie didn't want her to feel like she was being monitored.

Excitement welled up in Jaymie as they got to the intersection of highways 81 and 21, which was the north-south highway that followed the shore of Lake Huron past Pinery Provincial Park and finally through Grand Bend. It took her back even further than her school days to when she was a kid and her dad would take her camping to the Pinery. There was a smell and a feel that was unforgettable, of lake and sand, pine and poplar. It was somehow different from her cottage on the St. Clair River.

"Where do you want to park?" Jaymie said as they entered Grand Bend, a bustling town of two thousand that could easily swell to fifty thousand or more on a weekend in the summer.

"I looked it up online and there's a little pay-and-display parking area along Main Street where we can leave the van," Valetta said, checking in the rearview mirror. "I figured we'd mostly be walking, right? Shopping? Eating, etcetera? So . . . that's what we'll do."

They found a space, fortunately; it was already filling up. They were in the middle of a hot spell. Canadians and Americans in droves were there for the day, ready to play beach volleyball, swim, canoodle and drink their faces off. Grand Bend was good for all of that and more, a perfect venue for families and seniors all day, and students and young people all evening. They all hopped out of the van and retrieved their bags.

"I've got lunch and snacks in a cooler in the back," Jaymie said, hiking her bag on her shoulder and donning her sunhat and sunglasses. "But if anyone would prefer a restaurant, that's okay too. There's a great one called Sanders on the Beach . . . remember, guys?"

"So, what first?" Rachel repeated, turning in a full circle and hopping in excitement, her blue-tipped hair jammed under a sun visor and big gold sunglasses resting on peach-blushed cheeks.

"We're along for the ride," Bernie said, arm in arm with Heidi. "We'll go with the crowd, wherever you all go!"

"Let's walk," Valetta said. She snapped her sunglass add-ons on her glasses. "I've never been here before."

"Me neither. I'd like to see the town," Courtney, dressed in conservative Bermuda shorts and a golf shirt, agreed.

They wandered down Main Street, drawn by the view of a blue and sparkling Lake Huron at the end, but it was a longer walk than anticipated. Brandi lagged behind complaining her feet hurt and about the parking space Val had chosen; Courtney stayed with her, of course. Valetta, Heidi, Bernie, Rachel and Gabriela walked briskly on ahead as Jaymie and Melody sauntered, trying to bridge the lengthening gap between the two groups.

"Why do I have a feeling this is going to be a disaster," Jaymie fretted, looking behind at Brandi, who had her head together with Courtney. "I feel like Brandi is up to something." She told Melody about her midnight discovery that Brandi had left the cottage.

"You've done your best to plan a nice day, Jaymie. Stop worrying. You can't force people to enjoy themselves."

"I wish I could think that way. Brandi's bad enough—I'd forgotten how she can be difficult; I don't think she was on the last camping trip with us, so it's been several years—but there is something going on with Gabriela. Haven't you noticed? She hasn't been . . . *normal* since she arrived. She's worried and moody and . . . I don't know, *worried*. That's all I can say."

Jaymie and Mel joined Valetta and the rest on the beach. "This is nice," Val said, turning to her friend with a smile. She had dressed in sensible shorts and a golf shirt, with Vionic orthopaedic sandals on her feet, the only kind she could wear for her foot problems. "I'm glad you invited me along, though I feel like the den mother." She pushed her glasses up on her nose. "I'm not exactly the Grand Bend age, it seems like." At fifty, she was about fifteen years older than everyone but Melody, who was somewhere in between.

Jaymie took her arm. "My friend, there *is* no Grand Bend age." She pointed to a group of seniors sitting in low umbrella-covered chairs playing euchre, and to tiny toddlers digging sand castles, throwing toys and racing after seagulls followed by frantic moms and dads.

"Tell *them* that," Val said, pointing to some shirtless guys roaming the beach, pausing to eye Heidi, Rachel and Bernie with hope in their eyes.

"Grand Bend welcomes *everyone!*" Jaymie exclaimed, kicking off her flip-flops, raising her hands high in the air, turning in a full circle and running down to the waterside laughing the whole way.

They had brought a Frisbee and badminton set, and took turns playing. Heidi, Bernie and Rachel walked down the beach, while Gabriela sat playing on her phone and moping. Mel and Val sat at the water's edge digging their toes in the wet sand and chatting with Jaymie as she made drippy castles. Brandi and Courtney never joined them. There was no way they could get lost, so the general consensus was that they had stopped at a restaurant or bar. The friends gathered back together, got their feet wet in the lake, splashed about in the shallow water, people-watched for a while, then, as they packed up to walk back into the village, Jaymie made a bit of a detour and discovered that Sanders on the Beach, a lovely restaurant she had adored, was gone.

They strolled up from the beach to Main Street in search of food. There were bikini shops, where Heidi bought several bathing suits, and they stopped in the sweet shop, where Jaymie bought watermelon-flavored taffy for Jocie. She'd have to bring her daughter here someday, to tell her about being a kid and shopping here with her mom and big sister. A powerful tug of longing for Jocie and Jakob clenched her heart and stomach, but she fought it. Gabriela, though, was having more trouble. She dissolved in tears in the sweet shop as she bought a mix of candies for her little girl.

"I won't be surprised if Gabriela goes home early," Jaymie whispered to Valetta as her friend tried on a hat in a beach shop.

"If she does, please don't let it worry you," Val said, giving her friend a side hug. "You're doing all you can. You can't *make* people have fun."

"That's basically what Mel said," Jaymie said. Her writer friend was lingering near the door, staring out with a clouded expression. "I don't know what's got into *her* today. She *was* fine, and now she's turned off, like a light switch."

"Each person has their thing," Val said, eyeing herself in a mirror. "I don't think I'll get this. It looks goofy on me. I'll never be Heidi, who can put on anything and look stunning."

"Me neither, my friend. It's a good thing she's so sweet-natured, or I'd have to dislike her," Jaymie said. She frowned and shook her head. "I didn't mean that. I'm trying to teach Jocie not to judge people based on their looks, and not to be hard on myself for my own averageness, but I fall into it myself sometimes. I did that when I first knew about Heidi and Joel; I assumed because she is beautiful and slim that she was a snob and shallow, but she's neither."

Together, the group passed by a bar, loud music and drunken young people spilling out of the wide-open doors onto the sidewalk in front. Above the music, though, Jaymie heard a familiar laugh. "Aha! I think I found Brandi," she said to the group. "Let's check it out."

And indeed Brandi and Courtney sat at a large table with a group of guys. Brandi was clearly having fun, doing shots, a high five for each, but Courtney looked miserable. She perked up and waved to them as they approached.

"Figures," Gabriela said with a sniff, dragging behind. "She *would* find the one place to get drunk."

"Oh, there is more than one place to get drunk in Grand Bend," Melody said. "Don't you remember? We all had our moments."

"I never did," Gabriela said stiffly.

Melody stared at her. "Memory fades with time, I suppose."

"Still, she's a wife and mother. You'd think she could hold it together for one day," Gabriela snapped crossly. She took out a candy and chewed on it, tossing the wrapper on the floor as they approached their friend.

They made a deal with Brandi: they'd sit and have one drink with her if she'd come with them when they were done. Jaymie ordered an iced tea and checked her phone, sighing loudly in exasperation. Brandi had been doing social media, posting pictures and tagging new (younger) friends, and it must look to the rest of the world as if their day at Grand Bend was one long drinking game.

Rachel whispered to Jaymie that she, Bernie and Heidi were going to walk back down to the beach and grab some French fries along the way. Jaymie nodded and squeezed her friend's hand, happy that Rach and her two newer friends had bonded. Melody kept wandering to the entrance of the bar, which was wide open to the street. She looked up and down, and frowned, then returned.

"What are you looking for?" Jaymie asked under cover of the music, which was a loud EDM track.

"Nothing. Nothing at all." She drifted back into the shadows, but still glared out the door.

❦ Seven ❦

THEY FINALLY MANAGED to pry Brandi from the bar and strolled back down Main Street. They lingered in Archie's Surf Shop. Jaymie bought a cute sleeveless top for herself, a gray hooded sweatshirt for the fall for Jakob with *Grand Bend* emblazoned on it, and a couple of stuffy toys for Jocie. They stowed their purchases in the van, then walked down to the beach again with umbrellas and towels. They spent a few hours there in the sun, talking and relaxing, some with books and some, like Gabriela and Brandi, on their phones.

Gabriela's husband had not texted or called her back yet, and she was fretting. "Something's wrong," she said, gnawing on her fingernail as she stared at the phone on her lap, shielding the screen from the sun with her free hand.

"Is there anyone you can call to find out?" Jaymie asked.

"His mom, maybe, or his sister." She ripped the fingernail off with her teeth and spat it into the sand.

"His sister?" Jaymie dug in her bag and pulled out a nail clipper, handing it to her friend to tidy up the ragged edge.

"Tiffany, my sister-in-law," Gabriela said, snipping the nail's edge. "She and Logan are close."

"Call her," Jaymie urged, accepting the nail clipper back and tossing it in her bag. "Tell her what's upsetting you."

Gabriela nodded, her expression clearing a bit. "I'll do it once we get back this evening. If I haven't heard from Logan by then I'll message Tiff."

"I'm going to get a soda," Brandi said, standing and brushing the sand off her behind.

"I'll go with you," Courtney said, jumping up.

"No, stay here!" Brandi said irritably, picking up her sandals. "I'll be right back. Jeez, you'd think I couldn't have two minutes to myself." She stomped off like a teen in a bad mood.

"Someday she has to grow up," Melody said gloomily, her gaze shifting back and forth along the beach.

Jaymie eyed her author friend. Something had happened, but Mel wasn't talking about it. Maybe if she left it alone her friend would confide in her.

Of course Brandi never came back. Finally, as the sun began its

55

descent across the lake, they had idled as much as they could. "I guess we ought to round up our things and set out to look for Brandi."

"Or leave her behind," Gabriela sniffed.

"Some of us can take the stuff back to the van and wait there, if you'd like," Valetta said, eyeing Jaymie. "That way we won't all be trudging along Main Street with beach towels and blankets and the cooler and umbrellas."

Jaymie nodded. "Why don't all of you go and I'll find Brandi?"

"We can't leave you to do that all alone," Melody objected.

"I'll go with you," Courtney said. "I think I have the best chance of prying her away from the dudes."

Nodding, Jaymie agreed. "That sounds like a plan."

"I'm going with you," Melody said. "You might need help."

They parted ways and the others crossed the street, heading toward the parkette, pulling the cooler on wheels and laden with all of the towels and other beachy items. Jaymie, Courtney and Mel carried their sandals up from the beach to the road and paused to dust the sticky sand off their feet and put their footwear back on, then trudged along the sidewalk, stopping to gaze into bars. Courtney volunteered to ford the crowd at one to make sure Brandi wasn't in the depths, drinking. Jaymie and Mel stood on the sidewalk.

"It's nice of Courtney to take care of Brandi like that. It was rude of Bran to abandon her friend with virtual strangers. I don't know why Courtney is her friend. She seems like a nice girl, and Brandi's been a witch to her all day."

"Can't you guess why Courtney is so caring of Brandi?" Melody said with a quizzical side smile.

Jaymie stared into her eyes and caught on. "Do you think she feels *that* way about Brandi? I never got that idea."

Melody shrugged. "It seems like it to me. Maybe I can't see any other explanation for why any woman would put up with so much crap. I could be wrong."

"If you're right, Brandi doesn't deserve her," Jaymie groused.

Courtney came out and shook her head, and they continued. As they strolled they found out more about the woman. She was older than Brandi. They had met at a bar and become fast friends, but she admitted they fought often. She was a hospital equipment salesperson and single, though she had been married. She was a smoker and drinker, and considered Brandi to be the sister she never had.

As they passed by one place they had already checked, though they hadn't gone inside, they heard voices raised in an argument. "*That's* Brandi!" Courtney said and led the way inside.

Brandi was indeed in the dim interior, and she was face-to-face arguing with a guy Jaymie knew slightly; it was Brandi's ex-husband, Terry. Both were red-faced and furious, arguing at the top of their lungs as a bouncer, muscles straining the sleeves of a bar T-shirt, came toward them. "Take it outside, folks!" he said, clutching both of their shoulders. "This is a fun place. No fighting allowed."

Terry took a swing, missed, and the bouncer easily doubled his arm behind his back and marched him outside, followed by Brandi, Courtney, Jaymie and Melody.

Jaymie's face was hot with embarrassment as they emerged, watched by the barflies; they were all too old to be thrown out of a bar. But Terry wasn't done, nor was Brandi. Once on the sidewalk, with the bouncer retreating, the two kept fighting about his behavior (stalkerish) and her behavior (childish), calling each other names.

Terry, a balding, slightly overweight fellow in belted shorts and a golf course T-shirt, was red-faced and spittle foamed at the corners of his mouth. He called her a string of terrible names, then said, jabbing his finger in her face, "You're fooling around with guys, getting drunk all day, and left me with three kids to look after. What kind of a mother are you?"

"The kind who needs a vacation," she shrieked. "What the frick are you *doing* here? I'm gonna get a restraining order against you the minute we get home."

"Go ahead. Then I'll tell the court how you dump the kids on me every chance you get and go out drinking with your bony-butt friend," he said, flipping one hand at Courtney. "You've been gone one day and you're sleeping with some random dude. Don't try to deny it, Brandi! I know you."

"Get out of here," Brandi said, her cheeks flaming and tears streaming down her face. She was tipsy, but not so drunk that she couldn't walk, and she followed Jaymie and the other two along the sidewalk. "Leave me alone, Terry! There's a reason I'm divorcing you, and you *know* what it is!"

"Go, leave," he yelled. At least he didn't follow them as the group of women retreated toward the parkette. "Go ahead and bed every guy you find," he shouted. "But don't come home to me with some new disease of the month."

On their way to the van Brandi broke down weeping and Courtney held her arm close to her and tugged her along, murmuring to her the whole time. Jaymie and Melody exchanged looks but stayed silent. They reached the van, where the others were all packed and ready to go.

"Let's go home," Jaymie said, exhausted and near tears herself. The plan had been to stop along the way for ice cream, but stopping anywhere seemed like a bad idea. "Next time we won't go to the Bend, we'll go to Bayfield," she muttered, naming the town some miles north that was more quiet restaurants and jewelry stores than bars and surf shops.

After a day of sun, sand, booze and drama, the car filled with the aroma of tuna fish sandwiches and suntan oil, weariness led to quiet. They returned to Johnsonville and caught the ferry over to the island, cleared customs, then Heidi and Bernie hugged Jaymie, but stayed on the ferry.

"I have to go to work tomorrow," Bernie said, hugging her hard. "Or I'd hang out longer."

"I'm sorry, Bernie."

"For what?"

"For . . . for . . ." Jaymie flapped her hand at Brandi, who was slumped on the park bench by the dock in the twilight, crying. "For *all* of this; the drunkenness, the drama, the tears, the . . . the *drama!*"

Bernie snickered and Heidi laughed. "This is nothing," Bernie said. "Heidi and I had fun. We've never been to Grand Bend. We enjoyed it! It reminded me of this little surf town in Cali that I used to go to, to visit a guy I was dating. Stop worrying. We *love* your friend Rachel! She is *such* a sweetheart."

"I know, isn't she? You didn't get to know Melody, though; she's awesome too."

Heidi shivered and looked over at the author, who was staring off into the sunset frowning. "Melody seems like she's . . . like she's trying to figure you out when you talk to her," she whispered, leaning in toward Jaymie. "Don't get me wrong, I like her, but . . . she asks a *lot* of questions." Eyes wide, she said, "I told her the story about Grandpa Lockland and how he died and the big inheritance, and she asked me, did anyone think it was murder! I thought you said she was a *romance* writer! I pictured someone . . . someone *fluffier!*"

Jaymie laughed, her mood brightened by talking to her Queensville friends. "Melody is interested in everything. You cannot bore her, and her mind works in weird ways." She hugged and released them both as the ferry captain indicated he wanted to pull away. "I wish you could stay, but I understand."

Val, who had left the van on the ferry to take across to Queensville, trotted over to Jaymie and squeezed her arm consolingly. "Hey, kiddo, you look stressed. Are you okay?"

"I guess," she said, sighing heavily. "Today was a nightmare, no matter what Heidi and Bernie say." She looked over her shoulder, to Brandi, Rachel, Gabriela and Courtney, sunburns glowing golden red in the sunset light. They awaited her to head back to the cottage. "And I'm stuck with them."

Val hugged her, then looked into her eyes, her own filled with concern behind her heavy glasses. "I could take the van back, go check on Denver, and come back out to spend the night. Would you like that?"

Jaymie's heart swelled with love. "Would you do that? *Really?* That would be great, Val! If you like, we could spend the night in the new trailer. I haven't been able to do that yet!"

"I'd love that. Let me go home, take care of Denver, get my PJs, and I'll be back in a couple of hours."

• • •

HOPPY WAS, OF COURSE, overjoyed to see Jaymie. But he had to go piddle so badly he didn't stop to greet her. He trotted right out, down the deck and to his favorite spot in the bushes. Home at last, Jaymie switched to dinner mode; it was late, and because of the drama they had not stopped at a restaurant as she had thought they might. She was hungry, but didn't want to suggest a restaurant, not after the tiring day they had endured. She stared into the fridge and got an idea, assembling ingredients: new potatoes, sweet onions, baby carrots.

"You know, you don't have to do all the cooking, Jaymie," Rachel said, standing beside her in the kitchen. "Tell me what you're making and I'll help!" She nabbed a Tansy butter tart from the baker's box on the counter. "I'm *starving*!" she said, then bit into the tart. Her brows went up, her eyes widened and she moaned. "Oh, my goodness, sweet baby Jesus! This is *delicious*!" A dribble of filling leaked out of the side of her mouth and she licked it up. "Wow, you said these were good," she said, "but this is marvelous!"

"And those are the stale ones! Wait 'til you taste them fresh."

"Girlfriend, I'm there." She gobbled down the rest and rinsed off her gooey hands. "I'll go tomorrow and nab a dozen. Now, I've had enough to sustain me, how can I help?"

Jaymie slid a glance over at her friend; Rachel, always dependable, always sweet, always ready to help. But— "Since when do *you* cook?" she asked. "At school your idea of a meal was a block of ramen in the microwave. When you wanted to gourmet it up you added chopped scallions."

"I'll have you know I've gotten pretty good in the last few years. I go to visit Mom and Daddy in Jamaica and visit my grammy. She's teaching me. I got interested and now it's my main hobby. I will make you a jerk chicken dish that will make you *weep* with joy, girl." She had copied her mother's Jamaican accent for the last sentence.

Jaymie laughed. "You're on! We'll go grocery shopping one day and you can make it for me."

"You should *know* all this. Don't you ever check social media? I'm *always* posting photos of my food."

Jaymie set down the package of chicken breasts she got out of the fridge, leaned against the counter and stared at her friend. "Those were meals *you* cooked? I thought they were restaurant meals!" They laughed together. "Okay, so . . . I'm doing what are called Hobo Packets. You take whatever meat you want and put it in a heavy foil packet with potatoes and veggies and some seasonings . . . like this," she said, showing on her tablet a recipe she had found on Pinterest. Not much of a recipe, just a method that you tailored to your own tastes.

"Ooh, that looks *good*. I've done something similar in the oven. I can help. I know what we like and don't." After that Rachel took over at the kitchen counter, slicing potatoes and carrots and thick chunks of zucchini, so abundant local gardeners were giving away club-sized monstrosities by August. Jaymie left her to it. She descended to the firepit, balled up some paper, poked some fire-starter cubes into the paper folds, then crisscrossed kindling over it. She finished by propping some long sticks in a pyramid, then, flicking the barbecue lighter, she touched the tiny flame to the paper and fire starter.

The flame caught, and she blew gently as a breeze danced in the trees overhead and Hoppy sniffed at the rock garden slope. She took in a deep breath and glanced around at her tiny vintage trailer and the patio area. It wasn't quite camping, but it was close. The fire needed to get good and hot and burn down to coals to cook properly, so she added more wood, and then layered on some charcoal briquettes.

Rachel came out at one point and wandered in the rockery, plucking things here and there, then returned to the cottage. As the sun set, the others, who had been changing their clothes, tidying themselves up and rearranging their luggage, wandered down to the fire to sit and stare and yawn. Wine was opened, tequila was poured. They talked in soft tones. Jaymie did her best to bring them together in conversation. She asked a bunch of questions. Brandi loved her kids, but hated the job she had recently quit. She was hoping to get into an aesthetician course in her town. Courtney, who sat beside her, nodded and smiled, batting her eyelashes in the vivid gold sunset light that found a spot to peek between the cottages and pines; Brandi had apparently done eyelash extensions for her.

"Who knew that was a thing?" Jaymie said. "I've never heard of eyelash extensions before!"

"*You*, my dear, don't need them," Brandi said, examining her lashes closely. "You've always had the most gorgeous lashes. Your eyes and hair have always been your best features."

"My husband loves my hair long," Jaymie said.

"And who wouldn't?" Brandi said, lifting Jaymie's ponytail, which was heavy and long. "Your hair is naturally gorgeous. Let me French braid it for you one day."

Jaymie leaned down and hugged her; this was the Brandi she remembered, the one who would spend hours helping her friends get ready for special occasions, and who had a knack for making everyone feel beautiful.

Gabriela, wrapped in a red shawl she had crocheted for herself, was excited about an addition she and Logan were planning on the house, and maybe an addition to their family. She was hoping— trying, she said, with a smile—to get pregnant again. "You should have a baby, Jaymie! You'd make such an *awesome* mother!"

"I *am* a mother," Jaymie replied gently. "I'm a *good* mother."

"No, but I mean of your own baby, you know . . . a child of your *own*."

Jaymie took a deep breath and moved over closer to her author friend. Gabriela's insistence on viewing Jocie as not Jaymie's child was upsetting, but she chose to keep the peace for now. The day had been dramatic enough. She stirred the fire; the coals were almost ready. She took a low stool by Melody, but her friend was the only one who didn't talk. She stared gloomily into the fire and glanced around uneasily, jumping at rustling in the bushes and odd noises. Jaymie frowned; her friend was still moodier than usual, and seemed anxious.

"Are you okay, Mel?" Jaymie murmured as Courtney, Brandi and Gabriela chatted.

"Yeah, I'm . . . I'm all right. I thought I saw Andrew in Grand Bend, that's all."

"Andrew? Your husband? Why would *he* be there?"

"I don't know. But why would he friend Brandi online? That's what I can't figure out. The trouble is, she posts so much you can tell where we are and where we've been."

Rachel yelled out the back door, "Jaymie, can I use these peppers in the fridge?"

"Use whatever you find!" she called back. She tried to get Melody to talk more, but she shook her head.

Rachel carried out a full tray of the neatly folded and sealed packets, and Jaymie, using tongs, nestled them in the bed of coals she had created. The packets sizzled on the coals, and Jaymie made a pot of tea from a blackened kettle she had always used on the fire. Valetta joined them, duffle bag in hand, right then. Jaymie jumped up and hugged her friend. "We'll sleep in the new trailer tonight," Jaymie said, giving her friend the tour. "You gals don't mind, do you, Val staying out here tonight?" she asked. "You can all have a turn sleeping in the trailer, if you'd like."

"Not me! No offense, Jaymie, but I'll take a cottage over camping any day," Brandi said. "I've slept on the ground too many times. And Val's a welcome addition," she added. "Better company than some people." She shot a hostile look at Gabriela.

Her group of friends was low-key. Melody, cup of tea in hand, still stared into the fire, her gaze clouded. Gabriela was twitchy and anxious, near tears at times, brooding at others. Brandi lay back in a recliner lawn chair and snored, while Courtney sat beside her nursing a bottle of Coors and smoking her Capri Magentas.

Jaymie shrugged, sighed, and opened the door to the trailer. It was a snug fit, but there was the sofa that pulled out to be a double bed, and the dining table that flattened down, and the cushions from the seats that laid out to make another double bed. She had worked hard to get rid of the musty odor of the trailer from its years in storage.

"You've done a great job!" Valetta said, putting her duffle bag down on the sofa and looking around. The interior was all shades of turquoise and red, even down to a turquoise enameled teapot, with turquoise and red melamine Boontonware teacups and mugs. "I saw it in the planning stages, but you've done a great job!"

"Jocie is excited about it. She was disappointed we didn't get to spend a night in it before she and Jakob went off to Poland, but I said we'd have a girls' weekend adventure here in the fall, when the cottage is closed up and before we winterize the trailer."

"How are they doing?" Val said, sitting down with a happy sigh. Hoppy scratched at the screen door and Jaymie let him in. He begged to be let up, and Valetta took him onto her lap. He sniffed her all over, detecting Denver's scent.

"Good," Jaymie said, sitting down at the dinette table and turning on the little sconce light above it, set in the bulkhead that held additional storage. "Jakob sent me pictures today. Jocie is having a ball getting to know cousins, grandparents and great-grandparents. It's going to be hard to settle her back down when school starts, I think, after this."

"She's a good kid, and she loves school."

"You're right. I can't wait to see them. It already feels like forever, and it's only been a few days."

They returned to the fire. The hobo meal packets were done. It was late, but they ate; or at least some of them ate. Brandi was ill after a day of sun, humidity and drinking. She picked at her food. Valetta raved about the unique meal, and Jaymie loved it. The packets turned out better than she anticipated.

"What spices did you use, Rach?" she asked.

"The secret to flavor is balance," she said. "I used to put Old Bay on everything, and I still use it, but I noticed everything tasted the same because—duh—I was using the same spice on everything. You have herbs in your rockery garden, so I used rosemary—chicken's best buddy—thyme, sea salt and fresh ground pepper. Oh, and a squeeze of lemon! And oregano . . . kind of a Greek feel to the seasonings, when I think about it."

They got into a discussion about food, which Val entered with enthusiasm. She and Rachel talked about how hard it was to get motivated to cook for one. Val said that what she did was cook something on the weekend, like a pasta salad, that would serve if she didn't feel like cooking or wanted a quick side dish to go with a piece of chicken. Rachel said she had taken to doing meal prep on the weekend, creating slow-cooker freezer packs that she could throw in the slow cooker before she headed out to work.

Jaymie eyed her friend with interest at how Rachel lit up as they discussed food in a way she didn't when she talked about her day-to-day work. But as she glanced around, she realized that the others had a glazed look. Maybe they could come up with a conversation that was more interesting to the others.

"Courtney, you said you're in hospital equipment sales," Jaymie said. "How did you get into that?"

It worked to turn the conversation more general.

Jaymie sighed and drew her feet up under her on the sling chair she was sitting in. This moment right now—the crackling fire, the wind in the trees overhead, the sounds of night—this was finally getting to feel more like their vacations of years gone by, getting to know her friends again after time apart. Brandi had roused herself and only mentioned Terry's behavior three or four times in a row.

Courtney gave her a look, and she calmed. Melody had cheered up some, and entertained them with an impersonation of her husband, who seemed stiff and creepy at the same time. Jaymie snorted in laughter as Melody, using a faux deep voice and deliberately running the words together, said, *"That snot how we do things in my family!"*

And speaking of husbands, as the others did . . . Gabriela seemed to be the only one who, like Jaymie, had a good marriage. Unfortunately her worries about his silence came back as she talked about him and their daughter. "I miss them like crazy. My Fenix is a real little angel!" She sobbed. "Something is wrong. Something *must* be wrong or Logan would have texted or called by now!"

"Why don't you call someone right now?" Jaymie asked. "Set your mind at ease. Surely someone at home, maybe someone from Logan's family—you mentioned his sister—would know if something was wrong?"

"I should," she said softly. "I just—"

There was a rustle in the darkness. A voice, calling soft and low, said, "Hello?"

Jaymie leaped from her chair. "Who's there?" she called out.

A woman emerged out of the velvet darkness and strode toward them. Hard-featured and rail thin, she had short sandy brown hair—perfectly and elegantly feathered and curled—and a scowl that appeared to be her natural expression. A neighbor? A lost vacationer? Jaymie opened her mouth to ask, when Gabriela cried out, *"Tiffany!"*

The woman paused at the edge of the ring of lawn chairs and stared at Gabriela. "Gabby. How you doing?"

Gabriela jumped out of her seat, her face a mask of confusion and fear. "Is . . . is everything okay? What are you doing here? What's wrong? Is Logan . . . is something wrong with Logan?"

"Nothing's wrong. Everything is dandy. Why would you think otherwise?"

"Logan is okay?" Her eyes were wide, and she still looked worried.

"He's fine. He sends his love. I missed you, that's all. I thought I'd surprise you and drop in on your girls' vacation for a few days. That's okay, isn't it?"

Her mouth open, Gabriela shrank back to stand behind her chair. "Of . . . of course. It's cool to see you, sis."

Jaymie looked from one to the other of the two women; their gazes were locked. Something passed between them. "What's going on, Gabriela—?"

"This is Logan's sister, my sister-in-law, Tiffany." Gabriela turned to Jaymie with a brittle false smile. "Isn't this *fun*! She just . . . dropped in."

Brandi, from the shadows, said, with a snide tone, "Hey, Gabriela, Tiff is here! Your favorite person in the *world*. How *nice* for you."

✑ Eight ✑

JAYMIE, THOROUGHLY PEEVED, tossed things around in the cottage. Val had followed her in and stood, watching her, a sympathetic look on her face. "This must be annoying."

Tears of frustration welling in her eyes, Jaymie turned to her friend. "Is it too much to ask that if people are bringing people with them, or having them drop in, that I be told ahead of time? As the host? I mean, really . . . am I being a witch for getting annoyed?"

Tiffany had made it plain that she expected to crash at the cottage for a few days. She didn't seem apologetic in the slightest. She said she had a cooler of beer, bottles of wine, and another cooler of steaks in her car, which she had brought over on the ferry, though parking at the cottage was limited and cars were discouraged on the island.

"You have a right to be angry, kiddo. I get it. But . . . you have to live with them all for a while. How you handle this may determine how the rest of your vacation goes." Valetta hugged her. "I'll go back out and babysit the happy campers."

Jaymie made sure there was space for Tiffany, and room on the dresser for her toiletries. The woman entered with an enormous suitcase, suitable for a three-week cruise, and another bag of toiletries and hair appliances, which she plopped on the floor by the dresser and unpacked. She had shampoos, conditioners, a flatiron, a blow dryer—one of the five-hundred-dollar ones—a curling iron, mousse and assorted other hair products. She pushed the others women's stuff aside to make more room for her own.

"When you're done, come on back out to the fire," Jaymie said stiffly.

"Yeah, okay." Tiffany meticulously lined up her hair products on the dresser, then positioned her bag of hair appliances on the floor. She pulled out an extension cord and plugged it into an outlet. She did it all silently.

Nothing else. Not a word of *Gee, I hope I'm not inconveniencing you* or *Thanks for letting me stay,* just a grunt. Jaymie stalked back out to the fire and joined Valetta. She didn't often get angry, but when she did, Jaymie found it hard to shake the mood. This time she felt her anger was justified. However, as she sat by the fire, staring into the dancing flames—Rachel had added a little more wood and it flared up—she reasoned with herself. This was not right, but Valetta had a good point: if she let it spoil her whole vacation that was on her. Surely Tiffany wouldn't stay long.

She took a deep breath and let it out slowly, then looked up with a smile on her face. "Everyone likes s'mores, right?" Some nodded, but there was a distinct lack of enthusiasm from everyone but Rachel and Melody. "I've got a cast iron pan variation I think you'll all love!" She retrieved the food and cast iron frying pan from the trailer and sat down by the fire, resting the pan on the bricks surrounding the pit. She had prepared the crumble mixture of graham cracker crumbs and butter ahead of time; she pressed it into the bottom of the pre-greased pan, then layered chocolate chips and half marshmallows on top. She covered the pan with nonstick foil, then found a hot spot in the fire and set the pan on it.

Once done, she looked up. "You must be relieved, Gabriela, to know that Logan and Fenix are all right?"

"I am. *So* relieved," Gabriela said. Her sister-in-law joined them and dragged a chair close, popping open a bottle of beer and sitting back with a sigh. "Tiff, I've been worried sick. All these girls can attest to that. I've been worrying nonstop. Where is Logan? And Fenix? Why didn't he answer my texts? I was *frantic!*"

"Logan thought he'd surprise you," Tiffany said, watching her sister-in-law closely. "There was . . . a little problem with the house, and he figured it was a good opportunity to have a break with Fenix, so he brought her to stay at the Queensville Inn."

Gabriela, her mouth open in surprise, stared at her sister-in-law.

"That way you can visit with them." She took a long drink of her beer. "He figured you'd be missing Fenix."

"I . . . I am, of *course*! *And* him. Of *course*. You mean Logan and Fenix are *here*, in Queensville?"

Tiffany nodded and smiled, a slow, sly smile.

"She's been talking about nothing but her little girl," Jaymie said, feeling like Hoppy did when there was a skunk in the brush, her hackles rising, the hairs on the back of her neck feeling prickly. Something about Tiffany's expression was wrong; it was a smile but there was no *happy* in it. "And she was deeply worried about Logan."

"Was she?" Tiffany asked. "Was she *really*?"

Jaymie stared at Tiffany. Somehow, she didn't think she was going to like the woman much.

They all ate some of the s'mores crumble, which turned out okay, but it was late and no one was hungry after such a late dinner. She wrapped the remainder in foil, then set the cast iron pan on a table to soak with hot water, too tired to deal with it that night. Cast iron was wonderful, but it did need proper care, and she hoped she wouldn't regret setting it aside.

They all turned in about midnight with murmured "good nights" echoing softly in the dark.

It was very late . . . or very early. Maybe it was the upsetting day, maybe the unexpected visitor, maybe sleeping in the new trailer, or maybe Hoppy begging to go out. Or maybe it was Valetta's snoring. Jaymie couldn't sleep. Fortunately, she had prepared a whole thermos of tea for just such an eventuality. She took the thermos and a couple of Boontonware melamine teacups outside and sat in a lawn chair near the firepit, letting Hoppy roam and piddle and chase critters. "No skunks!" she whispered to the little dog, and he softly yipped.

She sat by the dead fire, smelling the aftereffects of the drowned charcoal, the bitter acrid scent that was soothing to her. It took her back to camping as a kid, and her dad, who was meticulous about attending the fire and dousing it properly at the end of the evening, the plumes of smoke and steam from the water and the hissing sound of the scalding embers familiar. The moon had climbed across the sky and was now descending, peeking between pine trees. She couldn't see it, but she knew from long experience that the river would be silvery and quiet, gleaming with a moon trail, sliding and slipping between the banks of Heartbreak Island and the Queensville shore.

It had been a long, dreadful day, but it had been rescued by her Queensville friends, Heidi, Bernie and especially Valetta. Rachel had been a bright spot too, their friendship reviving with a bright spark over a shared love of cooking, and even Melody had been a soothing influence in her own inimitable way. She knew Melody was suffering through a bad patch in life, married to a husband she no longer loved but not sure what to do about it. Andrew was difficult, demanding, suspicious and slightly creepy (to Jaymie), and it was making Melody's work nearly impossible. How could she summon delicious dukes and attractive earls when all she wanted was to ditch the man she had married?

Was she right, though? *Had* she seen Andrew in Grand Bend? It didn't seem likely, but . . . Jaymie didn't know Andrew well. Maybe he *was* following Melody. After Brandi's encounter with Terry in Grand Bend and Gabriela's husband Logan showing up with baby and sister-in-law in tow, anything was possible. She remembered Melody's alarm when she realized that Brandi had accepted Andrew's friend request online, and how copiously Brandi posted to social media. It had made them easy to follow.

The back door of the cottage opened. Melody wandered out, yawning and sighing. She softly closed the door behind her, then quietly padded down the steps, her flip-flops slapping out her timing, and joined Jaymie to sit by the firepit. She gladly took some of Jaymie's thermos tea and stared, brooding, into the dead fire.

They sat in silence for a few minutes, but Melody finally murmured, "What do you make of that whole scene? Tiffany showing up, and all?"

"I don't know. It felt . . . weird, like there were things going unsaid between them. Did you get that?"

"Big-time. I think we need to take Gabriela aside and find out what's going on." Melody shook her head and knit her brows, looking slightly like an angry poodle, her curly mop in her eyes. She swept her hair back. "It feels like whatever it is involves them all: Gabriela, Tiffany, Brandi, and Courtney. They all live in the same town and Brandi and Gabriela have been sniping at each other since they got here."

"I thought it was just that Brandi brought Courtney with her, but maybe you're right."

Hoppy yipped softly. He had finally learned that all-out barking was not tolerated at night. But there was a rustling in the bushes, and some distance away someone was yelling.

"What *is* that?" Mel asked, frowning nearsightedly into the bushes. She always forgot to wear her glasses—they were prescription, but not an absolute necessity since she didn't drive—so her vision at a distance was poor.

"Probably a drunk leaving the Ice House."

"Isn't it a little late for that?"

Jaymie checked her light-up watch, a gift from Jakob for her birthday. "I guess you're right. I didn't realize it, but it's almost three thirty." She paused, but then said, "Mel, where do you think Brandi was last night when she went out? She must have been out pretty late. Where would she go? I know we said maybe a walk, but we both know that girl does not walk unless she has to." She didn't tell her friend what Courtney had said about Brandi going to a bar on the mainland; it was clearly a lie and pointless to share.

"You know how she's on her phone all day every day?"

"Yeah. So is Gabriela."

"I'd bet Brandi met a guy online and took off to hook up with someone local."

"You think so? I know those dating sites and apps are popular, but it seems . . . I mean, those are strangers from the internet! They could be anybody, hiding behind a fake photo and ID." She shivered. "It gives me the creeps. Not to judge . . . I mean, I got lucky. Not everyone does." She cast a quick glance at Melody, hoping she hadn't given offense, but Melody was frowning still, lost in thought.

The sound of a door closing startled them both.

"That sounded close!" Jaymie said. In fact, it had sounded like her cottage door, but the front door, not the back. Was Brandi sneaking out again? She stood up, grabbed her flashlight from the table and swiftly, silently, raced up the hill and to the front of the cottage. She shone the powerful narrow beam of light down the road and thought she saw a flash of red, but there was nothing else. She came back. "I guess I was mistaken. We'd better both try to go back to sleep," she said. "Or we won't be fit for anything tomorrow. Though I thought maybe we'd spend the day here, today, reading and talking, after our long Grand Bend day today . . . yesterday, I mean."

"I'm up for that," Mel said, draining the last of her tea and setting the cup aside as she stood and stretched. "I have a book on Victorian death rituals I'm dying to read."

Jaymie almost broke out laughing, but then realized Mel wasn't joking . . . or she was and had meant the punning joke. Her deadpan delivery made it hard to tell. "See you in the morning," Jaymie whispered. "Come on, Hoppy. Back to bed."

But it was a while before she could sleep. The trailer was not as soundproof as the cottage, even less so with the windows open. She did finally fall into an uneasy sleep, but there were more shouts, and once, someone walked or ran close to the trailer. Footsteps woke her up, and Hoppy stood to attention, his whole body quivering, his ears alert. Valetta murmured *What was that?* once, but Jaymie said she didn't know, and wasn't about to go exploring, since she didn't want to meet a skunk.

Finally she slept again, but she was awoken before dawn by the sound of the island emergency alert and sirens. She shot out of bed and flung herself from the trailer, followed by Hoppy and a sleepy Valetta, muttering and rubbing her eyes.

"That's the island fire warning siren!" Jaymie yelped. She slipped flip-flops on, grabbed a wrap for her top half and a scrunchie for her hair, and headed out to the road, and down it, toward the far end of the island near the Ice House, where she could see a plume of smoke rise over the trees.

"Let it not be the Ice House," she muttered. "*Please*, let it not be the Ice House!" Her friends the Redmonds were still not home, though they would be the next day or so, but the loss of the Ice House would mean devastation to the local economy. *And don't let anyone be hurt,* she added to herself.

The Ice House restaurant was silent and closed up tight in the pearly predawn light, but a few houses away there was noise and fire and people gathering. She scuffed toward it, wiping sleep grit out of her eyes. A heavy boat motor echoed, and the shouts of men coming closer, on the shoreline on the other side of an A-line cottage that was aflame, cut through the crackling fire. The slanted roof caved in, and a plume of sparks and flames shot into the sky along with black smoke that was in sharp relief as search beams flicked on from the river side.

Did someone live in the tiny cottage? Did they get out? Jaymie sobbed in fear as others clustered in groups, chattering and backing away as more of the cottage disintegrated, with a crash of boards and tinkle of breaking glass.

Valetta joined Jaymie and hugged her close. "Oh, my heavens, this is the cottage that Brock sold a couple of months ago!"

"To who?"

"You know, that handyman Mario. He's living in it with his girlfriend."

"Oh *no*! So there *are* people living there. How can we help?" Jaymie cried, breaking away from her friend and jumping from foot to foot. "What about Hallie and Mario? And their friend, Kory! Brock said he lives there too!"

"Hon, the firefighters are there, on the other side," Val said, grabbing Jaymie's arm.

"I know. I can hear the boat motor!"

"Look, there's Constable Ng!" Val said, pointing at the young man.

There was always one local police department constable who lived on the island, and it was now Constable Ng. Still dressed in gray boxer shorts and a dark maroon T-shirt — his PJs, no doubt — he grabbed a blanket from someone who had the foresight to wet it down until it was dripping. He pulled it over his head and dashed down the lawn on the side of the building away from the worst of the fire.

"Oh no! I hope he doesn't get hurt!"

A frantic woman in a long sleeveless T-shirt-style nightgown ran, barefooted, to a huddled group of cottagers. She screamed questions at them, then, shrieking and wild with fear, had to be physically restrained from dashing after Ng.

"Who is *that*?" Jaymie said.

"I don't know."

She was crying, her hysterical screams heard over the crackle of the fire and the voices around them. The boat on the other side of the home *was* the local fire department, as they had conjectured, swiftly on the scene. Heartbreak Island had a fire plan. When the emergency siren sounded it triggered a rapid response; the ferry operator, who lived right near the dock, would be up in a flash and have the ferry ready to go. The volunteer fire department had portable pumps stored in a building on the island. Those would be retrieved by the trained volunteers, some brought over to the island on the ferry, who would set up the pumps to draw water from the river to pour on the fire.

Because the pumps were stored close by, in an outbuilding by the restaurant — storage space donated by the Redmonds — the island fire crew had them working in seconds and swiftly poured water on the fire, the heavy throb of industrial generators fueling the pumps. Shouts of the firefighters, and the hissing squirt and gush of water, announced they had started. There was a crackle and a plume of gray smoke and ash.

"Look!" Jaymie cried, as did others. Ng led a coughing, weeping Hallie, filthy and smoke-smudged, followed by a choking, breathless Kory, who staggered behind. The woman in the nightgown broke away from the group and raced to Hallie's side. Maybe it was the pregnant young woman's mother.

Others surged forward and helped Hallie to a bench nearby, making her sit, getting her water, wiping her face with a cloth. Clusters of islanders circled her and her mom, helping in any way they could as the cottage crumbled, the fire sizzling and hissing to an end. Searchlights flashed and moved as the firefighters looked for remaining fire or embers to extinguish.

Where was Mario? Jaymie covered her mouth against the cry of fear that erupted from her unbidden, and clung to Valetta, who was shivering, too, in the misty predawn. Was Mario still inside? How awful if he was!

Hallie screamed his name. Ng looked ready to dash back in but the fire chief, who had arrived, held him back. Hallie wept on her mother's shoulder, holding her bulging belly, as Kory stood, helpless, swaying unsteadily, staring at the wreckage of the little A-line cottage. You could see through it now, to the pearly light of dawn.

Melody, rubbing her eyes, joined Jaymie and Val, and soon Rachel and Brandi did, too. There was a shout, and a commotion. *"Found someone!"* a man yelled. There was a stir among the gathered neighbors. Hallie cried out, loudly, shouting "Mario!" and doubling over as Kory staggered back and forth, clutching his wild hair and pulling at it, tears streaming down his cheeks, making mucky trails in the soot on his face.

Brandi, tears in her eyes, said, "Oh that poor, *poor* girl!"

The fire chief, an older man, looking weary, bustled out from around the other side of the now smoldering cottage and took Constable Ng aside. Ng stumbled back but swiftly got himself under control. He took someone's proffered cell phone and made a call, moving away and gesticulating as he spoke.

Moments later the wail of police sirens on the shore caught their attention. Minutes after that the ferry chugged away, then ten minutes later chugged back, as the whole American side of the island gathered in little groups. Police officers arrived, along with a grim-faced chief of police, Deborah Connolly, and her homicide detective, Angela Vestry.

Mario's body must have been found in the fire. There was no rescue, no heroic carrying of his living, breathing body out to his grieving pregnant girlfriend. Jaymie's heart clutched; Mario was Hallie's baby daddy and presumably she loved him. They had a home together and were expecting a baby, and no matter what their relationship status, no matter how bad his behavior had been, this outcome was tragic. Ng moved among the onlookers, asking questions, taking notes. The bartender from the Ice House was among those he spoke with, as were some regular barflies and a few tourists Jaymie didn't recognize.

A murmur swept through the crowd. Jaymie saw Sammy Dobrinskie and motioned for him to join them. He knew Valetta of course, and ducked his head in greeting, his tousled blond hair wildly mussed.

"What's happening?" Jaymie asked him. "It looks like Constable Ng is asking a bunch of questions."

Sammy shifted uneasily from foot to foot. "Yeah, he talked to me. I was working at the Ice House last night. I've been picking up shifts as barback and dishwasher for the summer, to help Mom out," he said of his widowed mother. "They were all there last night—Kory, Hallie, Mario—and there was this huge fight."

"What time was this?"

"Near the end of the night . . . about two-ish?"

"What was the fight about?"

He shifted uneasily and glanced over at Jaymie. Locally she had a reputation for solving murders, and she had, in fact, solved his dad's murder a couple of years before. He trusted and liked her, but he was not a gossip. However . . . he glanced both ways and leaned close. "Mario and Hallie got into it, and Kory stepped in the middle. Mario told Kory to butt out, and Kory said he wouldn't stand by and see Hallie abused."

"Abused?" Valetta interjected.

He shrugged. "I don't know if he meant, like, physically. Anyway, Kory was thrown out — matter of fact, they all were thrown out — but not before Kory said . . ." He sighed heavily and shifted his shoulders. "Not before he said he'd kill Mario if he ever hurt Hallie."

There was a stirring among the crowd; Constable Ng took Kory's arm. On a wafting breeze floated the words *You have the right to remain silent.* Kory was being taken into custody. After what Sammy said, Jaymie wasn't surprised. Was the fire set to conceal a crime? No doubt it would all come out in the following days. Kory was led away. Shortly after, Hallie retreated with her mom as the police cordoned off the burned-out smoldering shell of the cottage with police tape. The firefighters remained, as hot spots were detected and snuffed.

Jaymie and her friends walked back to the cottage. She made coffee. Dawn had broken, the sun rising to cast long shadows over the grove, where a damp chill hovered, mist clinging to the trees as the humidity of the day built. Valetta headed back to the mainland to check in on Denver and feed him, and make sure his catio was open so he could get outside, after which she was coming back to the island. Courtney and Gabriela were both late sleepers, so Jaymie couldn't bustle around in the cottage much. Tiffany, apparently, had her half-hour shower — leaving little hot water for the others — and had moved on to her hair, which took a solid hour to coif. She seemed sturdily incurious about the morning's affair, simply saying the fire was *too bad.*

Melody, with her book on Victorian death rituals, retreated to the shaded seating area in the grove with a blanket wrapped around her and a cup of coffee in hand. Brandi sat on the back deck of the cottage with her phone in hand and scrolled and tapped. Rachel, too, texted and scrolled.

Jaymie cleaned. The s'mores pan from the night before was sticky and congealed, with an edge of rust along the damp remains. It was going to take forever to clean. She scrubbed it, then set it out to dry thoroughly. It would need to be reseasoned, which reminded her . . . the pie irons had been cleaned, but it was necessary to season the cast iron one. Cast iron anything needed to be regularly seasoned, rubbed all over with oil, heated for a good length of time and allowed to cool. It was a pain, but in general cast iron cooking implements were worth it, lasting a cook's lifetime and beyond.

Where had she put them? In the trailer? No. In the cottage kitchen? No. She stood by her friend on the cottage back deck. "Brandi, do you remember where I put the pie irons when I was done cleaning them the other night?"

Brandi looked up from her scrolling and shook her head.

Jaymie returned to the trailer and stood outside of it, looking around with a frown. "Mel, do you remember where I put the pie irons when I was done with them the other night?"

Melody looked up from her book. "Each one has a leather thong tied to a hole through the wooden handle. When you were done cleaning them you hung them from a nail on that pine over in the spot where the sun hits in the late afternoon."

Jaymie bit her lip. Even on such a solemn morning, she couldn't help but smile from her author friend's habitual quick eye. "I remember now. Thank you." She went to the pine and there they were. Or . . . at least two of them. The aluminum ones were there, but not the cast iron one she needed to season. Odd. Maybe a raccoon had absconded with it. She hoped not; it was the oldest of the vintage lot!

A cell phone rang and Brandi, on the deck, answered. Her eyes widened and she said something quickly, then jabbed the screen to hang up, but sat staring at her phone. She appeared upset.

Jaymie bustled over to her friend and looked up from the grassy slope beneath the back deck. "Bran, you okay? What's up?"

Brandi shook her head and opened her mouth, but as Tiffany, perfectly coiffed and dressed in a trim pair of khaki shorts and a puff-sleeved blouse, stepped out of the cottage, she shut it again.

"I had the worst night of sleep in my *life*," Tiffany announced. "That bed is too soft. And everything feels damp. Your air-conditioning sucks."

Jaymie, taken aback, stared up at her. Was she supposed to apologize to an unwanted guest who had a bad night's sleep?

"And that shower thingie! I mean, first you have no real shower," she went on, hands on her hips. "And then . . . it has *no* water pressure! You should have that looked at. I wouldn't stand for it. And the air conditioner is noisy. Maybe that's why I didn't sleep." She stretched. "What's for breakfast?"

"Whatever you make," Jaymie snapped and whirled, descending the lawn back to the trailer. Out of the corner of her eye she caught Melody laughing and giving her the thumbs-up.

But inevitably, the payment for snapping was that she felt bad about it. Even an unwanted and uninvited guest was a guest. She compensated by making eggs and bacon over the fire in her largest cast iron frying pan, the one she could hardly lift.

As they finished up, Melody volunteered to wash dishes, since she didn't cook and wanted to contribute in some way. After saying this, she shot a wicked look at Tiffany, who sat on a chair at the kitchen table, but that woman was checking her hair in a purse mirror and didn't seem to notice. Gabriela wandered out of the bedroom, rubbing her eyes.

"Oh, hey, you're all up? I guess I overslept."

Rachel rolled her eyes and looked annoyed. She was not one who tolerated laziness, but she should cut Gabriela a break, Jaymie thought; it was vacation, after all, and being a mother was exhausting.

"Of *course* you did," Tiffany said with a wide smile. "Like Logan always says, *Gabriela could sleep through a hurricane or a brass band rehearsal!*"

Gabriela blinked and slumped down in a chair.

Rachel jumped up. "I need to do something, go for a walk. How about I head over to Tansy's Tarts and get some fresh-made butter tarts for today's dessert? So *you* don't have to do anything about that, at least," she said to Jaymie, also shooting a look at the oblivious Tiffany.

"Would you mind some company?" Courtney said with a hesitant smile.

"I'd love it," Rachel said.

ϰ **Nine** ϰ

THE TWO SET OFF, and Jaymie and Melody did dishes while Brandi stalked back and forth out on the grass, talking on the phone.

"Who do you think she's talking to?" Jaymie asked.

Melody squinted. "Offhand? I'd say Terry. Online she is always complaining about him. It's getting tedious."

"Hmm. This surprises me. I thought they'd make it."

Melody cast her an incredulous look. "Don't you know . . ." she started, but then shook her head and closed her mouth.

Jaymie rolled her eyes and sighed. "I know what Brandi's like, but I just . . ." She shrugged and sighed again. Brandi finally stabbed at the phone and slumped down in a chair, lolling with her legs over the arm.

Tiffany, sitting at the kitchen table drinking her fourth cup of coffee, checked her own phone and frowned at it, stabbing at it repeatedly. "Your wifi sucks," she grumbled.

Jaymie and Melody exchanged looks. Jaymie was grateful for her friend; the writer's bemused looks and laughs were helping her stay sane. She wouldn't have minded all the changes in the vacation—from a week in the middle of August camping to a week to ten days at the end of August in her cottage—but it seemed that the few years when they had not been able to do their yearly trip had changed them all so *very* much. Or was she misremembering?

Tiffany exited, mumbling about going for a walk, and Gabriela, with a cup of coffee and her phone, went out to sit near Brandi, the two pointedly not talking.

"Was it always like this, or did we all used to have a lot in common and have fun?" Jaymie asked, handing a dripping plate to Melody to dry.

"A little of both. I guess I see it differently. I'm a few years older than you all, and I was never one much for partying, or hanging out, or talking about guys. I always sat back and watched, and I could see that for most of you, your similarities were superficial. Rachel was the super-studious one, but she went to parties with the rest because you all shared a house. *You* were more into reading and cooking and spending time with your family, but you also partied with the others because . . . *house*. Brandi partied harder than anyone else, but I don't think any of you thought that made her different . . . but it *did*. She partied not for you all, but for herself."

Jaymie gave her a quizzical look.

"I'm not judging her," Melody said with an irritated sigh. "I'm *not*. She can do whatever floats her boat. I write romances, so I get it, the dirty looks when women talk openly about sex. No judgment from me. But it's true. Brandi is who she is, a party animal, and I think time tends to" — she frowned, looking for the right word — "*harden* our tendencies."

"What do you mean?"

Mel shrugged. "The introvert becomes more introverted," she said, pointing to herself. "The party girl parties harder," she went on, pointing out to Brandi.

"I don't know if you're right about that. Some seek change. Rach, as you pointed out, was always studious and work-driven, true, but I think she's questioning her career-life balance now, and maybe her career choices."

"You've got a point," Melody admitted.

"And Gabriela . . . she used to party as hard as Brandi, but she's now a stay-at-home mommy. And she misses her husband and kid."

"So much that she's not rushing into town to see them, now that she knows they're here?" Melody said with a cynical tone.

"She just woke up. You know how she always was; it took a lot of coffee to get her motivated in the morning."

Her friend leaned back against the counter and wiped a plate. "I guess you're right about that . . . some people do change. I've seen a lot of changes in *you* over the years."

"How have I changed?" Jaymie glanced at her, curious.

"You were mousy, a bookworm. That's why you and I got along. We could sit in the same room and read books and not need to talk. But you've gotten a lot more outgoing. After that loser, Joel, ditched you for that bimbo — "

"Heidi is *not* a bimbo! She's a lovely person and my friend."

" — and you did some soul searching, you had this burst of energy . . . you identified what you wanted and began to go after it. I'm proud of you, all the progress you've made."

"Thanks, Mel. It started then, you're right about that." She turned the tap for more hot water. "I think before that I was grateful a guy wanted to be with me. But living alone after Joel left made me realize I'm good company even for myself and I'm a pretty good catch."

"That you are. Jakob's a lucky guy."

As they finished the last dish, Jaymie heard raised voices outside. She hung the damp dishcloth over the tap and walked out back with Melody to find Brandi and Gabriela arguing.

"What's up, guys?" Jaymie asked, leaning on the deck railing and looking down at them. The railing creaked and she straightened.

The two women looked toward them, but neither spoke, their faces both red, expressions mulish. There was something going on. "What's wrong?" Jaymie asked.

"Nothing," Gabriela said. "We were just—"

"Hey, all," Courtney said, strolling toward them from the laneway and joining Gabriela and Brandi. She carried two bakery boxes.

"Where's Rachel?"

Courtney looked up at Jaymie. "She's still at Tansy's Tarts. Hallie and Tansy had a fight yesterday and Tansy fired her, but forgot that her husband, Sherm, has a medical appointment in town today. Rach explained about Mario dying in that house fire this morning, and that even if she hadn't let her go, poor Hallie wouldn't be working today. Tansy was *really* upset; I guess she liked the girl, even though she fired her. She had been giving her advice, like to get life insurance on Mario for their baby's sake, and so on."

"Tansy seems like a tough nut, but she's a softie inside," Jaymie said.

"Anyway, Rachel and Tansy got on like a house afire, pardon the expression," Courtney said with a rare smile. "Rachel offered to stay and help out for a few hours. She sent me back with an apology, but she didn't think you'd mind because there wasn't anything planned for the day."

"No, I don't mind. Of course." Jaymie felt a welling of pity, remembering poor Hallie. She had lost so much, it seemed unfair that she had also lost her job. But she had not been cut out for the service industry, and how much longer could she work anyway, as close to her due date as she must be? Rachel, smart, efficient, and with her bright smile and winning ways, would be a much better fit, for the moment, anyway.

Brandi's phone rang again, and she looked down at it. At the same time Gabriela's chimed, her ring tone a snatch of John McClane's profane yell in *Die Hard*. She looked at the screen, her eyes widened, and she took the call, but moved away. All they heard her say was, *"Hello, hello?"*

Jaymie frowned, examining her friends. Brandi and Gabriela . . . both seemed distracted and upset this morning, or was she projecting her own deep sadness on them? She watched Gabriela, who was standing staring down at her phone now, with a look of apprehension on her face. Was everything truly okay between her and Logan? She seemed no happier now, with her husband and child close by in town, than she had been when she was worried about not hearing from them. Jaymie was about to go to her to try to find out what was wrong when she heard, from behind her, a familiar voice.

"Hello, all!"

Jaymie looked over her shoulder. Bernie, in uniform, strolled toward them, a neutral look on her face. "Hey, Bern. What's up?"

She had a notebook in her hand and flipped it to a fresh page. "I'm doing some canvassing in regard to the fire and death this morning."

"What's that about a fire?" Gabriela said, pocketing her cell phone and rejoining the group. She frowned and looked around at each person.

"I guess you didn't hear," Jaymie said. "You were sleeping." Gabriela had a long history of not paying attention, so she had missed Courtney's explanation of why Rachel was still at the tart shop. "Early this morning, before dawn, there was a house fire, a cottage near the Ice House. Someone died."

"Oh, that's *terrible!*" Gabriela, with her ready warmth, said. "Who was it?"

"Some guy named Mario something?" Brandi said.

"I came by to ask if anyone saw or heard anything unusual last night," Bernie said, glancing in turn at each face.

Her gaze was assessing and level, but Jaymie noticed something in her eyes, some flare of interest. She glanced around at her friends, to see what had sparked that expression, but didn't see anything. She turned back to Bernie. "I was sleeping in the trailer, and so was Valetta. She slept pretty soundly, but I kept hearing noises all night: shouts, banging, and it sounded like someone ran through my property, too. I got up and Mel and I had a cup of tea sitting outside."

"What time was that?" Bernie asked.

"It was three thirty; I looked at my watch."

Bernie nodded and jotted the info down.

"Did you hear anything, Mel?" Jaymie asked. "Other than what you've already said?"

"Besides Tiffany snoring despite her contention that she didn't sleep at all?" She shook her head. "Nothing much."

Bernie turned to her friend. "Jaymie, are you missing anything around here?"

"No, I don't think so." She watched her friend, head cocked to one side. Bernie was attentive but still waiting for more. "Like what?"

"Anything at all, even something inconsequential," Bernie said. "Something you don't think is stolen, you just think it's missing."

Jaymie stood for a moment, then slowly said, "I *am* missing a cast iron pie iron."

Bernie nodded and walked away a few steps. She radioed her partner. It was almost impossible to hear all that she said, but the words that stood out were *missing a pie iron*.

Jaymie remembered that the police knew immediately that Mario had been murdered and she felt a wave of sickness. *Please, don't let my lovely vintage pie iron be the weapon,* she prayed. But if she had to bet, she would have bet that her prayers were too late to do any good.

Bernie returned to them and took Jaymie's arm, pulling her aside. "I hate to do this, Jaymie," she murmured, "but I'm going to need you to talk to the detective in charge. Detective Vestry is here investigating. She'll come to your cottage shortly."

It seemed as though her worst fears were being realized. "Don't tell me my pie iron was the weapon!"

"We don't know anything yet," Bernie said, her tone soothing. "That's what we're going to try to figure out."

"Was one found on the scene?"

"I can't tell you any more than what I already have, Jaymie, I'm sorry." Bernie's dark brown eyes were kind and full of sympathy, but her words were firmly said.

Jaymie took a deep breath and nodded. "I can show you where they were; the other ones are still there. But I don't know when the cast iron one went missing; I discovered it was gone this morning when I decided to season it. I used them two nights ago, cleaned them, and hung them on the tree to dry."

"Can you describe the missing pie iron?"

"Sure. It was square, on a long handle, about thirty inches, and it was a Rome Industries pie iron."

"Okay. One sec while I see when the detective will be here." Bernie walked away and used her phone again.

The others had gathered in a cluster, heads bent, murmuring. Brandi was the first to straighten and stalked away from them. She confronted Jaymie, hand on her hip, one of Courtney's cigarettes in her quivering fingers. She periodically gave up smoking and went back to it in times of stress. "What's going on? We overheard; some detective is coming here? Why?"

Taken aback by her brusqueness, Jaymie examined Brandi's face, her cheeks red, her eyes narrowed, her nostrils flaring.

"Slow your roll, chica," Melody said, strolling over and putting one hand on Brandi's arm.

"Don't *touch* me!" Brandi said, pulling her arm away.

Gabriela, tears welling in her eyes, joined them. "Jaymie, I can't believe you've gotten us involved in one of your murders."

"One of *my* murders?" Jaymie yelped. "What do you mean?"

"We know you're always getting mixed up in them and you're used to it, but we're *not*!"

"That's not fair, Gabriela," Jaymie said, her voice shaking. "This has nothing to do with me."

"Calm down, everybody," Melody said, her tone edgy. "Gabriela, shut up. Jaymie didn't do anything, and you know it. She was good enough to invite us all here to stay at her family cottage at no cost. What have any of you done but gripe?"

A chorus of protest broke out among them, and it devolved into a squabble, with tears, shaken fingers and trembling voices. It reminded Jaymie of the old days in ways she had not anticipated; there was one memorable fight in their school days that had resulted when Brandi stole some guy Gabriela was interested in. Melody had exacerbated it in that case by joking that you could steal a wallet and you could steal a sweater, but you could not steal a man.

Jaymie retreated to the grove to sit and sniff back her indignant response. Melody hadn't helped, all she had done was irritate everyone. She did that too often, occasionally with ill-timed humor and often with her impatience at the others' emotional spats. Right now Jaymie was weary of the lot of them. An old adage about fish and houseguests and three-day limits came to mind. This was the third day.

"A man is dead, you bunch of jerks! Not you, Court," Brandi finally said, stalking away from them and joining Mel in the grove. She lit another cigarette. "I need a drink."

"It's a little early," Jaymie commented.

"It's noon somewhere."

Jaymie couldn't sit still, she had to move. If she didn't, she would either break down or berate her friends. She jumped up and retreated to the shady rock garden they had constructed on the hill that led to the Redmonds' home above. She spent a few minutes pulling weeds, tossing them into a pile she was collecting that would have to be moved to the composter at some point.

It didn't make any sense to her that her cast iron pie iron had been stolen to murder some guy she barely knew. How random was that? And how would anyone know about the availability of the pie iron except for her friends?

If it was her pie iron at the scene of the crime, it was unlikely the person who used it happened to wander through her property, stole it, and attacked the victim. She dusted her hands off and sat down on a rock, watching her friends from the shadows, trying to gather her thoughts. Melody sat in a lawn chair reading her book; she was observant most of the time, but oblivious to how her brisk manners sometimes hurt feelings. Courtney and Brandi sat together smoking and drinking coffee. Gabriela was inside, getting ready to go over to Queensville to visit with her husband and child. Tiffany, back from her walk, had apparently decided to go with her. They couldn't do anything, though, until Detective Vestry had spoken with them all.

She went back to the first evening, their dinner at the Ice House, and frowned. What stuck out to her was how efficiently Courtney headed off Mario as he walked toward Brandi. What did she say to the guy to put him off? That was the one single thread she could find that tied their group to Mario, but that was flimsy, more a wisp than a thread.

Was there more she didn't know?

• • •

DETECTIVE VESTRY, a slim, serious-countenanced woman in her forties, arrived, glancing around at them all. She beckoned to Jaymie, who went with her to stand in the lane and explain.

"So, the second murder in three years on Heartbreak Island and you're mixed up in both of them?" she said, referring to the murder of Sammy Dobrinskie's father, which Jaymie was instrumental in solving.

Jaymie stiffened. "I'm *not* mixed up in this."

"You merely provided the murder weapon, is that it?"

"So it *is* my pie iron?" She cleared her throat, trying to get past the tears. This was too much, and the detective hadn't helped with her finger-pointing.

"Pending positive ID, it's a pretty good chance. We'll be taking the other two to see if there are any prints on them." She signaled to another officer, who nodded and headed to the pie irons. "How fortunate that you've given us such a good description of your missing one. How do you remember so much about it?"

Ignoring the accusatory tone, Jaymie squinted at the sun that angled down into her eyes and said, "You know I specialize in vintage kitchen stuff. I could tell you perfect details about any of my kitchen stuff. I have a red Pyrex bowl that has one scratch in the finish and I'd know mine in a second if you lined up a dozen red Pyrex bowls in front of me. I can tell you about one of my graters, which is a WonderShredder. It has a patent number. Want to know what it is?" She smiled. "I could go on. And on."

Vestry's eyes widened. "Beats me why anyone is interested in kitchen crap. I use whatever is handy."

"You're not a collector, I'd assume. I know people who feel the same about their cat figurines, or Lionel train collection. My brother-in-law could tell you in detail about his Bakelite radio collection."

"It's funny, I'd never heard of a pie iron before this," Vestry mused, "and suddenly I'm knee-deep in them. Every islander Bernie canvassed seems to have one. Or more than one in most cases. Who needs more than one?"

"Detective, let me guess: you've never camped before?"

"What does *that* mean?"

Jaymie bit her lip at the defensive tone. The detective, despite Jaymie's best attempts, appeared to think her a troublemaker, and everything Jaymie said seemed to irritate her. She made a little progress occasionally, but then something like this happened and it felt like they were back to square one. "I meant that most campers are familiar with pie irons. But I get that not everyone is a camper. You do need more than one if you have multiple people, or you're left waiting for one pie to cook before you can make another."

Melody approached and had heard most of the conversation. "Detective, why did Jaymie asking if you'd camped before irritate you?"

Giving her a look, Jaymie attempted to stave off Melody's feistiness, ill-timed as it would be at this moment.

Vestry's gaze swiveled to Melody and she opened her mouth to respond, but stopped and stared, then said, "You look familiar. Who are you?"

"This is my friend, Melody Heath."

"Melody Heath." The detective squinted. "The name doesn't ring a bell. You *look* like someone else."

"Mindy Howe? Mercy Hall?" Melody said, giving her pseudonyms for contemporary and medieval romance novels. When Vestry shook her head in puzzlement, Melody twisted her mouth, glanced over at Jaymie, and then looked back to the detective. "How about Megan Hunter?"

"Megan Hunter!" Vestry exclaimed. "You're *her*?"

Melody smiled. "I am."

Jaymie glanced back and forth between the two. "Who is Megan Hunter?"

"You don't know? She writes the Jade Torrence Private Dick series! I *love* those! Jade Torrence kicks butt; she's awesome. Hey, when are those going to be made into a movie . . . or better yet, a TV series!" the detective babbled, gray eyes wide, cheeks flushing with pleasure. "I can see Cameron Diaz playing Jade. Your books would be ideal for Netflix or Amazon Prime; probably too much swearing and sex and violence for network TV."

Jaymie stared at Detective Vestry, who had turned into a fangirl in front of her eyes. Then she swiveled her gaze to stare at Melody. "A new pseudonym?"

Mel colored faintly. She shrugged and waggled her hand. "Newish. I've written two so far, the first out last year and the second a few months ago. I keep the Megan Hunter books separate. Different website, different social media . . . everything separate. They're action mystery, not romance. There's more . . . mmm . . . blood and guts in them."

"And sex," Vestry said with a wink.

"But . . . but you're a *romance* author!" Jaymie wailed, staring at Mel.

Melody rolled her eyes. "I'm an author, full stop."

"But I'm your friend, and you never told me. Why didn't you tell me?"

"Jaymie, can we talk about this later?" Melody said, her tone edgy.

"Maybe *we* can talk later," the detective said to the writer. "I have some great ideas for plots."

Melody's eyes lit up. "I'd like that. Maybe we can grab a drink at the Ice House."

"You're on." She turned back to Jaymie, all business, but in a self-conscious trying-to-impress manner. "Now, you say you don't know when the pie iron went missing. Maybe someone else noticed?"

No one had. Vestry moved among the others, asking questions, following up on Bernie's notes. Brandi seemed alarmed by the whole affair, while Courtney appeared ambivalent, though worried about Brandi. Tiffany and Gabriela, after being questioned briefly — neither knew anything — headed to the ferry to go to the Queensville Inn to visit with Gabriela's husband and daughter. Jaymie sat in the shade and brooded. She watched her remaining friends, Melody reading her book as Brandi and Courtney sat together whispering.

Brandi was upset about something, but when Jaymie had asked

her what, she had shaken her head. Melody had conjectured that the first night, when Brandi disappeared, she had gone off for a tryst with a local guy. Why would she hide that? It was her personal life, and no one else's business. However . . . maybe her friend feared the others would be judgmental, as Gabriela appeared ready to be. Brandi's behavior, while her own business, worried Jaymie.

Brandi knotted her burgundy dyed tresses into a bun and stretched a scrunchie around it. Jaymie watched and something occurred to her in that moment. Melody had conjectured that Brandi had hooked up with some local guy she had met online. Mario's words haunted her, about a flame-haired love interest he was thinking of dating more seriously.

Could that be Brandi? "Mel, *Mel!*" she said, scooting into the shadows and crouching down by her friend. "Listen to this." She shared her hypothesis.

"Makes sense. But don't you think she'd be more upset by his death? I mean . . . if I sleep with a guy and he dies, I'm gonna be cut up."

Jaymie gave her a look. Her attempt at humor wasn't appreciated. "But she is upset about *some*thing, and she won't tell me what. I'd say she looks more nervous than sad. You'd think she'd be crushed, and we've all heard his name repeatedly today. Unless . . ." She frowned.

"Unless what?"

"Unless she's upset about something else. Maybe she doesn't connect Mario with the guy she was with. He probably didn't use his real name on the dating app." She plunked down on the ground and wrapped her arms around her knees. "Is that possible?"

"Yeah, I guess. Maybe he used a screen name, like, oh, Hot Dude 27, or something like that."

Jaymie glanced at her, frowning; she remembered at the Ice House mistakenly picking up Brandi's phone and seeing a message from someone with a screen name . . . what was it? It was 1BuffDude, or something like that. She explained what she had seen on the phone.

Melody nodded. "So, she could have been with Mario and not know at this point that the guy is dead. How would we find out?"

"It would be a heck of a coincidence."

"Maybe not. I know there's a hookup app that tells you if someone who wants to hook up is close by, so if she checked in on that and Mario or whatever his screen name was came up? You already know the guy's slept with lots of random women. Not so big of a coincidence, I'd say."

"You may be right about that." Jaymie watched Brandi and Courtney. "I wish I knew what to do."

Melody's eyes had narrowed. "There's something else I've been wondering about, something that would make the explanation simpler. Jaymie, when Brandi told you that our campsite booking had been canceled, did you check with the site owners?"

"No, why?" Mel raised her eyebrows and waited while Jaymie puzzled it out. She thought about what her friend was asking. "Are you suggesting that Brandi faked the booking being canceled so she could come here and meet up with a guy? I don't know, Mel . . . if it was Mario, then she had met up with him before." She told Mel about him bragging about the hot redhead he had met up with a few times. "Why would she need to cancel our camping trip and rearrange it to be here if she was seeing him whenever she wanted?"

"I can think of a few reasons. She wanted to see him more often and the camping trip was going to get in the way. Or maybe she was planning to take it to the next level, like, become boyfriend/ girlfriend, and she wanted time to make it happen."

Jaymie remembered what Mario had said, about kicking Hallie out and moving in his hot redheaded lover. "But she wouldn't get serious like that without knowing his name, would she?"

"You'd be surprised," Melody said. "Even a screen name . . . I read about one case where a guy and gal who went beyond screen names used fake real names — if that makes sense — to text."

"Huh?"

Melody shifted impatiently. "Okay, say a guy texted as Hot Dude and the encounter went beyond screen names. Maybe his name is really Frank, but he wants it to be more . . . romantic, sexier, so he calls himself Brick, or Stone, or some other stupid soap opera name."

"For a romance writer you're impatient with people looking for romance."

"Romance. Huh. It ain't romance guys like Mario are looking

for." Sighing, Melody nodded and shook her head awkwardly. She shrugged her shoulders, like she was trying to release tension. "Maybe you're a little bit right. In the present moment I *am* having trouble summoning up the romantic feels, you know?"

"I'm sorry, Mel. I hope you sort things out."

"Me too," the writer said gloomily, then glanced at Jaymie. "You're not really mad I didn't tell you about the Megan Hunter books, are you? I didn't think you'd be interested in them."

Jaymie thought for a moment. "I'm not mad, Mel. I'm hurt, I guess. I don't only want to know about the writing I want to read. I want to know how your life is going. These books . . . were you excited about writing them?"

"Yeah, I am. It feels fresh. That's good."

"Then tell me about them. I'm interested in your life. We're friends."

"Okay. I get it. We'll talk. Now . . . back to Brandi and Mario, if any of our suppositions are true."

"I *just* don't know. All I *do* know is, Mario was thinking of dumping Hallie for a hot-to-trot redhead. And we know one of those." Jaymie watched Brandi. Should she ask her? Should she probe if her friend had been meeting up with Mario the first night? And if it was true, should she tell the detective?

It wouldn't have anything to do with Mario's murder—it *couldn't* have!—but . . . what if it *did*?

ಜ Ten ಜ

HOPPY PERKED UP AND BARKED, one happy yip of excitement. He danced in a joyful wobbly circle, then took off up the hill, zigzagging dizzily through the ankle-deep bed of dry pine needles, yapping in elation the whole way. Jaymie peered up through the shadowy trees to see Ruby Redmond, moving chairs around on the back patio of their rustic cottage. The couple was back from their sailing trip.

She went to the bottom of the hill and shouted out, "Hey, neighbor! Don't mind my doggie who is dashing up to see you; he's been missing you."

"I have bickies for my favorite doggie friend," Ruby called out. "Come up. I have something for you, too, Jaymie!"

Jaymie climbed the hill along the obscure path; it wove between clumps of hostas and hydrangea and dogwood, along a path mulched for tidiness and with logs in strategic spots to act as steps. In the dark it was virtually impossible to find unless you knew how to scale it. She crested the hill and saw Hoppy waggling and wiggling around Ruby's feet while she fished the doggie treats he loved out of her shorts pocket. "Come, sit!" Ruby said, motioning to the Adirondack chairs that lined the back patio of their cottage. She squatted and ruffled Hoppy's fur, caressed his ears and gave him a couple of crunchie doggie biscuits.

"Are you talking to me or Hoppy?" Jaymie asked.

"Both. Wait here; I've got something for you." Ruby disappeared into the cottage.

Jaymie sat down in one of the chairs and leaned back, closing her eyes. The questions she had about Brandi were worrying her; if her friend was mixed up with Mario, then how long before the police made the connection? The guy would have a cell phone and he and Brandi would have texted or spoken . . . surely the police would be wanting to speak with her again once they looked over his phone.

Ruby returned and held out a paper bag to Jaymie, joy lighting up her visage. She had a sailor's face, deeply tanned, angular and lined from time spent in the sun and the wind, with a shock of short white hair that stood straight up most of the time. "Got this up north. We did a bike trip on Mackinac Island. Enjoy!"

Jaymie opened the bag and inside was a three-slice box of famous Mackinac Island fudge: Traverse City Cherry, German Chocolate, and Butter Pecan. "Oh, Ruby, *thank* you!" She teared up, which she thought was a strange reaction—it was just fudge, after all—but it meant a lot that her friends thought of her while they were away.

But Ruby jumped up and put her arms around her. "Aw, honey, it's okay."

"I don't know why . . . I mean . . . *tears!*" She shook her head as her voice became clogged. "It's all that awfulness this morning."

Ruby put her forehead to Jaymie's, holding her face in her long-fingered hands for a moment, then she sat back down, staring at Jaymie earnestly. "I know you saw the fire this morning. We *knew* Mario; it's terribly sad, especially with poor little Hallie expecting any day now!"

"You know them?" Jaymie said, sniffling back her tears.

"We had Mario and Kory do some work at the Ice House this spring, before Kory's jail stint. I know he got out again a while ago." Her deep-set eyes sad, she shook her head. "It's a terrible thing. I worried at the time, you know . . . Hallie visited the job site from time to time, and I *saw* how Mario treated her."

"Not good, I've heard."

"Not good. He was dismissive of her, casually cruel. He often said nasty things about women: their intelligence, that they talk too much, that they aren't sensible, that they complicate things unnecessarily. She's too young to be putting up with that nonsense," Ruby said firmly, her tone angry. "Not that there's a good age to put up with nonsense, but you know what I mean. She's got her whole life ahead of her." She lifted Hoppy up to sit on her lap and she leaned back in the chair, scruffing the little dog's ears. "I told Garnet, if she leaves him it might be the best thing to happen to her and that poor child she's carrying."

"They've arrested Kory; did you know that?"

"What?" Ruby bolted upright, disturbing Hoppy, who whined and rearranged himself. "No, I didn't! Garnet is down at the restaurant right now checking in. Maybe he'll know something. I can't *believe* that Kory would kill Mario. He *idolized* the man!"

"I know. It's weird. But I heard that Kory threatened Mario last night at the Ice House. He was angry that Mario was treating Hallie badly."

Ruby narrowed her eyes. "You know, from my observation when they've all been together at the restaurant, Kory *did* seem protective toward Hallie. He was the one who made her sit down, got her some water, watched over her."

Garnet, tall and lanky, weathered and brown like his wife, strode around the corner of the cottage. "Hey, Jaymie, good to see you, kid!"

Jaymie jumped up and hugged him. Garnet patted Hoppy's head, but insisted Jaymie sit back down while he sat on the end of a lounge chair facing them. He said to Ruby, reaching out and taking her hand, "It's bad, hon. Mario was hit repeatedly with a blunt instrument."

Jaymie felt her stomach clench. "They think it may have been my pie iron."

"*Your* pie iron?" Garnet said, his thick salt-and-pepper brows knit together with two pinch marks between them. "How would anyone get your pie iron?"

"Stolen, the police think. I had three of them hanging on a pine tree to dry. Val and I were staying in the trailer last night, and I heard noises, and footsteps through my property in the middle of the night."

"Footsteps?"

"Yes . . . *heavy* footsteps, like someone running."

Garnet and Ruby exchanged looks. He met Jaymie's questioning gaze. "You may not know this, but Kory has a history of stealing from the cottagers. Even when he was a kid he would rifle through coolers, steal beer. And then he graduated to petty theft: tools, bikes, anything not nailed down."

"No, I didn't know that. We have had stuff stolen from time to time."

"I'd bet that was Kory . . . or one of his buddies, some of whom are now serving time. He was behind a rash of break-ins last fall, after folks closed up their cottages. He got out of jail a few months ago. Spent a bit inside for theft."

"I knew some of that, that he had been in jail." Jaymie processed that. "We've often blamed renters for missing stuff, maybe unfairly. I suppose it *could* have been him."

"Or, like I said, one of the guys he knows. He's not the only one, he just gets caught more than the others. He's the kind of guy who will steal something and sell it for beer money. He hasn't got a mean bone in his body, though." Garnet shook his head. "Or I didn't *think* he had."

"What are the police going on?" Ruby asked. "Why did they arrest Kory?"

Garnet was once a police officer, and then worked private security. He knew the police force locally, and had kept in touch with some police officers after his and Ruby's troubles of a couple of years past. They were friendly with the new police chief, Deborah Connolly, and her partner, and had them both out sailing before. If Chief Connolly was on the scene she likely spoke to him. "There was a big blowup last night between Kory and Mario in the restaurant. Kory threatened Mario, and Mario threatened Kory. Ng was called in; he was going to take them both in because there were fisticuffs, but Hallie begged him to let it go, and he did. They left. Now, this next part is not common knowledge, and I expect you both to keep it quiet."

Both women nodded.

"Hallie told the police that when they got back to the cottage Mario threw Kory out of the house. But he apparently came back, and neighbors heard the yelling, then everything quieted down again for some time. But Kory's got bruises and cuts on his face and knuckles, and they recovered a weapon on the scene." He sent an apologetic look to Jaymie. "I suppose it's your pie iron. The working theory is that he went away again, stole the pie iron and came back, confronted Mario, and killed him."

"Oh, no," Ruby said, hugging Hoppy close. She buried her face in his neck fur and jingled his tags. "That's so sad."

Jaymie sighed. It was a good theory. Probably true. There was plenty of bad blood, it sounded, between Mario and Kory. "I should get back to my guests," Jaymie said, standing and tugging down her shorts hem.

"Ah, yes, your group of friends!" Ruby said, looking up at Jaymie. "It must be nice to see them all again. How is it going?"

Jaymie summoned a smile and said, "It's okay. It's only been a few days and it always takes some time to get used to each other again, you know?" She turned to Garnet. "Say, I have a weird question for you . . . do you know, are the police looking at Mario's cell phone?"

Garnet frowned. "Why do you ask?"

"I heard him bragging about meeting women, you know . . . hooking up with them. I was wondering if there could be a jealous husband in the mix or anything? Or . . . I mean, Hallie *had* to have been hurt by his behavior."

"That girl didn't kill him," Ruby said, quick to anger. Garnet watched her carefully, his gaze steady and alert.

"No, no, Ruby, I'm not suggesting that. Maybe there were other guys involved. Maybe Kory *didn't* do it. Have they been looking at Mario's cell phone? Do you know?"

"Actually, they can't find it," Garnet said slowly, watching Jaymie's eyes. "Hallie told the police he lost it late Wednesday or early Thursday, she's not sure which. It was another irritant. I guess it's a pricey phone, the latest version, and of course he does all his business on it and it has all his contacts."

All his contacts; if it was missing, and if Brandi had been texting him, the police wouldn't know about it. They would get his phone records, but that took time. She took a deep breath and shook her head. What was she thinking? Brandi was *not* involved in his death. Even if she was seeing him, she had no motive for wishing him dead. Though . . . Terry, who had been following her yesterday, most certainly *did* have a motive, if he knew who she had been with. She felt the pit in her stomach deepen. "I'd better get going," Jaymie said with an apologetic smile, avoiding Garnet's watchful eyes. He was far too perspicacious. "Come on, Hoppy, let's let these folks get settled back in their home. I hope you had a good vacation."

"We did," Ruby said, taking her husband's hand. "It was good to get away from it all and sail!"

Garnet squeezed and smiled down at her. "I came back to get a lightbulb. One of the security lights on the Ice House patio burned out last night, and they've run through their supply." He was assiduous about keeping the big surrounding patio of the restaurant brightly lit. It discouraged vandalism and thefts, which had plagued them before the light system had been installed.

"Okay, both of you desert me, and your little dog too," Ruby said with a laugh.

"Thank you for the fudge," Jaymie said. "I'll share it with my friends!"

• • •

LUNCH WAS WHATEVER ANYONE WANTED; Jaymie made cold cuts, bread and sandwich fixings available, with little chunks of Mackinac Island fudge and Tansy tarts for dessert. Courtney prepared sandwiches for her and Brandi, and they ate in silence inside, in the bedroom, both on their phones. Jaymie, who checked in on them, glanced around the room, noting how Tiffany had taken over a substantial area on the dresser, her hair appliances and various liquids overwhelming the space. She wondered if Gabriela was enjoying her visit with her husband and little girl. Then she wondered if Gabriela would even return. Maybe the lure of family would be too great and she'd stay with her husband at the comfortable Queensville Inn.

She turned and watched her friend for a moment. "Brandi, did Tiffany ever say what the issue was with the house that made Logan and Fenix come here rather than stay at home?"

"I don't think so," Brandi said, looking up from her phone. "Why?"

"No reason. Just wondering."

"Knowing Tiffany it's a huge exaggeration. That woman is hateful."

"I thought she and Gabriela got along. You said Tiffany was her favorite person."

"I was being sarcastic, darling Jaymie; you never did get my humor."

"Oh." She retreated, leaving Brandi and her friend in peace.

Melody insisted on making Jaymie her specialty, a peanut butter and lettuce sandwich. It was actually not bad, Jaymie thought, as they sat in the comfy Adirondack chairs in the shaded grove. The salty goodness of the peanut butter contrasted nicely with the creamy crunch of Boston lettuce. But then, peanut butter went with almost everything. Melody certainly thought so, as she extolled the virtues of PB and bacon, PB and banana, PB and honey, PB and raisins, and went on to name the ones she had tried that *didn't* work for her: PB with sriracha, brown sugar, ham, and myriad others. She had even tried the Kinsey Millhone sandwich made famous in the Sue Grafton Alphabet series, PB and pickles, which Melody said was not nearly as bad as it sounded.

Jaymie laughed. "I'm sorry, but that sounds foul. I mean . . . PB and pickles?" She sipped her iced tea, finished her last bite of sandwich, and glanced over at her friend. "I have to ask, Mel, why do you want to talk to Detective Vestry? Is it because she was fangirling all over you?"

Mel looked shocked for a moment, eyes wide, bottle of water to her lips. Then she set the drink down. "Maybe if you'd read the Megan Hunter books you'd get it. Jade Torrence is a rule breaker, a kick-butt, take-no-prisoners loner who does not suffer fools gladly."

"And . . . ?"

Melody shrugged and set her plate on the grass beside her chair. Hoppy dashed over and licked the crumbs. "In the Jade Torrence book I'm writing right now—*struggling* through right now—I'm introducing an archnemesis, a frosty witchy police detective who is so officious and rule following that Jade wants to beat her with a rubber mallet."

"No, Mel!" Jaymie gasped. The description was spot-on. "You don't mean . . . but . . . how can you tell what Detective Vestry is like?"

"You think I don't listen to you when we talk? You've had run-ins with her before. And you keep trying to get her on your side, keep trying to bond with her. You're such a people pleaser you can't bear that she doesn't like you. But she never will; you're a nice girl, and though she is a rule-following fembot she *sees* herself in Jade Torrence, kick-butt break-all-the-rules hotshot detective. You, a wife, mother, food-blog-writing vintage-kitchen-collecting nice girl, are beneath her."

Jaymie felt a little hurt. "But I'm *more* than that."

"Of *course* you are," Melody said with an impatient twitch of her head. "You're smarter than she is, and that drives her crazy. The worst thing you could do, if you want to befriend Detective Vestry, is solve murders. Do you wish you hadn't solved the murders so you and she could be best buddies?"

"Of course not," Jaymie said sharply. "That's dumb."

"Then be *glad* she doesn't like you. Wear it as a badge of honor. As for my interest in her, I want to see what makes her tick. I want to dismantle her brain and turn it over in my hands and see where the on-off switch is. I want her to think I'm her new best girlfriend."

Jaymie sat and stared at Mel. "You're evil, you know that? But Mel, she obviously reads your Jade books religiously. She's going to hate it when you turn her into the enemy. And she'll take it out on me."

"Are you kidding? No one *ever* recognizes themselves in a character . . . or they *think* they do, but it's always the hero. Vestry sees herself in Jade, though Jade is probably the polar opposite of everything Vestry stands for." She winked at Jaymie. "I'll be able to tell you with more certainty once I've given her the Mel Heath treatment."

Jaymie still worried that Detective Vestry would recognize an unflattering description of herself. "Just go easy, okay? And make your character as physically unlike the detective as possible. Please!"

"Worrywart," Mel said affectionately.

"What *is* a worrywart, anyway? I hear that word often, but I've never known what it is."

"Someone who worries excessively. It comes from a comic strip from the fifties, but the meaning has been inverted." Melody stretched out on a lounge chair. "I'm going to have a nap."

• • •

VALETTA RETURNED FROM QUEENSVILLE with supplies and information. They sat together in the shade by the Shasta trailer, drinking iced tea, Hoppy curled up at Valetta's feet. "Brock came out to the island with me," she murmured. "He's showing a house, and he wanted to look at Mario's cottage. He is *sure* that Hallie killed Mario and then tried to cover it up by setting the place on fire."

"Why?"

"There's that life insurance policy that Hallie asked him to buy when she first found out she was pregnant."

"I knew about that already. Courtney said that Tansy is the one who suggested it to her." Jaymie digested that for a minute. "And that would be normal, though, right? To protect the child?"

"How many teenagers do you know who would follow an adult's suggestion, though?"

"I guess. But . . . that can't have been too long ago that they took out the policy. Isn't there a time before it kicks in?"

"Coverage generally begins immediately. However, there would be exceptions, like, if a premium hasn't been paid, or if the papers haven't been signed. One might think he was covered and wasn't."

Anyway, if Hallie *did* kill Mario—Jaymie thought it was unlikely—it wasn't necessarily for the insurance. She shrugged. "I can't imagine that girl stealing my pie iron and smashing her boyfriend with it. Mario is a . . . *was* a big guy."

"She could have done it while he was passed out," Val said. "He was drunk according to Sammy, right?"

"They were *all* drunk, Sammy said."

"Not Hallie. She's not been drinking because of the baby, right? And remember, Mario was talking about dropping her. What if she found out? Maybe Hallie figured if he did drop her, he'd cancel the life insurance policy, or make someone else the beneficiary."

"Do you think that's what happened?"

Val thought about it for a moment, pushing her glasses up on her nose and peering up at the cottage. "Not really. I mean, they've arrested Kory. In most cases the person arrested is who is eventually convicted."

"But not always."

"Not always," Val agreed.

Jaymie told Val what the Redmonds had told her about Kory's past. "He and Mario fought; Mario ended up dead. It's the most likely solution."

"Especially since Brock says that he heard that Hallie and Kory were fooling around. Maybe the baby isn't Mario's. Maybe he found out."

"Wow. How reliable is that gossip?"

"I don't know," Val admitted. "Let's call it a conjecture and leave it at that."

"In that case, let's go further: what if Hallie and Kory were in on it together? I could buy Kory whacking him with a pie iron over Hallie doing it, but she could be behind it."

"It doesn't have the feel of anything planned though, does it?"

"No. Doesn't mean it wasn't, though."

They heard raised voices from inside. It was Brandi and Courtney arguing. After a minute of shrieking, Brandi stomped out, down the back porch step and toward them, flinging herself in a chair and sobbing, clutching her phone in both hands. Jaymie exchanged a look with Valetta.

"Bran, what's wrong?" she said. Courtney stomped out and down the lane toward the road.

"It's . . . I can't say!"

Jaymie took a deep breath, glanced over at Val, then back to her friend. "Did you . . . did you, by chance, find out some news about the guy who died in the fire?"

Brandi gasped and stared at Jaymie. "You *knew*? How? I didn't know it was him until now, when I saw his picture in a news article online; we never . . . I mean, we didn't share our real names. It was . . . we . . . how did you know I was with someone?" Tears welled in her eyes. "We read the news stories, and found out . . . I didn't know . . . I mean . . ." She shook her head, tears still streaming down her cheeks unabated. "It's awful. Then C-Courtney said with the way he treated women, maybe he was better off dead."

So Brandi did *not* know that her lover and Mario were one and the same. There was no way Brandi could have killed Mario if she didn't know who he was. "I knew you were with someone that first night. You told Courtney to say you had gone to the mainland to go to a bar to review it, but then you said you came back on the ferry about two. The ferry stops at eleven."

Brandi looked a little scared. "Have you . . . have you told anyone?" She flicked a glance at Val, then back to Jaymie.

"No. But you have to tell the police that you were with Mario Wednesday night, Brandi. You *have* to! I've heard they don't have his phone yet, but when they do, they'll figure out you were one of his contacts, right?"

"It was a fling. It didn't mean anything. He wasn't *anything* he said he was."

"What do you mean?"

She rolled her eyes, back to Brandi mode, which all the friends knew meant she was disappointed in a guy. "He acted like he was this hot marine dude, you know, all jacked up and tattooed . . . everything I like in a guy. He shared a photo of a bicep with a Marines tattoo. And then we meet and he's this fifty-year-old handyman with a pot belly and gray stubble. Never a Marine in his life. So *not* hot."

"How'd you get to know him?"

"There's this gaming app . . . LiveLoveLife, it's called. Court plays. Terry plays. We *all* play it on our phones. You enter, and create an avatar and have a screen life and . . ." She shrugged. "You get to do whatever you want."

"What does that mean?" Val asked with a frown.

"You know, you can live a boring life, get married, get a job, have kids, or you can spice it up . . . have threesomes, kink, whatever, you know?"

"Kind of like real life without the consequences?" Val said dryly. "No broken vows, no hurt feelings? No kids?"

"Some people don't understand," Brandi said, sending her a look of disdain. "Some people don't want any adventure in their lives, any excitement. But so what? I like it. *Life is dull; spice it up.* That's the LiveLoveLife motto. We began talking on the messaging part of the app, and we flirted and had virtual . . ." She stopped, red-faced. "*Anyway*, he suggested we meet and we made a date for here, the first night."

Jaymie frowned. Mario had apparently lost his phone Wednesday night or Thursday; Brandi could potentially help pin down the timing. "Did you message him or something?"

"No, we had already made a date. I was to meet him down at the dock at midnight."

So he could have already lost his phone or . . . Brandi could have stolen it. But what would be the point? "Anyway . . . so you met. And you were disappointed."

"Yeah. At first."

"Where did you go?"

"He's renovating a cottage on the island that's empty; we went there. It was fun . . . like sneaking out of the house when you were a teenager. We . . . we kinda role-played . . . just a couple of lusty kids sneaking into an empty house. He had made a little love nest, with beer and candles . . . we had a good night."

"Though he wasn't your hard-body dude."

Brandi teared up and sniffled. "No, but he was sweet, and needy, and he said he could *talk* to me. We talked for an hour afterward. He was *so* unhappy, and grateful. He . . . he told me I was the most beautiful woman he'd ever been with."

Jaymie sighed. Having heard Mario talk, and knowing what he thought of the women he cheated with, she could have disillusioned Brandi real fast. She frowned. So . . . was Brandi his hot redhead lover that he was thinking of hooking up with on a permanent basis? It didn't sound like it, since this was their first meeting, according to Brandi. And who knew how many other women he had on the line? She had heard from his own mouth that it was more than one, though with his braggadocio it was hard to know how much was real and how much fantasy. "Did you know he had a pregnant girlfriend?" Jaymie asked.

Brandi shook her head, but then stopped. "I knew he had a girlfriend. He told me they had an open relationship. She was cool with him finding some fun away from her."

"It was only open from his side, apparently," Val said dryly.

Brandi blinked and swallowed. "I didn't know his girlfriend was so young, and pregnant."

"You had never met Mario until the first night you were here, on the island?" Jaymie asked, wanting confirmation.

Something flickered in Brandi's eyes, but she jutted her chin out and said, "Yeah."

Jaymie felt a pit of anger burn in her stomach. "So . . . you *didn't* make up the campsite being canceled so you could suggest we use my cottage and meet your guy friend here?"

Brandi's eyes widened. "Uh, no, I mean, it's not exactly . . ." She sputtered and fell silent. Her eyes, though . . . in her eyes was calculation. "No, I didn't," she said, but her gaze slid away.

Lying or telling the truth? Once Brandi committed to a lie,

shaking her from it was impossible, so if she was lying, she'd *never* admit it now. "Okay, I get it." Jaymie said, standing. "Val, do you want to go for a walk with me and Hoppy?" At the word *walk*, the little dog perked up and yipped once.

"Sure. Let's go," Val said, jumping to her feet.

Jaymie turned back to her friend. "One question, Brandi . . . how did Terry know you had been with a guy here? He accused you when we were in Grand Bend; how did he *know*?"

Her expression clouded and she shook her head. "I don't know. He's been stalking me lately. He had a tracking app on my phone. I thought I got rid of it, but . . ." She shrugged. "I blocked him online, but I suppose he could have friended me as someone else."

"But still . . . how would he know you'd been with a guy? You didn't post that on social media, did you?"

"No, of course not . . . not exactly."

"What does that mean?"

She sighed and rolled her eyes. "I may have hinted. In broad terms. You know . . . in emojis . . . *eggplant peach*."

"I don't know what that means," Jaymie said. Though she *could* guess, but she didn't want to go there.

"Is it possible he followed us back here, do you think, to Heartbreak Island?" Val asked.

"Maybe." Brandi looked alarmed. "You don't think he . . . but he *wouldn't*." She shook her head. "No, he *must* have gone back home to look after the kids." She clutched her phone and swallowed hard.

Interesting, Jaymie thought, that she would go there, that she would conjecture that Terry could do such a thing. "He followed us all the way to Grand Bend. Who did he have watching your kids then?"

"We have friends, ones who babysit," she said, her tone defensive. "And his mom is cool . . . she likes having all the kids with her. I'm a good mom, you know, not some delinquent."

"I know you are," she said. And she did. Brandi's kids were important to her, Jaymie knew it, but her life was full tilt; Brandi liked drama, and being a mom didn't offer much drama. She clearly needed an outlet. Too bad she hadn't taken up poker. Or bingo. Or competitive roller derby. But . . . what she said was alarming. Terry could be on the island right now and he *could* be responsible for

Mario's death. Her skin crawled and she glanced around. His could have been the footsteps she had heard in the night. "You've *got* to tell the police," she said, looking down at her friend. "About being with Mario, and Terry following you."

Brandi, looking stubborn, shook her head. "No, I can't do that. Terry's got *nothing* to do with this, I swear."

"*Please*, Brandi . . . they'll find out you were with Mario. Someone will know something, and if you don't come forward voluntarily, it'll look weird. Tell them the truth, tell them it was just once, and you didn't know the guy's name until you connected the dots." Jaymie would be sure to tell the police all she had heard, Mario's bragging about all the multiple women he was stringing along. Val had likely already told them, but she would reiterate. They had to know there were likely many more women and their partners who could be angry with Mario.

"I'll think about it."

"No, do it! Or I will, I swear."

"All right, I'll tell them. Later." She fingered her phone, turning it in her hand.

Sure; she'd talk to the police. After she called Terry, Jaymie thought, *to see where he was.* She took in a deep breath. That wasn't up to her. "You do what you need to do." *And I'll do what I need to do,* Jaymie thought.

ଟ Eleven ଟ

JAYMIE AND VAL WENT FOR THEIR WALK with Hoppy. "I don't know what to think," Jaymie said as they walked. "Knowing Brandi slept with Mario the first night we were here . . ." She shook her head, at a loss for words. "She couldn't wait to meet up with him," she complained, knowing she sounded bitter. "I rolled with it when she brought Courtney, but now it looks like this whole vacation was about her hooking up with a guy she claims she'd never met before."

"Who is now dead."

Jaymie took in a sharp breath, then let it out slowly. "I know I'm focusing on the wrong things."

"I'm not criticizing," Val said as they paused to let Hoppy sniff a clump of grass. They had walked away from the cottage and up to the farthest south end of the island, where the land had risen above river level and overlooked the waterway toward Lake St. Clair, not visible from where they were except as a widening of the river toward it. They were circling around on their way to visit the tart shop. "I get why you're upset; you feel like it's a betrayal of the purpose of the vacation, which was for you and your friends to reconnect, to bond like you did when you were younger."

"I can always trust you to get it."

"But—"

"Uh-oh."

"You're going to have to come to terms with the fact that you all have changed some, that you have different priorities, different needs. You're not twenty now. The Brandi you knew has evolved. She's a mystery to you probably, this new Brandi, but you're still thinking of her as she was at twenty."

Jaymie nodded and climbed the bluff to a stone point that overlooked the river. A breeze wafted her bangs away from her forehead, and the hot morning sun beat down on her. She turned back to Val and shaded her eyes. "I'm worried. Beyond my own feelings, my hurt that I think she arranged this whole thing so she could hook up, what if the cops want to check all our phones? I've heard that even if you delete phone messages, a forensic analyst can retrieve them. They could find out she was texting Mario, right?"

"You'll have to cross that bridge when you burn it down, as my mom used to say." Val smiled.

"I keep thinking I should be telling Vestry about Brandi and Mario. I mean . . . isn't that information they should have? Maybe he said something to her, or . . . or . . ." She shrugged.

"I can't answer that question for you, Jaymie. I can't give you advice," Val said, her expression sympathetic. "This is between you and your conscience."

Nodding, Jaymie turned away from the spectacular view. "I'm working on it. Right now, I want to give Brandi a chance to tell the detective herself."

Val nodded. "I think that's wise."

Jaymie linked arms with her friend and they walked on, with Hoppy tugging at the leash. "I'm lucky I have you here."

The day was humid, with the kind of dampness that stayed in the linens and beaded on the forehead. They stopped in to check on Rachel at Tansy's Tarts. She was happily wearing a white apron and selling ice cream to families.

After a happy vacationing family exited, licking their cones, Rachel turned to her friend. "You *have* to try this!" she said, her dark face radiant, her cheeks glowing. "Both of you! I'm going to sell you the best dessert in the world." She got out two cardboard cups, plopped a butter tart in each, and dished out one scoop of chunky, creamy ice cream. "Look at those chunks," Rachel said, pointing her scoop at some crusty tan and caramel bits. "This is Tansy's new ice cream, Butter Tart Blast, made with real Tansy butter tarts! On top of a Tansy butter tart it is a menace to the waistline, girls, but mmmm, *sooo* good! Look . . . we've gone environmental, and you get a real old-fashioned wooden paddle to eat it with! It's like a vintage disposable spoon!"

Val grinned. Jaymie laughed and said, "Rach, you have *literally* never looked so happy in your life!"

"I know," she said with an enthusiastic hop and nod, her springy curls bobbing like little blue-tipped waves. "I've found my bliss." She put the scoop back in the ice cream and closed the cooler with a slam. "I'm quitting my job and moving here to work. Tansy offered me a job until October — she's going to train me in pastry making — and then when things slow down for winter I'm going to find more work at a restaurant or bar. I *love* this island!"

Jaymie, stunned, stared across the counter at her friend. "You're . . . omigawd, Rach, are you *sure*? You're, like, a six-figure project manager. This is, like, minimum wage!" She was so stunned she had descended to her teenage gibberish of *like* every second word.

"I'm sure."

"But are you *sure* sure?"

"I'm *sure* sure. I could live for five years on my savings. I'll cash in my retirement fund if I need to. I *hate* my job, I *hate* my apartment. I want to live somewhere I like. Don't you want me close to you?" she said, clasping her fingers together and putting her fists under her chin, with a winsome smile.

"Are you kidding?" Jaymie hopped in excitement. "You *bet* I'd love you closer! Omigawd, Rachel, it'll be, like, the best!"

"You got it, bella!" Rachel came out from behind the counter and the friends hugged.

"I've got to go," Jaymie said finally. "We've got Hoppy, and I don't want to leave him tied up outside for any longer. I'll see you later."

Jaymie and Val ate their melting treats as they walked on, away from the tart shop. They briefly talked over Rachel's news, but then were both silent, eating the butter tart ice cream on the butter tart. It was so sweet Jaymie's teeth hurt, but it was delicious. She paused, finally, and crouched down to give Hoppy the last scraps, enough to give him a taste. She then gave him some water in the portable doggie dish she carried; it attached to a water bottle and flipped down, filling when one turned it over.

"I like your friend," Val said as they watched Hoppy lap up the water.

"Rach?" Val nodded. "She's the best. She and Mel kept me sane in college."

"And Brandi and Gabriela?"

"They were the reason I was *in*sane at times."

"Melody is an odd friend for you, though; she's . . . insular."

"Maybe you don't remember how introverted I was when I was a teenager. I suppose she takes a bit of getting used to, getting to know. And she's withdrawn more. She's not herself right now." Jaymie brooded for a long moment as she flipped the doggie bottle closed and tucked it back in her small knapsack, shifting it back to her shoulder. "We bonded over books, and that never stopped. She was a history and lit major. I was the one who introduced her to Grandma Leighton's collection of Regency romances. She wrote three books before we finished school; it came naturally to her. Her grades would have been better if she focused more on school projects, but she had a purpose. She'd read me bits and pieces, and I'd give her critiques. She's never looked back. It was slow going at first, but she stayed with it."

Val nodded. "I get it now. You're her muse, in a way."

"Maybe. I like that idea!" Jaymie's smile fell. "But she's not happy right now. And she's writing different stuff. No gentle dukes or nervous viscounts for a while now. It's all cynical beauties, dastardly cads and now crime thrillers."

"You have to let her write what she needs to write."

"I guess. I hate to see her unhappy. Andrew is not good for her. She thinks she saw him in Grand Bend, and she's been looking around ever since like she's afraid she's being followed. I'm worried."

They walked on, with Hoppy stopping to sniff at every clump of grass and sapling, and disposed of their cardboard bowls in a public waste bin. They then circled along the dirt road close to the end of the island, near the restaurant. There was the cottage that had burned out, what remained of the A-frame stark against the hazy sky, blackened splinters jutting up, and littered glass and wads of insulation bats strewn about at the base. It smelled acrid, and the charred wood and broken glass all around was a terrible reminder of what had happened that morning. A uniformed officer stood guard inside the police tape.

Another couple stood staring at it. Jaymie recognized them and waved. Val knew them too, and they joined Fran and Dan, seniors who had settled on Heartbreak Island a few years before, after living in Wolverhampton for years.

"What a shame!" Fran said, leaning on her cane and staring at the burned-out wreckage. "We looked at this place for our daughter and son-in-law, but it was such a wreck. We were glad someone bought it intending to fix it up. That poor guy had barely started."

Dan, a lean octogenarian with a sunspotted bald dome under a safari hat, was more pragmatic. "If Mario had spent more time working and less time bragging and drinking, he would have gotten somewhere."

"You knew him?" Val asked as Fran bent down and rubbed Hoppy's ears.

"Yep," he grunted. "We hired him to do a couple of things at the cottage. Can't say I thought much of his work, *or* his work habits. Always on that damned phone. I expect that from young people, but he was too old to be fiddling with his phone like a teenager."

Jaymie and Val exchanged a look. They knew what he was doing on that phone—making dates to hook up. "I heard he was working on some cottage where the owners aren't around right now," Val said.

"Yep. Don't know how much work he was getting done," he said with the loud voice of the partially deaf. "I heard he was using it as his personal love nest, different girl alla time, in fact, there were two girls at once, I heard—"

"Dan," his wife said, touching his arm. She shook her head.

"What? Mario's *dead*. No reason to protect him now, not that I would. The guy was a cheating lowlife."

There was a faint sound from behind them, and they all turned to see Hallie there, clutching her distended belly, supported by a woman Jaymie recognized from that morning as her frantic mother. The woman gave him a venomous look, and Dan had the grace to look ashamed.

"Hey, now, I didn't mean—"

"Enough damage done, Dan," Fran muttered. "I'm sorry, honey," she said to Hallie. "He didn't mean anything by it. We're truly sorry for your loss." She led her husband, who was still grumbling apologies, away.

Her lip trembling, Hallie stomped away to speak with the young police officer who was standing guard.

"Is Hallie okay?" Val said to her mother, who stood, arms folded over her chest, glaring off into the distance. "This has to be awfully hard on her, young and pregnant."

The woman pursed her lips and ambled closer, watching Hallie intently as the young woman argued with the police officer. Hoppy danced over to her, and she crouched, petting the little dog, her expression softening as she did so. "She's taking it harder than I would have thought, given what Mario was like. That man . . . the one who spoke . . . he wasn't wrong. I tried to get her to leave Mario, to come home, but . . ." She shrugged.

"I know you're her mom," Val said. "But I knew you before this morning."

"You're the pharmacist," the woman said, standing. "I've been getting Hallie's prenatal vitamins and such from you." She turned to Jaymie. "And I've seen you around town many times. You serve at the Tea with the Queen event and work at the historic house."

"Yes, I do! Wait . . . we've met before, too, haven't we? You brought a group of kids once, through the historic home."

"I did! Ellen Granger," she said, introducing herself with a trembling smile. That expression cost her and she choked back a sob. "I brought my Girl Scout troop through." She cleared her throat, shook her head and returned her gaze to her daughter. "Hallie always was the lost one of my daughters."

"Mrs. Granger, do you think Kory did it?" Jaymie blurted out.

"I wouldn't have thought it before this morning, but . . . he was trouble. Mario *tried* to help him, tried to *guide* him, but he was always getting into these fixes and Mario was always trying to get him out." She saw the look Jaymie and Val exchanged. "Oh, don't get me wrong, I was no fan of Mario's. He's older than *me*, for pete's sake. And with my daughter . . ." She shook her head. "But at least he was always polite and kind and he tried so hard. And he was looking forward to being a dad again."

Val blurted out, "Again?"

"Sure. He has a son, thirty-something. Didn't you know?"

"No. I don't think anyone local did."

"It was from his time away from here. He left after high school, moved to Ohio, and then came back here a few years ago."

Hallie returned to her mother, who put her arm around her shoulders and hugged her close. "He wouldn't let me look for my purse," she said, shooting a resentful glance at the police officer. "Everything important is in there, my driver's license, my insurance card, *everything!*"

"How are you, Hallie? I'm the pharmacist, remember me?" Val said. "Are you doing okay? How's the little one?"

The girl smiled, weakly, through tears. "She's okay . . . little Ariele." She rubbed her stomach.

"Please don't worry about your insurance card. If I can help with the hospital, I think I have a copy on record at the pharmacy until you get a replacement. Let me know if you need anything."

"Okay. Thanks. I don't know how I'm going to deal, with Mario gone, and Kory in jail, and . . ." She hid her face in her mom's shoulder.

"I didn't know Kory well," Val said, "but I *have* met him. He didn't seem a violent sort; I know that doesn't always mean anything. And yet I heard there was quite the blowup at the Ice House last night."

"It wasn't that bad," Hallie said, sniffing back tears, a defensive edge to her tone. "People are making it sound *way* worse than it was."

"We heard Officer Ng was called in," Jaymie said. "And that you all were asked to leave."

"Kory was . . ." She sighed, a much-put-upon teen. "Mario was being a jerk, and Kory was trying to make me feel better. He put his arms around me and gave me a kiss, and Mario got mad. That's *all*. They got into a big fight, and Kory said . . . he said he'd kill Mario if he hurt me." She shrugged with a helpless expression and sniffed back tears. "He didn't mean . . . Mario never *hurt* me, you know . . . he never hit me. He hurt my feelings all the time. He could be a real jerk, you know? And Kory wouldn't hurt a flea. It's been blown way out of proportion. *Way*."

"But it continued when you went home? The neighbors heard quarreling."

Hallie went rigid and stony. Her mouth clenched and she looked off into the distance. That was all the answer they needed. There was clearly much she wasn't saying.

But Jaymie had concerns of her own involving her friends, and she felt the need to seek information, so she pressed on. "I heard that Mario's cell phone went missing. Maybe it burned up in the fire?"

Val sent her a surprised look. It was an awkward question, bordering on insensitive.

But Hallie, appearing unconcerned, said, "He must have left it somewhere. I tried to help him find it. I phoned it from my phone, but nada. It wasn't in the house anywhere or we would have heard it ring. I don't know where it is, but either he lost it or it was stolen."

"When was that?"

Her mother eyed Jaymie narrowly, but Hallie blinked. "I . . . gawd, I don't know. Wait!" She stopped, slack-mouthed, then said, "That was one of the things that started the fight back up when we got home. He had been looking for his phone all day and couldn't find it, and blamed me. He said I was snooping again—"

"Again?" Jaymie interjected. "Did you often look at his phone?"

Stony-faced, she said, "Yeah, I did. He was cheating on me, the louse." Her mother gasped, and Hallie looked up at her mom. "I know, I never told you. But he had girlfriends all the time. He couldn't keep it in his pants."

Jaymie was silent; the infidelity, which she clearly knew about, gave Hallie a reason to kill him, for sure, along with the insurance and the possibility that Mario was going to dump her any day and leave her with a baby and no money.

"But I said, frick no, I wasn't looking at his phone, duh, and that he was so clueless that he prob'ly left it at the Ice House Wednesday night. He should have checked with them while we were there. He said, why didn't I say something earlier, because since he was kicked out he wouldn't be able to go back until morning. And I said it wasn't *my* job to remind him to look for his frickin' phone. He didn't remember when he had it last, but he'd been moaning about it all day so . . ." She shrugged. "Yeah."

"Was he careless about it?"

"No, not actually. I mean, he was secretive. That's why I got suspicious and scoffed the phone once and looked at it when he was in the shower. He was cheating with all kinds of women." She glanced at her mother. "That's why Kory was mad at him, because he was cheating."

"Do you remember the girls' names?" Val said. "The ones on his phone?"

She shrugged. "They weren't *real* names, you know? It was, like, HotRedhead22, and he was, like, BigStud30. Or she was Sexxxy-Mom," she said, spelling it out, "and he was HawtMarineBoy."

"So what happened next?" Jaymie asked. Now that Hallie had opened up, she wanted to find out as much as she could, hoping to get enough information she could be sure her friend, or her friend's husband, was not involved. "I mean, you guys were fighting, and the police came to the house, right?"

Hallie shot the police officer a dirty look. "Cops are always coming out for something. We've got cranky neighbors."

"Hallie!" her mom said. "Those people were *kind* to you this morning. And Officer Ng saved your *life!*"

"I know, I know!" Hallie said, sniffing. "It's been terrible. Mario threw Kory out, but Kory didn't have anywhere to go."

"What did he do?" Jaymie asked.

She stared at the burnt-out cottage. "It wasn't much — the house — but it was nice having a place on the river," she said wistfully. "When Mario was in a good mood, when we first moved in, he made this spot on the deck over the river, with a hammock for me to nap in when I was tired. Kory went there last night, to the hammock on the porch." She turned away from the scene. "He curled up there." Hallie looked teary. "I took him out a beer and he said he was sorry, that he never meant to cause trouble. I told him it was no big, Mario and I were . . . were going to fight anyway. We were *always* fighting."

Kory was close enough to kill Mario *and* start the fire, then. "When did you first notice the fire?"

Hallie looked pensive. "I don't know what time it was. I heard some noises. I got up to go pee, and I heard Mario talking. He was being real loud."

"He was talking *to* somebody?" Val asked. "Like maybe Kory?"

Hallie's mother was paying attention too, totally focused on her daughter.

"I think he was arguing with someone. He shouted, *'What are you doing here?'* . . . something like that. And he was mad, I could tell. He said, *'Get out or I'll call the cops,'* and then I heard a struggle."

"Was it with Kory, do you think?" Val repeated.

"No! It can't be. I mean . . ." She shook her head. "It wasn't Kory he was talking to," she said, but didn't offer any proof or reason.

And yet it would be exactly what Mario *would* say if he discovered Kory sleeping on the hammock after being thrown out. Jaymie wondered what Kory's version of events was. How would she be able to find out? "And then?"

Her gaze slid away. She shook her head. "I don't remember what happened next."

She was lying, Jaymie thought. There was something she didn't want to say.

"You don't remember?" her mom said. "What do you mean?"

"I don't *remember*, Mom!" she said, aggrieved. She pushed her two fingers to her temples and moaned. "I feel crappy. That smoke . . . I'm nauseous."

Pressing her on the point was going to aggravate her more. "And then the house was on fire?" Jaymie said.

She nodded, tears in her eyes. "I lost everything, *everything*! I lost all the stuff I'd saved for the baby, and . . . I even lost the sonogram!" She wept.

"Honey, we can get a copy of that," her mom said.

Val and Jaymie exchanged looks. As badly as they felt for Hallie, this might be the one chance to get her version of events. Jaymie asked, "Did you ever meet Mario's son?"

"Sure," she took a deep gulping breath and calmed. "In fact, I seen him the other day."

"He's here? On the island?" Jaymie blurted.

"Yeah. Or he was, anyway. He came to visit, I guess, random-like." Her face blanched. "He's going to be upset when he finds out! Crap." She sighed.

"I thought maybe he and Mario didn't have a relationship."

"They don't . . . didn't. But he was hoping to get to know his dad, he said. That's why he wanted to know what he was working on, and where we lived, and what we did."

Jaymie and Val exchanged looks. Nothing needed to be said; a stranger out to kill Mario would be doing that research too.

"Why didn't he walk up to him and talk to him? Or did he?"

"Not that I know of," Hallie said.

Jaymie frowned. The girl didn't know then if his son had found his dad. Maybe the son was unwelcome. Maybe that's who Mario was shouting at and saying *What are you doing here* and *Get out or I'll call the cops.*

"What does he look like?" Val asked.

"Nothing like Mario, I can tell you that. He came into the tart shop, scoping me out, prob'ly, an' asking those questions. He's tall with wispy hair . . . almost bald." She snickered, but her laughter died. "Not much like Mario. Mario was real proud of his hair."

"What is his name . . . Mario's son?" Jaymie asked.

"Terry."

℘ Twelve ℘

"T-TERRY? Are you . . . are you *sure*?"

Hallie stared at Jaymie. "Yeah, he told me. Why?"

"No reason," Jaymie said, her voice faint.

"Can we go home? I want to lie down," Hallie said to her mother.

Hallie's mom led her away, her arm over her daughter's shoulder. Jaymie watched them disappear around a bend in the road, happy that at least the girl had family, then turned to Val with consternation. "What are the chances that Mario's *son*, Terry, is Brandi's *husband*, Terry. The description is right."

Val shivered. "How awful if Brandi's husband found out that his wife was inadvertently sleeping with his father. It's pseudo-Oedipal in some weird way I can't wrap my mind around. And that kind of weirdness could easily lead to murder."

"But Terry is a common name, right? How many Terrys do *you* know?"

"I know three or four, at least, probably more," Val said. "It's like the name Chris, so common. But if the two Terrys are one and the same it would give Brandi's husband a powerful double motive for killing Mario."

"Hallie knew about Mario sleeping around. That gives her a motive too, beyond what we already knew. Kory's definitely got a motive, and he was right there. People keep saying he's nonviolent but . . . what do we know about him?" She glanced down the road and saw Sammy walking toward them, hand in hand with a girl about his age. "Sammy!" she called out.

He came closer, but his gaze was on the burned-out cottage. "Wow. I saw it this morning when it was on fire." He stared at the blackened timber, long charred boards pointing skyward. "Somehow this is worse."

The girl was glancing at Val and Jaymie and trying to get Sammy's attention.

"Sammy, maybe you could introduce us?" Jaymie said.

His cheeks pinked. "Yeah, sure. This is Ashlee; Ashlee, this is Jaymie and Miss Nibley, the Queensville pharmacist."

"Val," Valetta said, putting her hand out to the girl. "I'm just Val when I'm not at the pharmacy counter."

Ashlee shyly shook hands with them both. They made brief small talk, discovering that the girl was in college too, and had been home all summer, babysitting and sometimes working with Sammy on landscaping jobs, which he took on in addition to his barback job at the Ice House.

"Were you working at the Ice House last night, Sammy?"

He nodded. "It was hopping. We had a different band there last night, 2B-Tru, and they brought in a whole lot of their friends from Wolverhampton. But most of them cleared out before eleven to catch the last ferry. After that it was locals."

"What time was the trouble between Mario and Kory?"

Sammy watched Jaymie's eyes and nodded once, acknowledging that he knew why she was asking; her help in solving his father's murder was something he was never likely to forget. "That was about one or so. I know he was arrested, but I don't think Kory would have killed Mario. For one, he was dead drunk. And for another, if the cops think Kory killed Mario, then they must think that he set the fire to cover it up, right? But he would *never* have risked Hallie's life like that. He loves that girl. He'd never do a thing to put her in danger."

Jaymie was struck by Sammy's firsthand observation. It was a point that had not occurred to her, but it was logical.

"Kory is the one who took her for all her doctor's appointments." Ashlee, who had been watching Sammy, now turned her gaze to Jaymie. "I'm friends with Hallie's half sister, and she says that Kory acted more like the expectant dad than old Mario ever did."

Val was nodding at what both the young people said. "We were talking to Hallie, and I think you're probably right. Do you think Kory was *in* love with Hallie, or was it the love of a friend?"

He turned pink and ducked his head. He was used to Valetta as a figure of authority, and to be questioned by her on such a subject appeared to make him shy. But he looked back up and met her gaze. "Oh, he's in love with her, all right," he said, taking Ashlee's hand. "And I may be wrong, but I think she loves him too."

As they walked away, Jaymie asked Val, "But is Kory the father, or was Mario? And would the jealousy and anger possibly lead to murder?"

"I don't know. But the police should know about all of this."

"I'll make sure they do." Jaymie paused and let Hoppy sniff a tree trunk. "I can't stop thinking about what Hallie said. She said she heard voices, and Mario said 'get out' or something. But was Mario saying it to Kory or someone else?"

"And what is Hallie being evasive about?"

. . .

DINNER WAS BARBECUED BURGERS, raw veggies and pasta salad. They sat around the campfire after. As the golden sun set on another island day, Brandi was quiet and withdrawn, Melody read her book, but Rachel made up for the others, chattering nonstop about her new plans.

"I'm going to text my boss tomorrow and give my two weeks notice. I have more vacation time coming, so that can be in lieu of notice, actually."

"Are you sure about this, Rach?" Jaymie said, picking Hoppy up and cuddling him close. "You're throwing away your career!"

Rachel's cheeks got pink and her expression serious. Melody looked up. Brandi's eyes widened.

"Jaymie Leighton, who is the most responsible person you know from the old gang?" Rachel said. "Who always paid her bills on time? Who had a credit card, and worked to pay her tuition, and never stayed out late and partied?"

Jaymie bit her lip and could not hide a smile. "You, Rach. It was always you. I'm sorry for questioning your judgment. I should know better."

"I spent my twenties being responsible and doing what others said I should do. I think now, in my mid-thirties, it's time I did what I truly want for a change."

"You know, you're right. No more questions, and I'll be thrilled to death to have you close by." She jumped up—upsetting Hoppy, who toddled off to curl up by Valetta's feet—gave her friend a hug, then sat back down. "Now, I'm going to make proper s'mores; I've got the graham crackers, the marshmallows and the Hershey bar. Anyone can join me if they want." She made several of the treat and passed them around to anyone who wanted one, then got a couple of damp cloths so her friends could wipe the sticky mess off their hands and faces.

It had gotten quiet again. The next night they were going on a dinner cruise, but for tonight, it was just chill by the fire. Jaymie couldn't stop thinking about the notion that Brandi's husband was Mario's son.

"Hey, Brandi, you okay?" she asked. Her friend was gloomily texting and checking her phone, instead of engaging in conversation. Courtney was silent too, but she appeared worried for her bestie.

"Yeah."

Jaymie and Val exchanged looks, which Melody caught. She squinted at them, and became even more attentive than usual.

"I only know what I've heard from Jaymie about you all," Val said. She asked Courtney about her job, selling hospital equipment, and the woman launched into a detailed explanation of her day-to-day tasks. After, when there was silence, Val turned to Brandi. "I don't know a thing about your husband. What's his name again?"

"Terry."

"Where is he from? And how did you two meet?"

She shrugged. "We met at a bar. Where else do you meet guys?"

"You live in Ohio, right? Is that where you met him?"

"Sure."

"He was born and raised a buckeye, he always says," Courtney added, glancing at her friend, then looking to Val. "I knew Terry before I knew Brandi."

Melody glanced between Val, Jaymie, Courtney and Brandi. With an innocent gaze, she said, "Do you and his folks get along, Brandi? That's been a problem between Andrew and me. I can't stand his mom and dad," she said mendaciously. Andrew's mom and dad both lived elsewhere and were not often present, if at all. "How are his parents, Terry's mom and dad?"

She shrugged. "I don't know his dad. His mom is okay. She's pretty quiet, but she takes all the kids when I need her to."

"So his dad is alive? Dead? Absent?"

"I've never met him," she said. "Why the interest in Terry's dad all of a sudden?"

"No reason. Just making conversation," Mel said.

There was a noise behind them, above, on the laneway, and

Hoppy stood, yipping once. Gabriela, shadowed closely by Tiffany, joined them at the fire. For someone who had spent the day with her husband and much-loved child, Gabriela did not seem cheerful, and kept shooting unhappy glances at her sister-in-law, who also looked gloomy.

This was turning into the vacation from hell, Jaymie thought. But . . . it was *her* vacation from hell, so . . . tallyho. Pasting on a cheery smile, she said, "Hey, you two. How was your day? Gabriela, you must have been happy to see Logan and Fenix!"

She smiled, the first genuine smile in a while. "It was nice to see Fenix. I miss her already, coming back here to the cottage. I wish I was with her."

Jaymie narrowed her eyes. Was her friend preparing the way to go stay with her husband, cutting her girls-only vacation short? "I miss my hubby and daughter too. I'd love to have Jakob and Jocie here with me. If you want to go back to the inn, to be with Logan and Fenix, you can go, Gabriela. I want you to do what makes you happy."

Tiffany sniffed and looked perturbed. "One out of two ain't bad," she muttered.

Gabriela shot her a frightened look, and it looked like pleading in her eyes.

What was going on? Jaymie, troubled, didn't know what to say or where to go with the conversation.

But Mel had no such qualms. "Tiffany, you and Gabriela have a fight? You seem peeved."

The woman bridled, and shot the writer a dirty look. "Gabriela and I have our differences. It's private."

"Okay, so don't scowl and mutter then," Mel said. "Classic passive aggressive: act out, make people ask what's wrong, and then refuse to discuss it."

"I am *not* passive aggressive," Tiffany said, glaring at the writer. "I'll have you know, I have no *problem* calling you out. In fact, let's start with *you*; you're full of crap. You think you're hot because you're some author of sickly sweet fantasy romance. I've seen your stuff online. It's *junk*."

Oh, crap, Jaymie thought, eyeing her friend. Her work was the one thing Mel truly cared about.

But she perked up, looking like she was enjoying herself. Her eyes gleamed in wicked joy. "You've never read a romance novel, I'll bet. Certainly not one of mine."

"No, I read *proper* fiction."

"*Proper* fiction? What's that?"

The group had gone still, all watching the spat.

"Literary fiction," Tiffany sniffed. "You know, *real* writing."

"Like what?"

Tiffany sputtered, opened her mouth, but then closed it.

"No, come on; you said literary fiction," Melody goaded. "So, who? Alice Walker? Cormac McCarthy? Toni Morrison? Ishiguro? Naipaul? Fowles? *Who* do you read?"

Eyes wide, seething with anger, Tiffany was silent, her glare stony, but exhibiting uncertainty.

"Like I thought, you don't read at all," Mel said, contempt in her curling lip. "But this isn't about that; this isn't about books, and certainly not about *my* books. This is about you casting your gloom over everything and then acting passive aggressive when you're called on it. If you have a problem with Gabriela, why don't you say it out loud?"

"Melody, please," Gabriela said, folding her hands in a prayerful gesture. "Don't . . . just . . . don't." She choked back a sob. "It's been a long day. I'm going to bed." She jumped up and stomped off.

Tiffany rose more slowly, and glared around at them all, the firelight gleaming on her bronzed face. It looked like she had a tanning session during the day, probably at the Queensville Inn. "You think you know Gabriela, but you don't know anything at all. You have *no* idea what she's capable of. Except for maybe *you*, Brandi." She stomped off up to the cottage.

๙ **Thirteen** ๙

"WHAT DID *THAT* MEAN?" Rachel asked. "Brandi, you spend more time with Gabriela than the rest of us. What does that mean? And what is up Tiffany's butt?"

"She never liked Gabriela," Brandi said, rolling her eyes and sighing. "Tiffany is a pill. She's a self-righteous stooge. And she brags *constantly*. No one in town likes her. She's *petty*. If you look at her the wrong way she will get back at you, find a way to blacken your name. Trust me, she's tried with me, but luckily I have no name to blacken! It's already coal."

They all laughed, and Jaymie appreciated the comic relief, but the encounter left her unsettled. "What do you think she meant, what she said about Gabriela? About one out of two ain't bad, earlier? And that we don't know what Gabriela is capable of?"

Brandi shrugged and didn't answer.

"Brandi, Tiffany actually singled you out as someone who *would* know what Gabriela was capable of," Jaymie said.

Brandi shook her head and shrugged again. What had Gabriela done that was worthy of such disdain? Mel and Jaymie exchanged looks. Their friend, if she knew anything, was not about to divulge it. Maybe it was some cruel town gossip that she didn't wish to spread.

"Tomorrow evening is the dinner cruise, folks," Jaymie said, standing and stretching. "An all-you-can-eat perch dinner, or chicken for those who don't like fish, and entertainment. I bought tickets a couple of weeks ago, but I need to buy two extra tickets, for Tiffany and Courtney, at the Emporium tomorrow. Anyone want to go to Queensville with me and see the town, such as it is?"

"I hope you don't mind, but I promised Tansy I'd work again tomorrow. But I'm on for the dinner cruise! I wouldn't miss it; it sounds lovely," Rachel said. She got out her cell phone. "I'm going to send you the money for the ticket, though. There is no way you should be on the hook for that."

"I appreciate it, Rach. And if you're working for Tansy tomorrow that's okay, sweetie. How about the rest of you?"

They all agreed that Queensville sounded good, and turned in for the night.

• • •

THE NEXT MORNING they let Rachel shower first, as she had to dash to work, and the rest took turns. Tiffany, as before, took an inordinate amount of time showering, then even longer doing her hair, her makeup, and ironing her clothes.

Ironing. Her clothes. While vacationing in a cottage. It was bizarre to Jaymie, but she reminded herself that not everyone has the same standards. Maybe she appeared slovenly to Tiffany, but vacation was a time for flip-flops, tank tops and shorts. Though she supposed she'd look a *little* more decent to go into Queensville, like . . . best walking shorts and a clean tank top.

Fortunately, Tiffany's extended toilette, while the others relaxed with their phones or books, gave Jaymie time to have a face-to-face with Jakob and Jocie, where it was late afternoon. She retreated to a shady spot in front of the vintage trailer so she'd have a cute backdrop. "Hey, honey!" she said, trying to keep the tears out of her voice. "I miss you, my Jocie!"

Jocie waved and laughed, and then chattered nonstop. She had been to a zoo, and saw her first camel, she petted a giraffe, and kissed a hippopotamus. She sang a snatch of "I Want a Hippo-potamus for Christmas" — their favorite song to sing together — and then, in a solemn voice, told Jaymie that the zoo had been a hiding place for escaping Jews during the Second World War.

Then, in the lightning-fast shift of childhood, she chattered more about her cousins. She was learning Polish, and taught Jaymie how to say *What price is the Pączki?*

"Now what *is* a Pączki?" Jaymie asked.

"It's a doughnut!" Jocie said. "So good! We had an eating contest, but I didn't win." She named a boy cousin who won, Piotr, then made a face. "He can eat all day," she whispered, looking over her shoulder. Then her sweet round face, framed in blonde curls, got serious. "I miss you, Mama. I cried last night. Daddy says we'll be home soon, but it's only been a few days. How am I going to stand it?"

"You've got Daddy, and all your new cousins."

Jocie made a face, wrinkling her button nose. "I said I missed my mama, and my cousin Piotr said you weren't my real mama," she whispered. "That I only had one mom, and she was in heaven."

Jaymie took in a deep breath. How to handle this? "Sweetie, you tell your cousin that yes, your mom is in heaven, and you miss her, but that I asked if I could be your mama on earth so we could be happy together and I could take care of you. Okay?"

She smiled, a radiant, happy expression, which then fell. "I *still* miss you. I wish you were here. Daddy misses you too."

Jaymie choked back a fit of weeping, her heart aching. It was just ten days; she had to remember that. And they had only been gone a few . . . less than a week! "My sweet girl, think of all you'll have to tell me! Are you writing it all down in the diary I gave you?"

Jocie nodded and sniffed. "I am."

"Then write, every day. Write it all down so you won't forget it. Take pictures, too, and write about what's in the pictures. Then you can tell me everything. We'll come out here and stay in the trailer, just you and me, for a night. We'll stay up all night talking."

Jocie nodded. "Okay. Daddy wants to talk now and make kissy noises at you," she said, handing over the tablet with a giggle. She ran away, yelling at her cousin that she had talked to her mama, and had something to tell him.

Jakob's dear face appeared. A choking sob surprised her, and she touched the screen. "I miss you."

"I wish you were here. I miss talking to you every night. I miss holding and kissing you."

He looked tired. This must be taking an emotional toll on him, being with Jocie's grandparents. Inevitably Inga's sad life and fate would be the subject of much adult conversation. The pain would be fresh for the family. It was a lifetime for Jocie, but the passage of a very few years for them, having lost their daughter far too young. Jakob would be constantly trying to keep it light for Jocie, balancing letting her know that her mother loved her, and didn't intend to leave her, with the truth: Inga's life and death had not been easy.

The conversation was over too soon. Jocie had one more thing to say; she reappeared on-screen and reminded Jaymie to enroll her in dance classes for September.

After they all signed off, Jaymie shut down the tablet and set it aside. She closed her eyes, letting the emotion wash through her, walking through it, feeling it, missing her husband and daughter, but reminded herself they would be home soon. Missing them deeply meant she loved them deeply, and she was grateful for that. Ten days was nothing; military families all over the world had to bear separations of months, sometimes years. She was certainly strong enough to stand ten days.

Right now she had more to think about. She realized she had not mentioned any of it to Jakob. Normally they would discuss it all in detail; he never asked her not to try to figure things out when it came to murder. He trusted her gut and her instincts and knew she would be careful. But this time he was far from home; he would worry, knowing he could not be there in a minute if she needed him. It had not been a conscious decision and she had not purposely withheld it from him, but still . . . she'd tell him all when he came home.

"You ready, Jaymie?" Melody called from the back porch of the cottage.

"I am," she said, dashing away the last tears clinging to her eyelashes. "Let's go."

It was another ferociously hot, humid day, the heat clinging and cloying, perspiration a constant film on Jaymie's neck and forehead. It was worse the moment you emerged from the shade into the sun. They took the ferry, Hoppy on his harness, and ambled into the village. The Emporium was the first stop, since Jaymie had to buy two more spots for the dinner cruise. Val had to check in with the pharmacist who was taking her place, and then go home to spend some time with Denver, whose nose was out of joint from her absence. He was accustomed to Val's full attention. She would meet them in a couple of hours at the Queensville Inn for lunch.

The group visited Jewel's Junk, and the Cottage Shoppe, and then finished at Queensville Fine Antiques, Jaymie's sister and brother-in-law's store. Becca and Kevin were not there; they were both in London, Ontario, at the moment, with Jaymie's Grandma Leighton, taking her to visit family in a nearby town. Georgina, Kevin's frosty sister, who didn't much like Jaymie or anyone, it occasionally seemed, was looking after the shop alone.

After dawdling, they walked to the Queensville Inn, a few streets away. They approached along the road, and Jaymie glanced up a grassy sloped lawn to the modern part of the inn, built to create more rooms and suites to fit more guests. Mrs. Stubbs's son owned the inn and had created, for his mother, a ground-floor suite with a wheelchair-accessible bathroom, a kitchenette, and a patio that overlooked the street. The woman was sitting in her mobility chair in the open doorway, reading a book. Jaymie called out and waved. Mrs. Stubbs beckoned.

"Come up and see Mrs. Stubbs," Jaymie said, motioning to the rest of them.

They scaled the yellowing grassy incline up to the patio block terrace. The elderly woman regarded them all, a flicker of recognition in her eyes when her gaze passed over Gabriela and Tiffany. Hoppy danced around at the feet of one of his favorite people, someone who always had a cookie to share.

"You remember my friends, from the wedding?" she said to the woman.

"Of course I remember," she said. "Though I don't remember your names, and some of you have different hair." She squinted and frowned. "Mebbe I don't remember you *all*."

It wasn't surprising Mrs. Stubbs didn't remember them. The wedding was a year and a half ago, and her friends didn't mingle much, mostly sticking among themselves. After reintroducing them, she said, "Mrs. S., if you don't mind, can Hoppy sit with you while we have our lunch in the restaurant? I didn't think about it when I brought him along. If it's trouble, I can take him back to be with Georgina at the antique store."

"Good lord, sentence him to time with Georgina Brevard?" Mrs. Stubbs said of Becca's sister-in-law. "My little doggie friend is more than welcome to visit for an hour."

"I can leave him with you now, then," Jaymie said. She unhooked his harness and set him inside with Mrs. Stubbs, and closed the screen door so he couldn't dash back out. "I'll be back in a little while to retrieve my fella."

Jaymie led the way as Tiffany, Courtney, Brandi, Gabriela and Melody trudged after her, an oddly assorted and discordant group. This vacation was going to be an endurance event; who could last the longest with sanity intact? Now that they had lost Rachel's inevitably cheery outlook for most of the day, Melody's sarcastic cynicism was the semi-bright spot.

They entered the front doors of the inn to the cool dim interior, and from the hall passed through the double doors of the restaurant. It had been redecorated a year ago to be clean, calm, and elegant. Jaymie was grateful for the air-conditioning. The hostess was leading them to a table by the big bay window overlooking the street when Tiffany said, pointing, "Oh, hey, Gabriela, there's Logan and Fenix. Let's sit with them."

The hostess paused and frowned, glancing over at the small table in the corner, where Gabriela's husband and little girl were sitting. "I'm sorry. There's not room for your whole party at that table."

"I'm sure Jaymie won't mind if Gabriela and I sit with our family," Tiffany said. She stalked away.

"I'm sorry, Jaymie, I am," Gabriela muttered. "But I ought to . . . I should . . . I'd better go sit with them."

"You do whatever you want," Jaymie replied, forcing a cheery note into her tone.

"It's not what I *want*, but it's what . . . I'll see you later."

"I can come over and say hi to Logan and —"

"No, it's okay, Jaymie, just go have lunch." She headed over to the table and picked up her little girl, kissing her face all over as the child giggled.

"Aaand . . . we've lost her," Melody said, watching the family reunion. "But on the bright side, we lost Tiffany too. I count that a win."

The hostess seated them, and a waiter soon arrived with menus. Val texted that she'd be a while and not to wait for her. The pharmacy delivery driver was off sick, and so her replacement pharmacist wouldn't be able to deliver until after hours, so she had volunteered to fill in for an hour. Jaymie texted back an okay. They took a few moments with the menus. Brandi ordered a Caesar drink and salad, saying she was going for a theme. Courtney ordered identically—of course—while Melody ordered the chicken tortellini salad and an iced tea. Jaymie, knowing the fish dinner on the cruise would be marvelous, ordered a green salad. The struggle to keep fitting into her summer shorts was real.

Brandi was in a thoughtful mood. What *was* she thinking behind her huge sunglasses, always perched on her nose? Jaymie wondered. Was she thinking about Mario? There was no telling, as she was being unusually circumspect. Of course, she had Courtney to talk to. Jaymie was actually glad of that. It felt like, as the years had passed, she and Brandi had less and less in common. Maybe their fun friendship of years past was based on an illusion, something Mel had intimated.

"How did your conversation with Jocie and Jakob go this morning?" Mel asked, sliding a glance sideways at Jaymie.

"*So* good."

"You cried, right?"

Jaymie nodded.

Brandi smiled. "I know how you feel. I miss my kiddos too." Her smile died. "I trusted Terry to be looking after them, for God's sake, and instead he shows up here. He needs to let it go."

"Maybe he's back there now?"

"I hope so." But she didn't look convinced, finally laying her sunglasses aside to reveal red-rimmed bloodshot eyes. "He hasn't returned my text."

"But *someone's* looking after the kids, right?"

"Oh, yeah, if the babysitter poops out on us, his mom will take over. She's great. Even my oldest likes her and calls her Grandma. His family is fine, *he's* the one who screwed up."

"Screwed up?" Until this moment, despite numerous comments she now recognized as hints, she had assumed that Brandi got tired of being married. "What did he do, Bran?"

"I don't want to talk about it," she said, her smile watery.

The waiter arrived with their drinks.

"This is what I need: vodka, and lots of it." She took a long, thirsty drink, then called out to the departing waiter, "Hey, another of these, please!"

He turned, nodded and headed back to the bar.

Brandi fished in her purse and got out her phone, bringing up pictures. "Here's some of the latest pics of my kids. I don't share them online because you never know, right?"

"That's why I don't share pictures of Jocie." Jaymie took the phone and scrolled through the photo gallery of Brandi's photos, most of her kids, but also many of her partying, a few of her and different guys and some of Courtney. There were, among them, older ones of Brandi looking happy with Terry. The best was one of Terry with Logan and Gabriela.

"Aw, I love a couple of these pics of you, Brandi," Jaymie said.

She swallowed hard, glanced at Melody, then looked at her friend. "Do you mind if I send a couple to my phone?"

"Which ones?"

"Uh . . . this one of you at Mardi Gras in New Orleans, for one. And a couple of others. You have some of my wedding that I didn't see."

"Sure, whatever," she said, draining the glass and reaching out as the waiter brought another. "Just don't post them, okay?"

"I wouldn't dream of it. In fact, I won't leave them on my phone," Jaymie said, sending the photos she had named, but also another of Terry, to her phone. "I'll off-load them to my computer as soon as I get a chance." She didn't know how, but she was going to take the photo of Terry to Hallie to see if Brandi's Terry was Mario's Terry. It was going to bug her until she knew for sure. Mel was looking at her weirdly. Jaymie made a face and handed the phone back to Brandi.

As they ate, Brandi talked about her kids. The oldest took music classes and was showing some remarkable talent. *Said every parent everywhere,* Jaymie thought with a smile. The child she was looking after finally slept through the night without waking up screaming, which was a big move forward.

"And my little guy baby . . ." Brandi's expression softened. "He's my last. I got my tubes tied. You know, I think babies are the one thing men don't make a mess of."

"I'm sorry your marriage didn't work out, Brandi," Jaymie said, reaching over and squeezing her friend's hand. "What was it about him that broke the marriage up?"

Courtney snorted. "What wasn't there?"

"Court, enough. He's a good dad most of the time, but he won't discipline the kids. It's left all up to me. And . . ." She sighed. "He cheated on me."

"Figures," Mel said darkly.

"Right?" Courtney added.

"I'm sorry," Jaymie said. She paused, but then said, "But you've moved on, right? Like coming here to hook up with . . . with a guy."

Melody raised her brows. Jaymie belatedly realized her writer friend had not been in on the conversation about Brandi and Mario, but it was too late.

Brandi sent her a narrow-eyed look. "I can do whatever I please. I'm a free woman, despite what you or Terry think."

"I'm sorry, Brandi, I didn't mean it to sound—" At that moment her phone pinged and she picked it up to look at the text. "Val says she'll meet us on our way back to the island, if we can stop at her house." She looked up from her phone. "I have to go retrieve Hoppy at Mrs. Stubbs's. Anyone want to go with me?"

"I'll go. And it's my turn to pay for lunch. You've paid for enough, Jaymie," Melody said, with a pointed look at the others. "Brandi, you can settle up with me for your Caesar drinks. I'm not supporting your booze habit."

Jaymie and Melody stopped at the cash desk to pay the bill, and then proceeded out to the hall and toward Mrs. Stubbs's suite.

"What was that about Brandi meeting a guy on the island? Not that I'm surprised."

Jaymie told her what she had figured out. "I shouldn't have brought it up, though. I think I hurt her feelings. But listen to this," she continued, and told her friend what she and Val had discovered about Mario's son being named Terry.

"So *that's* why you were trying to find out more about Terry last night around the fire."

"You caught on enough to help," Jaymie said. "Not that it did any good."

"Let me guess: one of the photos you sent to your phone is of Terry?"

Jaymie nodded. "But I don't know what to do next. I don't want to accuse an innocent man."

"If he's innocent, it'll all be fine."

"But it feels like I'm crossing some kind of invisible friendship line, you know?" she murmured as they headed down the carpeted, dimly lit hallway. "Taking the photo without asking, and maybe showing it to Hallie . . . and the police?"

"A man was murdered. Which is worth more: finding the killer or preserving Brandi's feelings, such as they are?"

"I don't know. Here is Mrs. Stubbs's place," she said as they came to the door. "You don't mind coming in to talk for a minute, do you? Mrs. Stubbs is an avid reader, and she'd love to talk to an author."

They entered to find Hoppy securely on Mrs. Stubbs's lap as she read *Elizabeth Is Missing* by Emma Healey on her reading device, a gift from her sons. She liked it because her sight was fairly bad even with thick glasses; books that had not been available in large print she could now read, with the font sizing capability.

"Mrs. Stubbs, this is Melody Heath, my writer friend."

"Ah, Jaymie has talked about you," she said, closing the cover on her device. "She keeps trying to get me to read your books. I haven't so far."

Mel laughed out loud, a hoot that echoed and startled Hoppy, who looked up, ears perked. "I respect that, Mrs. S. Not all books or all writers are for all readers."

Jaymie rolled her eyes. "That's before I knew you wrote the Megan Hunter books," she said to Melody. "Mrs. Stubbs reads mystery and suspense, not romance."

Melody's eye lit up. "Hey, I'll send the Jade Torrence series to your device."

"They're Detective Vestry's favorite books," Jaymie said with a hint of acerbity.

"That woman . . . ! I'd be interested in reading the books, young lady, to see if there is anything Jaymie's least favorite police detective and I have in common."

They sat with Mrs. Stubbs for a few minutes and talked books. She and Melody had many favorite authors in common, as it turned out, and both had a surprising penchant for true crime.

"We'd better get going," Jaymie said. "We're keeping our friends waiting."

"Who are the two girls you were with? Not the tall one with the purpley hair, or the one dressed like her, but the neatly dressed one and the other . . . the chubby girl?"

"That's my friend Gabriela—the one you call chubby—and her sister-in-law, Tiffany."

"I saw them; thought they were guests here at the inn. But they're part of your girls' week?"

"Gabriela is. Tiffany was an unexpected bonus," Jaymie said.

"The gift that keeps on giving," Melody added.

Mrs. Stubbs's arthritic fingers moved restlessly, turning her reading device over and over in her hands. "There was something . . . *wrong* in their interaction."

Jaymie's gaze sharpened. When Mrs. Stubbs talked, she listened. "What did you see?"

"It wasn't what I saw, it was what I overheard. There was something menacing. Something . . ." She sighed and frowned. "Do you know how someone talks to you when they know a secret, something they are holding over you?"

"I'm not sure I know what you mean."

"I do," Melody said. "It's like gloating; it's cruel, cold, calculating. There's a certain tone of malicious enjoyment, like they know something, and they *could* tell the world, but they'd rather hold it back and torment you with the knowledge."

"Exactly!" the woman said, pointing one crooked finger at Mel.

"Who was holding what over someone's head?"

"I first saw them walking along the grass; I was sitting on the terrace outside my window. It was a nice day, not too hot yet. I'm old, virtually invisible to some people. These two were deep in conversation, and the skinny one looked around and dragged the other off around the corner of the inn. But I hadn't heard their voices, so I don't know who was saying what." She closed her eyes, thinking.

Jaymie exchanged a look with Melody, who was totally enthralled in the old woman's method.

Mrs. Stubbs opened her eyes. "The conversation went like this: first woman said, *Why are you torturing me like this?* Second woman said, *Because you deserve it, after what you did . . .* and the first woman interrupted and said, *It was an accident. I didn't mean any harm.* Then the second woman said, *If you know what's good for you, you'll give up and let go, Gabby!*"

෨ **Fourteen** ෨

JAYMIE RECALLED THE FRIGHTENED LOOK on Gabriela's face when Tiffany showed up. "The first woman is Gabriela, the second is Tiffany. Tiffany is definitely holding something over Gabriela — I think you're right — but what?"

"Something that happened at home before Gabriela left. Or something that was discovered after Gabriela left Ohio," Mel said.

"What do you mean, something that was discovered after she left Ohio?" Jaymie asked her friend.

"I can think of a lot of possibilities: something wrong with the car that she didn't tell anyone about, or a dangerous situation with the house she ignored, maybe?"

"I can see that," Jaymie said. "Gabriela was never handy around the house. And she could be careless; she was notorious for leaving the door unlocked at night, if she was the last to come in."

"I remember cops coming around and warning us about that after a series of break-ins of student housing. And *still* . . . she kept forgetting to lock up."

"It sounds like Tiffany is threatening Gabriela, though . . . to say *If you know what's good for you, you'll give up* . . . what does that mean?"

"They have a child with them, don't they?" Mrs. Stubbs said.

Jaymie nodded. "Logan, Gabriela's husband, came to Queensville with their daughter, Fenix, and his sister Tiffany. Something happened at their house and they had to leave. We don't know what it was. What could be so wrong that it would force them out?"

"If that's his daughter, he hasn't been spending much time with her. I sit in the lobby often to people watch. I know for a fact from Edith's phone calls," she said, naming her son's partner, who manned the combined reservation concierge desk, "that he's had the Queensville Inn babysitting service on alert for the few days he's been here. There's a lovely girl; Allie or Ashlee . . . I can never remember her name. She's been here on and off for days taking care of their daughter."

"Where is Logan going, I wonder, when he gets a babysitter for Fenix?" Jaymie said.

Melody squinted, staring out the sliding doors and into the

distance. "Maybe following Gabriela? What a bunch of weirdoes we married . . . all except you," she said to Jaymie.

"I do know the babysitter, if it's the girl I think it is," Jaymie said. "Her name is Ashlee, and she's Sammy Dobrinskie's girlfriend. Maybe she knows what Logan has been up to. I'll find out." She texted Sammy to ask for his girlfriend's phone number then returned her phone to her purse.

"But *Logan*?" Melody said. "Do you suspect him of doing in Mario? Why would he?"

"I don't know," Jaymie said. "But something is going on among those three: Gabriela, Tiffany and Logan. I've got this feeling . . . is it possible that Tiffany is setting Gabriela up in some way?"

"I don't know how that would work out . . . they don't have anything to do with Mario, as far as we know, none of them."

"You're right. It doesn't make sense. It's time to find out, though, what is going on there. If they won't tell me, I'll have to be sneaky." She stood and snapped Hoppy's harness on him. "We have to go, Mrs. S. Dinner cruise tonight." She kissed her friend goodbye, and Mel asked if she could come back sometime and hang out with Mrs. Stubbs, who said *yes* in a surprised voice.

"I like her," Melody said as they left and headed down the dim hall. "A lot. In fact, she might become a character in the Jade Torrence books. I need some balance, someone older, or *someone* different. The list of characters reads like a who's who of a Midwest country club."

Jaymie laughed. "Is that how you decide a character's identity? You have a quota system for diverse ages and ethnicities?"

Mel gave her a look. "Of *course* not. In general I let the character tell me who they are but lately . . ." She shrugged. "Maybe it's because I'm surrounded at home with such suburbanality."

"Is that a real word?"

"Nope. Coined it. Or *maybe* I coined it . . . who knows? Maybe I heard it from someone or somewhere and stole it." She grimaced. "There is nothing new under the sun. Isn't that a saying? Is it from the Bible? I don't know. I feel like I don't know *anything* anymore." She sighed. "I've been . . . *off* lately." She flexed her shoulders, an uneasy expression on her plain face. "The writing is suffering. I end up creating the same character over and over again and they're all miserable straight white people in horrible marriages."

Jaymie bit her lip, trying not to laugh at Melody's predicament, since her friend was clearly in distress, but it *sounded* funny, the way she said it.

"That doesn't reflect real life, does it?" Mel said, glancing over at Jaymie, anxiety on her face. "I mean, all the people in my work in progress are alike. Or it feels that way to me. I don't always do that, do I?"

"No, of course not. You're good at having a varied cast of characters." They walked on down the hall toward the front of the inn. "I guess I don't understand writing," Jaymie said.

Melody sighed. "I don't mean to be a pain. But I usually *am* a pain when the writing isn't flowing. Thank God for editors. Mine told me I needed a vacation, and he was right. I needed this." She stopped dead and put her arm around Jaymie's shoulders and gave her a side hug. "See, that's why this vacation is good for me. *You're* good for me. I needed to mix it up, to get out of my shell. I'm a natural born hermit, inclined to crawl into my dark cave and think too much. I needed time away from Andrew. Reconnecting with you and Rach and even Brandi and Gabriela has been good for me. And meeting Valetta, Heidi and Bernie . . . and Mrs. Stubbs . . . I *love* her! It's the best. I appreciate it."

"I'm glad you're enjoying it. I was afraid it was kind of a downer, you know?"

"I don't need perfect. Just being with old friends is good."

They continued on, emerged from the hallway, passed the reservation desk and threaded their way through the chairs in the lobby to the front doors, where Tiffany, Gabriela, Brandi and Courtney were waiting for them on a bench outside.

Together they walked to Val's place. She invited them in to visit and meet Denver, the "man in her life," as Valetta said with a smirk. Hoppy was overjoyed to see his old frenemy again and bounced around the cat, who eyed him, unimpressed by such an obvious display of emotion. Mel sat on the floor, back against the sofa, and Denver, after leisurely sniffing everyone, climbed onto her lap. She smiled and stroked the cat as he curled up and fell asleep. "This is what I need in my life. If only Andrew wasn't allergic."

"Ditch the husband and get a cat," Brandi said.

Mel laughed. "You've got something there, Bran."
After a cold drink they returned to the island.

• • •

FOUR HOURS AND MANY ACRIMONIOUS BATTLES over the bathroom
and mirror space later, attired in suitable summer dinner cruise
wear, they made the forty-five-minute trip north, Jaymie, Val, Rachel
and Melody in Val's car, and Brandi, Courtney, Tiffany and Gabriela
following in Brandi's. They parked at Desmond Landing in Port
Huron and got out of the vehicles, straightening dresses and shorts,
facing the humid hot air and retrieving purses from the two cars.

Jaymie, dressed in a cute tropical-patterned summer dress she
found at an end-of-summer sale at Target, spotted someone she
knew waiting by another car in the parking lot. She waved and
yelled, "Chief Ledbetter!" Val, who also knew the former chief of
police, followed her over to where he stood by an aging Buick,
accompanied by a gray-haired portly woman, her curls damp with
the August heat, fanning herself with a ticket for the dinner
cruise.

"Jaymie! How are you?" he said with a relaxed smile. He introduced her to his wife, Mamie, who smiled but stayed silent. She
resumed crocheting a baby blanket, the wool coiling out of the
depths of her capacious straw bag at her feet.

They traded tales, what they were up to, and how they had all
been, as more cars arrived and the dock became alive with the
sounds of laughter and chatter from the people looking forward to
cruising. Melody, who wore tan Bermuda shorts and a sleeveless T-
shirt, joined them and was introduced, her profession briefly noted
by Jaymie, who was proud of her friend's work. The chief's wife
perked up, eyes wide.

"Something tells me she recognizes the name. She reads a lot,"
he said, hitching his thumb at his wife.

"Horace!" she reprimanded. "Pleased to meet you all," she said,
continuing crocheting as she spoke.

Melody eyed her with fascination and sidled over to talk to her.
They were soon deep in conversation, but not about books; their
chat seemed to be mostly about grandchildren and crocheting.

"How is retirement?" Jaymie asked with a sly smirk. She knew the answer, but it came in an explosion.

"Boring! I've taken up lawn bowling," he said with a cross look at his wife, who smiled and kept crocheting and nodding, and talking to Melody. "Even *croquet*. Did you know there is a croquet league in Wolverhampton?"

"But I thought you'd buy a boat and fish?"

"I've *got* a boat, but it's a nuisance hauling it down to the boat launch every time I want to go fishing, and I hate paying to keep it in a slip. We'd like to buy a place on the island, matter of fact. If I had my own dock she'd never see me."

His wife looked up and smiled again. "I'd love that, too . . . to sit on the dock by the water with a cup of tea in the early morning. Heaven. But places on the island are pricey." Her voice was soft and velvety, and there was a sparkle in her blue eyes that hinted at a mischievous sense of humor. "When Horace is being a pain in the neck I could tell him to take a long walk off a short dock."

The chief chuckled.

"What would you think of a fixer-upper?" Val asked. "Not everyone is up for a project, but my brother has one or two Heartbreak Island cottages on his books. Brock Nibley, real estate agent; he handles most of the sales on the island." She fished out a card and handed it to the chief.

The chief took it and looked at it thoughtfully, nodding. "We had a fellow in Wolverhampton looking around for us, but he's no good. We're small potatoes and he'd rather cater to the rich folks. He took us to see one place on the island but they wanted half a million for it!" He handed it to his wife, who dropped it in her crochet bag. He looked up, pale blue eyes narrowed. "Heard there was a little trouble out there two nights ago."

"I'd call it more than a little trouble," Jaymie said, frowning. "It's a tragedy. And I'm not convinced the fellow the police arrested actually did it."

"Kory Jamison," the chief said. "I know him. He's been in and out of trouble a lot."

"For minor things like theft, though. He's not violent, is he?"

The chief shook his head. "Not to my knowledge. I've known him since he was a kid; friends of his family. He's been in trouble since he was ten. Mind you, it's always been petty stuff: breaking into sheds, stealing tools to sell." He turned to watch as the dinner cruise boat, a two-deck cruiser named the *Huronia*, motored toward the dock. "S'pose we'd better get ready to board. You got a whole crew of gals, huh?"

"College pals," Jaymie said. "We'll see you aboard."

"Ahoy," he said with a chuckle.

• • •

THE CRUISE WAS UNDER WAY. Jaymie stood on the open upper deck and leaned on the railing, watching the water splash along the hull, white froth lifting and falling as the boat cut through the waves. Seagulls—herring gulls, those squawky, begging, persistent pests that populate Great Lakes–area parking lots looking for French fries or other delicious scraps—screeched and wheeled overhead as the western sky turned a golden pink. The sun was a fireball sinking toward the horizon as the *Huronia* headed north into the lake. There was another hour or so of sunlight, but it was dwindling.

The air was fresher. A breeze lifted her bangs, drying the perspiration that had gathered on her forehead and under her heavy ponytail. She took a deep breath in, inhaling the clean lake air, then joined her friends. Families and couples strolled around them, everyone in a holiday mood, clearly happy with the weather and the evening.

The college friends sat on deck chairs in a circle with glasses of wine and laughed and talked about the old days: the parties, the guys, the classes . . . the *parties*. Hanging out at the Ceeps, the downtown London, Ontario, bar notorious among Western students through the decades, and the Spoke, the campus bar. They reminisced about their rented house, a ramshackle two-story barn with poor heating, uncertain lighting that flickered like in a horror movie—especially in the basement laundry room—and an ancient stove on which one burner worked.

And one bathroom for seven or eight girls.

"*That* was the real horror story," Brandi stated, leaning back in her chair. "Court, you should have been there! Trying to get ready to get to class in the morning, or to go out on a Saturday evening . . . it was torture! Worse than tonight."

"Poor privileged princesses," Tiffany said with a malicious snort. "Doomed to the horrors of a single bathroom." She took a long drink of her scotch and water, her coiffed and gelled hair not moving in the stiff breeze that fluttered the rest of their tresses. "Logan and me . . . we were raised in *hell*, with folks who didn't give a damn about us. We were happy to be together and lucky to have food to eat and a place to rest our weary heads at night, even if we *did* get beaten for stealing a cookie or asking for a drink of water."

"Isn't *that* a perfect conversation ender?" Melody said, shooting Tiffany a disgusted look.

"Says the woman who can end any conversation by saying, '*In my last book*' . . ."

Melody turned red and fell into a brooding silence, slurping down a long gulp of wine.

Brandi, glaring at Tiffany, said, "You can never let people be happy, can you? Can't you for *once* not be the death of the party? At least Mel doesn't try to out-misery everyone else."

Any hope of continuing peaceful communication effectively over, the group moved down the narrow steps, awkward for those in heels, and inside as the dinner bell clanged. The meal was served in a long room toward the prow, lined on all sides with windows. They had a round table to themselves. The chief and his wife were at the table next to them, seated with other couples of a similar age. Mrs. Ledbetter found an immediate friend in the woman next to her, and they began talking crocheting patterns and grandchildren, taking out their phones and comparing pictures. The chief, after eating his fill of all-you-can-eat perch and pickerel, served with lemon wedges, homemade tartar sauce, fresh coleslaw and hand-cut French fries, turned his chair slightly to rest his capacious belly on his lap.

Jaymie had seated herself right behind him, with Valetta on one side of her and Melody on the other. She enjoyed her dinner, which was delicious, though watching Tiffany pick at the fish and complain was annoying. Jaymie pointed out that if she didn't like fish she should have ordered the chicken but she said no, she liked fish all right, just not *this* fish. There were no complaints from the others, though Brandi spoke at length about becoming vegan, the pros and cons, how she had tried it and found it too much work, but as her oldest was vegan, maybe she'd go back to it.

Melody said, "You could always be pescatarian today, vegan tomorrow."

They laughed and ordered more wine, something they could *all* agree on. As Gabriela and Courtney both dawdled with their food, and Brandi ordered a Bloody Caesar from the bar, Jaymie turned and talked to Chief Ledbetter. Knowing it would go no further, she confessed her worries concerning Brandi's involvement with Mario Horvat. She explained about Brandi's jealous ex, Terry, and the Terry who was apparently Mario's long-lost son.

"Chief, what should I do? You know I don't have the best relationship with Detective Vestry. If I bring this up to her, and Brandi gets in trouble, I won't be able to intercede; she'd never forgive me." She hadn't realized how much she was worried about it until she said it out loud.

"I thought you were smarter than that," he said sharply, his heavy bushy brows slanting down, shadowing his pale eyes.

"What do you mean?" she whispered, leaning toward him, with a quick glance over her shoulder.

"If you're worried that your friend's ex is a killer, you're doing her no favor by not telling the police everything you know. And if it turns out he's not, you have a clear conscience."

She nodded and sighed. "Of course, you're right. I have to tell Detective Vestry my worries, right?"

"Do it, tomorrow morning."

"Okay." She sighed. "This week hasn't been going anything like I thought."

"What else is worrying you?"

His avuncular style always calmed her. When she first met him he intimidated her, but she saw through the façade now. He could be brusque. He could be curt. But he was a nice, smart man who cared about truth and justice. She related what Mrs. Stubbs had told her about the conversation she overheard between Jaymie's friend Gabriela and Tiffany, the sister-in-law. "I can't imagine what went down at home that would force Tiffany, Logan and Fenix to leave. I want to ask, but it's not easy."

"Isn't your friend Brandi from the same town? They must have acquaintances in common; all small-towners do. Mine those!"

"But then I'd have to tell Brandi my suspicions of Tiffany."

"And? You're worried about her reaction when she finds out you've told the police about Terry. If you ask her to find this out, she'll realize you're being snoopy, nothing more." He smiled and chuckled. "Kiddo, do all that and check back in with me. I'm heading out to the island tomorrow to go fishing with a buddy. I'll stop by the cottage. I have a hankering to see that cute li'l trailer you've posted online."

"You follow my 'Vintage Eats' blog?" Jaymie asked in surprise. She had begun posting some life moments on her food blog in response to her growing readership, who were enthusiastic about everything, it seemed, and pics of the vintage trailer were among them.

"Not me! But the missus does and she makes me look." He dropped a wink.

"I'm not sure yet if I'm going to leave the trailer at the cottage or take it home and use it as a tea trailer for special events."

The chief's attention was claimed by his wife, and a few moments later, Jaymie found her chance to talk to her friend about what was worrying her. Courtney had gotten up to go to the washroom, so Jaymie slipped over into her chair. "Hey, Brandi, you enjoying yourself?"

Brandi saluted with a full Bloody Caesar. "Booze and the open water, what could go wrong?"

"I do hope you're enjoying your holiday." She glanced across the table. Gabriela was still picking at her food and ignoring Tiffany, who was glaring out the window. "I have a question: do you know any of Logan and Gabriela's friends?"

"A couple. Why?"

Jaymie searched her eyes. "Do any know how to keep their mouths shut?"

"If I ask 'em. Why? What's up?"

"I'm curious." Jaymie hunched her shoulder so Tiffany couldn't see her mouth. "Tiffany keeps taunting Gabriela," she muttered, "hinting about something that happened to their house, like it's something Gabriela has done, or was at fault for. Can you find out what it was?"

Cocking her head to one side, Brandi eyed her for a long moment. "Maybe. Let me try." She texted a couple of people the questions, asking them to keep it between them, and that she was just curious. Quick texts pinged back, and the universal answer was, nothing had happened to the Offerman home. Not a thing. One negative response was from the Offermans' next-door neighbors. They thought it odd that the brother and sister Offerman had taken off to follow his wife to Michigan.

"That *is* odd," Jaymie said, frowning and staring off out to the dark sky beyond the deck outside. "Especially if nothing went wrong with the house."

"You, my friend, see mysteries everywhere," Brandi said with a slightly woozy giggle. "Even when there is nothing to be seen."

Was that true? Jaymie wondered. Maybe so. She hoped it was true, and, as bad as it was, she hoped the murder case was simply as it appeared, a drunken quarrel between friends that ended tragically. At least she could tell the chief what she had discovered.

• • •

DINNER WAS OVER, drinks had been consumed, and they were on their way back toward Port Huron. The sun was long gone, sunk beneath the western horizon of lakewater, and the fresh breeze lured Jaymie up to the top deck to get away from the Lite Jazz trio. Not her style of music, though they were competent. Val followed and they strolled, feeling the boat movement, the thrum of the motor faint under their feet, the slight heave as the boat cleaved through rolling waves.

They chatted for a few moments about Valetta's home project. She was still intent on making a bigger catio for Denver, but she had decided to build it herself. "I can learn how to use new power tools. I've done a lot of things on my house so I already know how to use a drill. I can do this."

"Good for you, my friend."

Around the corner from them, on the other side of a raised partition, they heard the sound of familiar voices raised. Rachel joined Jaymie and Val and frowned. "Who is that talking so loud? Or arguing? Is that Brandi and Gabriela?"

"I'm afraid so," Jaymie said. Together they walked toward the voices in time to hear an exchange.

". . . never thought I'd say this, but Brandi, you're a loose woman. I swear, you'll sleep with *anyone*," Gabriela was saying with a sanctimonious sniff.

"Not *anyone*," Brandi shot back. "I wouldn't touch your precious Logan with a ten-foot pole."

"That was uncalled for!" Gabriela wailed. "You take that back."

"Take that back? You want me to say I *would* sleep with your husband?"

"At least I keep myself for my husband!" Gabriela said.

"Bull crap! You forget, G, I *know* the truth," Brandi said, her tone guttural with anger. "You may not realize it, but in our town people have big mouths. No bad deed goes un-gossiped about. Get off your high horse, Gabriela, and shut your effing yap."

There was shocked silence, then they bickered again, joined by the strident tones of Tiffany, who blurted, "Maybe you *both* oughta take a look at yourselves. You're hot messes, both of you."

As Jaymie, Val and Rachel came around the corner, they could see the shock and something else on Gabriela's face as she stared at her sister-in-law. But she didn't respond. Normally she would have snapped back at anyone who argued with her, but not her sister-in-law. Jaymie was reminded of the conversation Mrs. Stubbs had overheard and wondered again . . . what the heck did Tiffany have on Gabriela? She needed to find out.

The argument broke up as the principals stomped away from each other, Gabriela to stand by the railing gripping it tightly, Brandi pursued and comforted by Courtney, and the others in a group to talk. Chief Ledbetter was strolling with his wife, and he joined the women. Jaymie saw Gabriela bumble further away on her own, watched with a snide grin by Tiffany. She followed her friend, who stood alone, leaning over the railing as they came in sight of the harbor mouth.

She didn't have much time. "Gabriela, sweetie, are you okay? Please, don't lean over the railing; you're making me nervous." She looped her own arm through her friend's and held fast. "How did that quarrel with Brandi start? I thought you two were such good friends." She knew better, but she'd discovered over recent years that sometimes the way to elicit the truth was to say something outrageously *un*true.

Gabriela whirled, tears streaming down her cheeks. "Oh, Jaymie, n-no . . . we're not such good friends anymore. We don't think alike. At *all!*"

"Back in college you used to have the same fight, though, about Brandi's lifestyle," she said, letting go of her friend's arm and rubbing Gabriela's back, in what she hoped were soothing circles. "You were *always* critical of her choices. But they are *her* choices, hers alone."

Gabriela blinked but remained silent.

"Hon, I have to ask," Jaymie said, putting her arm over her friend's shoulders. "You seem unhappy. Is everything all right?"

"It's fine. Why wouldn't it be?"

Sighing, Jaymie watched her for a moment. "Everything's *not* fine. You've been on edge since you got to the cottage, more so after Tiffany showed up. You say you get along with her, but . . ." How could she approach the argument Mrs. Stubbs overheard? "But I know for a fact that you're *not* getting along with her."

Gabriela looked out at the water, the glistening lights of a town twinkling along the shore. "You're married now, Jaymie. How do you find it? I mean . . . how do you get along with his family?"

It seemed an abrupt departure in subject, but Jaymie went along with it. "We get along great."

"You're lucky, then. Do they tease you? Do they hate you for not being perfect? Do they pick on every *little* thing you do that they don't approve of?"

Jaymie's heart ached for her friend. She hugged her to her side. "Is it bad? What about Logan? Does he support you against his family?"

Her eyes filling with tears, she said, "No, he does *not*. But . . . he's Fenix's daddy, so I'll stay, and we'll work it out." She held back a sob. "I loved him once. I still do, in my heart of hearts. I *love* him."

"Of course you do. I believe you, Gabriela. Truly." She examined her friend's face, the misery that welled in her eyes, the pain that was evident. Something was deeply wrong. How could she ask about the conversation Mrs. Stubbs had overheard, and winkle out what Gabriela had done that Tiffany was angry about? The loudspeaker boomed right then, asking passengers to please return inside to allow the crew to work while docking procedures were undertaken. They gathered in a discordant and silent group, any hope for Jaymie of finding answers gone for the moment.

The day had been long and the evening had felt longer. When they got back to Queensville, Val said she was staying in her own home that night, and Gabriela surprised them all by saying she was going to the inn to spend time with her husband and daughter. Of course Tiffany tagged along. Val offered to drop them off at the inn after driving Jaymie and the others in her car to the dock to catch the last ferry over to the island.

✒ Fifteen ✒

THE NEXT MORNING Jaymie walked with Rachel to Tansy's Tarts to give Hoppy a nice long walk after being cooped up the evening before. Mourning doves crooned in nearby trees, and Hoppy paused to bark at something in the brush along the sandy road, a mouse or vole, likely. Rachel was quiet, not her normal bubbly self.

"So, my friend, what's up?" Jaymie said with a side glance.

"I didn't expect I could fool you," Rachel said. She scuffed at the gravel at the roadside and bit her lip, looking off over the misty pines. "I'm worried. I . . . I saw something . . . something that might have to do with this murder investigation. Nothing major, you get me, but some nagging little detail. I don't know what it means, and I'm worried."

"What is it? You can tell me, Rach."

Her brown eyes filled with trepidation, Rachel shook her head, her blue-tipped curls bouncing. "I need to think about it for a few more hours. I'll tell you later, okay? I want to think on it. Let's hurry a little; I don't want to be late. Tansy gets wired up. She had trouble with Hallie and doesn't know what to do with a reliable employee. She always thinks I'm going to let her down. Until I don't."

Waiting in the window, Tansy saw them coming and burst from the tart shop with a full box of mixed tarts that she thrust at Jaymie. She hugged her hard, squeezing with all her strength, crushing the corner of the box. "I can't thank you enough for bringing this treasure to Heartbreak Island!" she said, waving toward Rachel, who smiled. "Sherm's been sick, and I've been worried. It's all I can do to bake the tarts, much less work the counter, and Rachel is so *good*! The customers are raving about her. You don't *know* what a relief it is having her here."

Jaymie laughed, thrown off-balance by the tiny woman's enthusiasm. "I know she's a treasure, but thank you, Tansy, for bringing the sparkle back to my friend. You've helped her discover her calling, I think." She added, "I'm sorry to hear Sherm's ill. I hope he'll be okay."

Taking a deep breath, Tansy put out both hands and let the breath out, slowly. "It's a matter of balancing his health problems. Once they get his blood pressure down, and his diabetes under

147

control, we'll be good." She looked at her phone. "Oh, I have to run! Sherm's got to be in Wolverhampton by nine."

Jaymie stowed the box of fresh tarts in her backpack and walked on, making the big loop around the island that brought her around to the fire-damaged A-line cottage, Mario Horvat's house. Who killed Mario? And why? Chief Ledbetter didn't seem to think it was Kory either, if she was to judge by his cryptic words concerning the younger man.

"Tryin' to figure it out?"

She looked over her shoulder and there was the chief in person. "Chief, what are you doing here?"

"Thought I'd get in my walk while my fishing buddy has his fifth coffee of the morning. I walked past your cottage to see that vintage trailer, but you weren't there, so I had a quick look then continued on! The missus checks my fitness tracker watch and if I don't have enough steps I get egg whites for dinner," he said, patting his stomach. "I don't like egg whites." Hoppy was jumping around his feet yipping, so he bent over with a grunt, patted the dog's head while huffing and puffing, then straightened.

"She's trying to keep you alive, you know." Jaymie turned back to observe the cottage as Hoppy went to the end of his leash to sniff a clump of beachgrass. It was a sad wreck, charred black beams thrusting into the air like a double middle finger salute.

"Y'know, what I didn't say last night is, Vestry has a theory, and it's a pretty good one, for why Kory could have cracked and killed Mario Horvat." He eyed her sideways, folding his arms and resting them on his stomach. "Not sayin' he did, but he had motive. Now, you didn't hear it from me, and I expect you to keep this to yourself, but she suspects, and I think she's probably right, that Mario Horvat is the so-called mastermind behind all the thefts that happened on the island the last coupla years. M'wife calls him a modern-day Fagin; I guess that's some sorta character from a book?"

His blue eyes twinkled. Jaymie suspected he knew the character Fagin was the child gang recruiter from Dickens's *Oliver Twist*, but he donned the character of a hick cop when it suited him.

"He got others to do the thefts, Kory among them, and then sold the stuff outta his trunk. Kory kept getting caught and never ratted

Mario out, taking the fall. Vestry thinks it built up to a point, and when he saw Mario treating that little gal badly, it was the last straw, and in a drunken rage they argued. That much we know — that they argued — but maybe when they got back to the cottage it got worse and Kory killed his friend, then set the fire to cover it up."

Jaymie nodded. "I *have* considered the drunken argument idea, though I didn't know about the Mario-as-the-theft-ring-mastermind theory behind it. Not bad, but if you listen to Sammy Dobrinskie, and I think you should, he and his girlfriend say that first off, Kory was too drunk that night to walk, much less commit murder, and second, that he never would have set fire to the cottage with Hallie inside. He loves that girl. He may be her baby's father."

The chief's bushy eyebrows rose. "You don't say? I'd say that gives Kory *more* motive to kill Mario."

"But it still doesn't change the fact that Kory would never have endangered Hallie no matter how drunk and angry he was. She was caught in that fire. If it wasn't for Ng, they may have *both* died."

The chief nodded. "I'll pass that idear along to Vestry. She's a sensible woman and a good investigator, despite you two not getting along. They're looking for Mario's cell phone. They'll get the phone records at some point, but some cell carriers are sticky about giving up records and it takes a while . . . channels and all that. It would be easier if they could find the phone. Now, why do you think someone would steal it?" He glanced over at Jaymie. "Maybe to hide something that was on it?"

Brandi. They were back to her again. Did the chief know about Brandi and Mario? Impossible. She shrugged uneasily; she *would* ask Brandi about Mario and his phone. She had many questions, but they were mostly about things she wasn't prepared to talk to the chief about at this point. She saw Sammy and Ashlee approaching, waving to her.

Just then the chief got a call; his friend was asking where the heck he was. The boat was ready, the fish were jumping and there was no time like the present.

Good thing, Jaymie thought as the chief walked away, toward the marina, and Sammy approached. Chief Ledbetter was shrewd and a keen observer. She didn't have much confidence in her ability to hide her uneasiness about her friend's involvement with Mario

Horvat from him. Hoppy came bouncing back and begged to be picked up. Jaymie cradled him in her arms.

"Hey, I got your message," Sammy said. "About Ashlee's phone number. We were at your cottage to talk to you, but one of the ladies there said you were out walking with Hoppy. She seemed kinda grumpy."

"I felt bad, like we'd interrupted her or something," Ashlee said.

"Ah, that would be Mel. She's a writer, so when she's not writing she's grumpy. Though from what I've seen, when she *is* writing she's grumpy too, just for different reasons. She probably hasn't had enough coffee yet."

Ashlee reached out and scruffed Hoppy's head. He wiggled in Jaymie's arms, yipping, eager to make a new friend. "Isn't he the sweetest little poochie in the world?" she said, bending over and nuzzling him, much to his delight. She straightened and met Jaymie's gaze. "We were wondering why you wanted my phone number? What you wanted to ask me?" she said, her pleasant voice rising at the end of the sentence.

"You've been babysitting a child named Fenix for a few days off and on at the Queensville Inn, is that right?"

"Yes. O-M-G she is adorable! Such a cutie, and a little stinker."

Jaymie considered carefully how much to ask, and how to ask, and what reason to give if Ashlee or Sammy wanted to know *why* she was asking. Sammy was watching her; he knew how involved she had been in solving crimes locally, and would immediately know it had something to do with Mario's death. Maybe there was no way around it but to swear them to secrecy. Sammy she trusted, but she didn't know Ashlee. And Gabriela was Jaymie's friend. Maybe she should ask questions without explanation until one was demanded. "What is the father like?"

"He's cool. He's here visiting family. I haven't met any of them yet but his sister?" she said, that same questioning lift at the end of many non-question sentences. "She arrived with him."

"Is she there at the inn often?"

Ashlee cocked her head to one side. "No. Which is weird, right? Because I know she arrived with him and checked in at the same time?" She shrugged. "But maybe she's got other stuff to do, you know?"

"What about his wife; where is she?"

"I don't know." Ashlee frowned. "The last time I babysat, night before last, the little girl said she was going to see her mommy. I asked when, and she said 'today,' but I don't know if she understands time, you know?"

Sammy's laser focus was on Jaymie. "You can tell us why you want to know this, you know." He exchanged a look with Ashlee and put his arm around her. "I've told her to trust you, and I hope you trust us back."

That was a big ask, given that she was trying to figure out what was going on in one of her oldest friend's marriages. And why her friend's sister-in-law was threatening her. And what Gabriela had done that was so heinous Tiffany could hold it over her like she was doing. And that she didn't know Ashlee at all. But maybe there was a way around trusting too much information in the hands of someone she didn't know. "Okay. Logan is my friend Gabriela's husband; Fenix is her daughter. Gabriela is with us, our bunch of college friends, which is why she's not at the inn all the time with her husband and child. I worry about her, you know? I feel like there is something going on between them, but she's reticent. She doesn't want to ruin our vacation, I figure. I thought maybe if I knew some of what was going on, I could get her to open up. Is there anything you can tell me about Logan? Where he's been? What he's been up to?"

"It's about a friend?" Sammy said, his expression full of doubt.

"Sammy, you don't get it." Ashlee's expression had relaxed into understanding. "O-M-G, I would so *totally* do that for one of my friends," she said, reaching out and touching Jaymie's arm. "I *have* been wondering. You know, he came back the first night late? Like . . . I don't know what time. I was asleep on the sofa. He told me to crash, that he'd take me home in the morning, if I wanted, so I fell back asleep."

"You don't have *any* idea what time it was?" Jaymie asked.

She shrugged and grimaced. "I checked my phone, but I can't remember. I was groggy."

"Did he say anything the next morning?"

She shook her head. "Just asked if I could work steady, whenever he wanted, for the week. He promised me a bonus. In fact,

I'd better check my phone." She pulled it out and her eyes widened. "Ooops, gotta go!"

"Wait, I—"

"Sorry, *really* gotta go!" She kissed Sammy on the cheek and was already walking away, turning and walking backward as she talked. "I gotta get to the mainland, and the ferry will be coming any second. Text me if you've got other questions, 'kay? I hope your friend is all right?" She skipped off down the road.

"And I'm working at the Ice House, on the lunch rush," Sammy said, backing away in the opposite direction, toward the restaurant. "I'll text you Ashlee's number and you can text her, okay?"

"Sammy, wait. Do you know where Hallie's mom lives? It's on the island here, right?"

"Sure. She lives in number seven of the Sunset Cottages, that little circle of cottages off Port Road. I gotta go too," he said. "Mr. Redmond is back, and he doesn't like slackers!"

Jaymie sighed and Hoppy stood, looking back and forth between the two departing young people, bereft that they were walking away from him. He turned first one way, then the other, then looked up at her. It was time to move on. Hallie's mother lived moments from where she stood. What were the chances that they'd be home? Port Road was one of several short lanes connecting the two main roads on the American side of the island, and it was on her way home. She headed back the way she came, but cut down Port Road to Sunset Cottages. Number Seven was painted a bright blue with a pink door.

But she didn't need to knock because Hallie's mother was in front washing her car with a garden hose and bucket of soapie water while Hallie sat on a chair on the wood deck, feet up, hand on her belly, looking tired and uncomfortable. Jaymie approached. "Hallie, how are you feeling?"

The girl looked up. There were dark circles under her red-rimmed eyes and her mouth was turned down in a sullen grimace. She held one hand up and shaded her eyes against the morning slanting sun. "I'm okay."

Her mother looked over, saw Jaymie, waved and went back to her task.

Jaymie let Hoppy, the world's best ambassador, lead her to the girl, whose expression softened at Hoppy's approach.

"Aw, he only has three legs! How did that happen?"

Jaymie explained about Hoppy's birth in a puppy mill, and how as a little fellow he got his leg caught in the wire mesh of a cage. By the time he and his litter mates and mom were rescued, his leg was too far gone and had to be amputated.

Her sulky expression had softened. She picked the little dog up and rested him on her belly, touching his soft ears and giggling when he licked her face.

"Hallie, don't let that dog lick your face! It's not good for the baby," her mother yelled.

She sighed and her shoulders slumped. "Everything I do now is *not good for the baby*. Even drinking soda pop."

Jaymie commiserated. She sat down on the sandy wood deck and they talked for a few minutes. Then Jaymie said, "Hallie, I have a question for you. You said that Mario's son came into the tart shop one day asking questions about Mario. You thought you'd recognize him if you saw him again. Is it this guy, by any chance?" she said, turning her phone with the photo of Terry on the screen to the girl.

Hallie set Hoppy down on the deck and took the phone. She frowned, stared at it for a long moment, and then looked back up at Jaymie with a quizzical look. "Why do you want to know? And where did you get this photo?"

Jaymie hadn't expected the girl to ask questions and she wasn't prepared to answer them. She hesitated, then said, "Let's say, I may know him."

"But who is he to you?"

"No one, truly. I'm . . . asking for a friend."

✑ Sixteen ✑

THE GIRL HANDED THE PHONE back to Jaymie and sat back. "You can tell your *friend*," she said, sketching air quotes with both hands, "that this guy, whoever he is, is not Mario's son, Terry."

Jaymie swallowed, blew air out through pursed lips, and could finally acknowledge how nervous she'd been to know the truth. "Okay. Just wondering."

"Nah, not so much," Hallie said, with a slight upturn of her lips in one corner. Her gaze was focused and unexpectedly shrewd. "You were worried and you got me curious. Who is this guy?"

"I can't say; it's not my business. But he truly is no one to me."

She narrowed her eyes. "But he's someone to someone you care about."

"Maybe you're right." Jaymie stood, dusted off her bottom and tugged Hoppy's leash. "I'd better go. I have to go to the mainland. I think, though, Hallie, that you may be wise, if you think Kory . . . if you're sure he's innocent, you should tell the police about the guy who was claiming to be Mario's son."

She nodded. "Yeah, you're probably right. I don't think you'd have given me that same advice if the guy had been your acquaintance, though."

"I hope I would," Jaymie said. "Hallie, if there is anything I can do, I'd like to help. You're in a tough spot, and if I can help in any way —"

"Have this baby for me," she said, and grimaced, moving in her chair.

Jaymie smiled, and waved goodbye as she led Hoppy away, down Port Road and turning to the road home.

• • •

BACK AT THE COTTAGE Mel was hiding out in the trailer with her laptop, writing something, no one knew what. She merely waved Jaymie away when she approached. Brandi and Courtney were about to leave for a shopping expedition to a factory outlet mall near Port Huron. They'd be gone all day and might not even be back that night if they ended up late.

As they puttered, Jaymie sat by the firepit and checked her emails on her tablet. There was one from Poplar Bluffs Campground, and all of them in the group were cc'd; that was odd . . . it was the campground that had canceled their reservation this year. Maybe they were checking in to make sure all was okay.

She clicked on the email.

> *This is a little late – it's been a hectic summer so far – but we wanted to say we were sorry to hear of the death in your group that caused you to cancel your reservation with us this year. Please let us know if you would like to reserve for later this summer, or next year, and we will do our best to accommodate you. With condolences and all our best wishes . . . the Poplar Bluffs Gang!*

She sat and stared at it. A death in their group? What was that about? She fished out her phone and called the campground. Cynthia, one of the new co-owners, answered. Jaymie explained about the email and how she was wondering what it meant. They had no death in their group and had not canceled the booking. In fact, it was Poplar Bluffs that had canceled due to their plumbing situation that had shut the campground down.

There was a long silence on the other end of the phone, then Cynthia, sounding affronted, said, "Honey, I don't know what kind of garbage someone has been slinging, but we have *not* been shut down, we did *not* have a plumbing problem, and I have the email right here from Brandi Xylander telling us that due to a death in your group you were forced to cancel your booking." She took in a deep breath. "I, myself, refunded the deposit. I don't usually do that—we say right on the website that the deposit is nonrefundable within thirty days of the booking—but since it was a death I made an exception. Now, what's going on?"

"Good question," Jaymie muttered. "I don't know, Cynthia, but I hope to find out." Brandi and Courtney came out the back door of the cottage, dressed in clothes more fit for a nightclub than a shopping expedition. "I have to go. I'm sorry for the mix-up. I'll talk to you soon, and next time, I'll take care of the booking myself." She clicked off the phone and stared at her friend, trying to make sense of it all.

"We're off," Brandi said with a wave from the porch. "I'm not coming down there, not in these heels," she said.

Jaymie jumped up and raced up the hill to the driveway, to confront Brandi. "Have you checked your email this morning?" she said, feeling her face flush with annoyance. "Bran, if you didn't want to go camping, you could have said so, you know. You didn't have to pull a dirty trick like canceling our booking."

Brandi, her long narrow face colored with tanning gel, blush that created exaggerated cheekbones, and eye shadow the color of a Hawaiian sunset, looked at her with a puzzled frown. "I have literally no clue what you're talking about."

"Check your emails." It was the outside of enough for her to be pretending she didn't know anything about it. Jaymie remembered in that moment Melody conjecturing this exact thing, that Brandi had canceled the campsite booking to spend time with a guy.

Brandi took out her phone and read through the email, frowning, her face a mask of puzzlement. "I don't know what this is about either."

"Oh, come *on*, Brandi! How can you not? You're the one who made the booking and who then *canceled* the booking! I asked you about it; you could have told me the truth then. You could have told me about canceling the booking." She glared at Brandi. "I didn't know one of us was dead! Which one? Who's dead, Brandi?"

Melody, a grumpy look on her face, poked her head out of the trailer and glared up the hill at them. "What's going on out there? Why all the yelling?"

"I'll explain later," Jaymie yelled. "Go back to your writing!"

"Okay." She disappeared.

"So, who's dead, Bran?" Jaymie pushed. "Who'd you kill off to the campground owners? I mean, I totally get it now, the whole reason behind this charade. You canceled the booking when you figured out there was a guy here you wanted to meet up with, and you cajoled me into letting everyone come here, to the cottage, so you could be with him."

"It's not that at all, it's not what it looks like, Jaymie." Brandi exchanged a guilty look with Courtney, who shrugged.

"She lied to you," Courtney said to Brandi, touching her friend's back and rubbing. "I don't know why, but she did."

Jaymie looked between the two of them. "She? She *who*? Who lied? What are you two talking about?"

Brandi sighed and rolled her eyes. "Okay, confession time. You know what I'm like . . . I'm busy. I'm looking after three kids and trying to keep a job and getting divorced: it all takes a hella lot of time. So . . ." She sighed again and shrugged her shoulders. "I delegated."

"You delegated," Jaymie repeated.

"I did. To Gabriela. She's good at that kind of thing, scheduling and details; I'm not."

"Why didn't you say so? You *volunteered* to take care of the booking, Bran. Why do that if it was too much?"

"I wanted to do *some*thing. All of you are so organized and have lists, and . . . I wanted to help somehow."

"But then you didn't. Okay, okay," Jaymie said, tamping down her anger. She took in a deep breath. And frowned down at her phone. "I don't get it. So Gabriela used your email address to make the booking. Why?"

Bran shrugged. "So it would look like I did it all," she admitted. "That was *her* idea, not mine, by the way. She's been trying to suck up to me for a while now."

"Why? What happened between you?"

Brandi shook her head and didn't answer. "She created a new email address with one of those free servers in my name, and kept track of it all. I don't have a password for that address; my actual email must have made it onto their list when I checked out the booking a few months ago. I wanted to know the exact day."

"Of course. But Bran, why would Gabriela then cancel the booking, making up a lie that one of us had died, while making it seem like the booking had been canceled because of plumbing issues at the campground?"

"I can guess at that," Rachel said, from the lane. "Hey, guys . . . I'm just back for a few minutes. I got the email too and wanted to find out what was going on. I have to get back to Tansy's Tarts, but . . . Jaymie, this involves what I was going to tell you earlier. I suppose I'll tell you all now." She joined Jaymie. "You know how Gabriela's phone ringtone is that yell from that old movie?"

They all nodded; John McClane's profane "Yippee-Ki-Yay" yelp from *Die Hard* was familiar to all and they had heard Gabriela's phone go off more than once.

"I heard that in the middle of the second night, Gabriela's phone ringing. I tried to get back to sleep. But then I heard the front door close, and looked out the window. I saw Gabriela creeping down the road in the direction of the Ice House."

Jaymie vividly remembered sitting at the fire with Melody and hearing what sounded like her front door. She had rushed out to the front but had been too late to see Gabriela sneaking away. "Where was she going?"

"My guess? To meet someone. I mean, why *else* would she sneak out?"

Brandi, guilty of the same thing, flushed but stayed silent.

"I don't get it. Who would she meet?" Jaymie asked. She met each of their eyes, but all looked blank. "I'm going into Queensville today. I'll find her and ask." Among other things, she thought, but did not say, remembering her interrupted conversation from the night before on the cruise boat.

Rachel returned to the tart shop. Brandi and Courtney decided to still take their day trip. Jaymie, relieved at least that Brandi's Terry was not the Terry who was Mario's supposed son, hugged them both goodbye before they headed to the ferry—she had warmed up to Courtney, who truly seemed to be a better bestie than Brandi deserved—and planned her own day. She interrupted Melody briefly to tell her to help herself to whatever was in the fridge, and make coffee or tea as she wished.

Mel had already forgotten that Jaymie was going to tell her what they had all been talking about, and Jaymie decided that later was soon enough. Mel was writing; she hadn't done that for a while, she said, so this was progress. Also, Detective Vestry had texted the author; they were meeting for lunch at the Ice house. She set a reminder on her phone to loudly ping so she wouldn't miss it.

Jaymie headed, with Hoppy, to the ferry and across to Queensville. Though she had planned to go out to their home in the country to check on it, she decided to wait until her friends were all available, because she wanted to show them the log cabin that her husband had built. Today she would be taking care of business: checking in with Val, buying staples for the Queensville house and stocking the fridge for Becca and Kevin's arrival in a couple of days, and maybe checking in with Mrs. Stubbs.

And confronting Gabriela about her lies. Yes, that would be on her to-do list for the day. Who had she been sneaking off to see? And what had happened at her family home that had caused Logan and Tiffany to come so unexpectedly to Queensville?

• • •

VAL WASN'T HOME. Standing outside her house, Jaymie called her and found out that though the pharmacy was closed on Sundays she was there, doing inventory with her fill-in pharmacist, though he was out at the moment, running errands. It was a busman's holiday, Val said with a laugh.

"If that were the case you'd be working at someone *else's* pharmacy," Jaymie replied. "How about we meet at the oak tree outside the Emporium for a cup of tea? I've got something to tell you. I'll wait for you there."

Val agreed and said she had a thermos of tea with her.

Once Jaymie got to the Emporium, the outside deck of it filled with late-season sales on pool toys and sunscreen, she put Hoppy in the little doggie playpen that was outside of the store. It had been expanded to be big enough to hold several small dogs or one St. Bernard. The replacement pharmacist, Charlie Wojohowitz, had left his little Cairn terrier Maxie in the pen, and Hoppy and he yipped at each other for a moment, then became fast friends, playing a complicated game of *got your tail.*

It was nice to be alone, and in her village and waving at passers-by, her friends and neighbors. Had she outgrown the girls-only camping trips she so fondly remembered from college days and up until five years ago or so? Maybe not; maybe she needed to find a way to be with the friends from the old days that she enjoyed, like Rachel and Melody. And maybe add in her new friends like Heidi and Bernie and her oldest friend, Valetta. That was a thought for another year. She had to survive this vacation first.

As Val came out with a thermos and a couple of mugs, Jaymie

retrieved a plastic container with a couple of crumbling Tansy tarts from her bag. They drank their tea and ate their tarts in silence, then wiped up the crumbs, tossing them and chunks of leftover crust to the sparrows that hopped around in the grass looking for bugs.

Val stared across the picnic table at Jaymie and pushed her glasses up on her nose. "Okay, spill."

Jaymie first told Val the news that she had confirmed that Mario's supposed son Terry was not Brandi's Terry.

"That's good news."

"It is. I also met up with Ashlee and Sammy. Ashlee has been babysitting Fenix off and on. Logan was gone until the middle of the night Thursday night; that's the night he and Tiffany arrived."

"What time did they get here, to Queensville?"

"I don't know. That's one thing I need to find out. But why would he come here, and then go out again, and until the middle of the night? It's suspicious to say the least."

"He could have come out to the island with Tiffany."

"Maybe. But why?"

"Get out your notebook, kiddo. I think if you want to untangle this mess, there's a *lot* you'll need to find out."

"I know. Some of it feels like it might be connected to the murder of Mario, and a lot of it doesn't, but it's getting muddled in my mind. And this morning I found something else out, maybe something that would tell me why Logan might come out to Heartbreak Island in the middle of the night," Jaymie said, and told Val about what she'd thought were Brandi's lies and evasion about the campsite booking. "Why did Gabriela do what she did? I mean, the likely reason is that she was meeting someone, but she seemed happy with Logan; surely she wouldn't cheat on him?"

Val stared off down the road and waved at Mrs. Bellwood, who was walking her pug, Roary. "There is some reason she had to be here, on Heartbreak Island or Queensville. And you still haven't found out what happened at home that prompted her husband and sister-in-law to follow her. What's that all about?"

"I know. Trust me, it's on my list of things to discover. I don't get it." Jaymie sighed and fished in her bag for the notebook and pen she was never without. "Let's figure this out."

"First, who killed Mario Horvat?"

"Okay, let's start with who I think *didn't* kill him. I don't think Kory killed him."

"Why? There's plenty of evidence."

"Circumstantial; they had a fight and he didn't like how Mario treated Hallie. But Val . . . isn't it odd that he'd race down the island to steal my cast iron pie iron to bonk Mario over the head? A, he was drunk, and B, that is so *specific* . . . I mean, the pie iron was hanging on a tree on my property. How would he know it was there and why would he steal it to use it as a weapon?"

Val frowned. "You said yourself that you don't know when it was stolen. He was a thief. Maybe he stole it the day before and had it at the cottage and reached for the first weapon around when he was fighting with Mario and killed him."

"Okay, you have a possible point, but that's a lot of *ifs*. I think it's thin. He stole one pie iron from a nail where three were hung?" She shook her head. "I don't think Hallie killed Mario either. She's a small girl, and heavily pregnant, and she looked devastated about his death."

"But . . . that insurance payout, and he was going to leave her for his hot redhead. Maybe she's the mastermind and got Kory to do it for her. Some guys will do anything for a woman they love."

"Okay, so both have to stay on the list, but I still think there is no scenario where she did it by herself."

Val nodded. "I think you're probably right about that. Now . . . what about the husbands?"

"Husbands?"

Val sighed and frowned. "Logan. Terry. Andrew. How weird is it that three of your friends have husbands who have shown up here or close by?"

"I get that it's strange, but what are you saying?"

"I don't know. It's . . . odd. I don't suppose I should include Melody's hubby, but Terry and Logan *must* know each other, right, living in the same town and being married to two women who are longtime friends? Is their arrival a coincidence or something more sinister?"

"True. It's weird. I don't know enough about them, how close the two couples are, how Logan and Terry feel about each other." Jaymie considered it, tapping her pen on the wood picnic table top.

"Although . . ." She thought about what Rachel had said about Gabriela sneaking out of the cottage the second night, and her own thinking that her friend was cheating on her husband with some guy. Given what she knew about Mario, could he have been hooking up with her, too? "Oh . . . *oh!*"

"What?"

"I just remembered something." She told Val everything she had been considering, and then said, "Brandi was talking about this game she plays, called something like . . . what was it? LiveLoveLife, or something like that. You have online affairs, etcetera. What if that's how she met Mario? He was always on his phone, Fran and Dan said. Brandi said they all played the game; maybe both met him that way? I wonder if there's a way for someone to find out who you've been online with. Could someone snitch your phone and check it out?"

Her eyes, behind her thick glasses lenses, widened. "I know who I can ask, my nephew! Will is a computer whiz; he went to a tech camp this summer. Brock sent him because he was getting into trouble hacking into other people's devices."

"So Brock thought he'd send him somewhere to learn how to do it better?"

"No, dope. This camp emphasizes the *ethics* of computer science, AI, and social media."

"And now you're going to ask him if he knows how to hack into someone's phone?"

Val laughed. "You've got a point. However, I think I can talk to him about it in the right way, emphasizing that if someone did it, they were invading the other person's privacy."

"Brandi said that Terry put a tracker on her phone without her knowing about it, and she wasn't sure she had gotten rid of it. What if there is some other kind of program that can tell him who she contacted in this game? Brandi said she uses all kinds of methods to find dates: dating apps, cheating sites, and this gaming app. Apparently it's a thing."

Val nodded. "I've read about it," she said, pushing her glasses up on the bridge of her nose. "I read an article about the new problem of people meeting other partners within games and leaving their spouses for them."

"Okay, so . . . it is possible that Mario met both Brandi and Gabriela on this game both women play."

Val checked her watch. "I have to get back inside. But maybe I can do some research and come up with some answers."

"I don't have much of a list yet of potential murderers."

"Let's work on eliminating your friends and their spouses from the pool of suspects. That'll be a good start."

✄ Seventeen ✄

SHE HOPED IT WOULD BE THAT EASY. Jaymie and Hoppy headed off toward the Queensville Inn. She'd be back to the Emporium for eggs, bread and milk for the Queensville house, and maybe she'd have information by then for Val.

It was a bright and sparkling day. The humidity had burned off and there was a fresh breeze sweeping through, tossing the trees in the village green. She waved at Jewel and Cynthia, who were outside their shops planning something, maybe working on their ideas for fall displays. Whatever it was took a lot of hand waving and vivid discussion. Hoppy barked at Jewel's little dog, his best canine friend, Junk Jr., but Jaymie didn't stop to let them play. "Another day, Hoppy; we'll have time next week." They walked on.

The Queensville Inn looked tranquil in the morning sun. Her first stop was to Mrs. Stubbs's room, where she explained what she was doing there and let Hoppy stay with her friend. As she left the room, though, her cell phone pinged. It was Val.

"Guess what?" Val said.

"What?"

"Your friend Brandi's husband is still here."

"Here? Like . . . he didn't go back to Ohio? How do you know?" Jaymie asked, standing in the hall in a pool of light cast by a wall sconce.

"So, Charlie came back and told me where he had to go. Yesterday he had a guy come in with a prescription, and he couldn't fill it that moment and wanted to check with the prescribing doctor, so he said he'd deliver it to him, though we're officially closed today. He checked it out, the script is valid, so he delivered it to the guy out at the motel on the highway between here and Wolverhampton."

"Okay. So—"

"So, the guy's name is Terry Xylander, and he's been booked there since Wednesday."

"Oh, *really*? And he's still there. So . . . Terry has been local, and has been following Brandi. It's creepy that he followed us all the way to Grand Bend. Of course, Brandi makes it easy. Anyone could go into stalker mode and friend her on social media and she'd accept them."

"Wait, there's more," Val said. "Charlie was talking to the motel cleaner. You know what Charlie is like, gab gab gab."

Jaymie smiled and said yes. Charlie was a retired pharmacist who was in charge of the Emporium pharmacy before Val. She served an apprenticeship with him. He knew everyone and everything local, and whoever he didn't know he *got* to know. Quickly. By asking copious questions of and about them.

"It turns out that Terry has a boat trailer parked at the motel. He had to get permission for an extra space, and he rented a spot at the Queensville Marina for a week for a Starcraft with an outboard motor. Said he's been doing some fishing, but Charlie didn't see any of the normal fishing gear."

Jaymie's heart sank. Terry had been furious in Grand Bend when he had accused Brandi of hooking up with a guy. He was jealous, and jealousy was a strong motive to kill Mario Horvat. With a boat to go anywhere, he could have been on the island following Brandi the night she was with Mario. He'd know who the guy was, what he looked like, and if he followed him home, he'd know where he lived. He could have been the person Jaymie heard skulking in the bushes, and he easily could have stolen the pie iron, using it to kill Mario and then leaving it there because . . . why? Maybe, if he knew about Kory's penchant for theft, it was to implicate that young man, but that was a little overly complicated.

The simpler explanation was that he left the pie iron at the scene of the crime to implicate Brandi. Her heart thudded. It all went together too easily. Something occurred to her in that moment . . . Brandi on her cell phone the morning after the fire, looking scared. Did she know, then, that Terry was at the motel? Jaymie would bet she did. But what did that mean? She wasn't thinking that Brandi had anything to do with the murder. At that point, as far as she knew, Brandi didn't know Mario's real name and who he was.

"Are you there, Jaymie?"

"I am," she replied. She had strolled down the hall as they talked and came out to the lobby and stood, wondering what to do next. This was important news, news that the police must have. She explained what she had been thinking, that Terry's motive was jealousy, but also to implicate her friend. "I have to talk to the police, don't I?"

"We have to give them the opportunity to solve this, no matter who is impacted," Val said.

"What about the LiveLoveLife app and the possibility of snooping on who someone knew or was meeting in real life?"

"I haven't gotten ahold of Will yet, but soon."

Jaymie saw, out of the corner of her eye, Gabriela, Logan, Fenix and Tiffany heading into the restaurant. "I have to go," she murmured. "I'll talk to you soon. Hopefully I'll have more information."

Jaymie waited until they were settled at a table and had ordered, then entered the restaurant. Good; they were at a table with four chairs. Fenix was in one of the high chairs, pulled up to the corner of the table between Gabriela and Logan. Jaymie entered, got a takeout coffee and turned, "seeing" them for the first time. "Oh my *gosh*, Gabriela, I'm happy to see you here," she said, weaving between the tables toward theirs. As it was Sunday afternoon, people would have brunched at the big Sunday Brunch Buffet, which the inn was famous for, and were now cleared out. The restaurant was virtually empty. "You don't mind if I sit here?" she said, taking a page out of Tiffany's playbook, assuming she was welcome. "Great, thanks. Nice to see you all!"

She sat down and brightly observed the faces around the table, which, apart from Fenix, who was chewing on Cheerios, were a study in varied aspects of unwelcome. They did not look happy; it was either they were not happy to see her or they were not happy being together. To get past the awkwardness she felt butting in, she focused on the child. "Oh my gosh, this little munchkin!" she said, jumping up and circling the table to crouch down by Fenix, who was a cherubic darling with blonde hair and chubby cheeks. "Sweetie, you are growing so fast!" She looked around at the adult faces above her. "At my wedding she was just a baby; she's growing like a bad weed. That's what my Grandma Leighton used to say about me. Growing like a bad weed."

She took her seat again as the waiter brought the food and left them to it. She examined Logan, a nice average-looking guy, then switched her gaze to Tiffany. The resemblance was plain now that she saw the siblings together. Their features were similar, and both were sandy-haired and rigidly proper about their clothing and grooming. Logan's hair was perfectly coiffed, and his tailored short-sleeve shirt wrinkle-free, as were his chino pants.

"It's nice to see you again, Logan," she said. "I don't think I've seen you since my wedding."

He nodded. "How is your husband?"

"Jakob is great. He and my daughter are in Poland right now on a family visit. My stepdaughter's mother was Polish."

He nodded but had clearly lost interest in what she had to say as he cut up some chicken for his daughter. She told him she didn't want chicken, she wanted a hot dog instead. He said no, she was going to eat the chicken.

"You're such a good father," Jaymie said, watching him.

He smiled, the first genuine expression she had seen on his pale face. He watched his daughter spoon macaroni and cheese into her mouth. "It's easy when you've got the world's best daughter," he said, wiping her hands with a cloth.

"Tiffany, I'm curious," Jaymie said finally, turning to Logan's sister, who was silently eating a club sandwich and checking her cell phone. "You hinted while you were my guest about something happening at Logan and Gabriela's house that forced you and Logan to come here and stay at the Queensville Inn. What was that?"

Gabriela's breathing was shallow, her gaze pleading. "It's something minor," she said, answering for her sister-in-law. "A little problem that they could have solved *easily* without upsetting me."

"You call the house almost blowing up something minor?" Tiffany said, glaring at her sister-in-law.

Jaymie was genuinely shocked. "What do you mean? Gabriela, what happened?"

"You hate me, Tiff . . . you always have, and I don't know why," Gabriela sobbed. "I never did *anything* to you!" There were fat tears in her eyes.

Fenix stared at her mother, one little fist holding the spoon of mac and cheese, alarmed by her mom's tears. She whimpered. "Mommy, you okay?" she asked.

Distracted, Gabriela patted her little girl's cheek. "I'm fine, honey. I'm good. You eat up your yummy lunch." She turned to

Jaymie. "You saw how worried I was about Logan, right?" she murmured, leaning toward her. "I wondered why he hadn't texted me? Apparently there was some problem with the gas in the house. I left, and . . . and there was some *problem*, the pilot lights were all out. The house could've blown up. If Logan's mom hadn't come to drop Fenix off, I don't know *what* would have happened."

Logan, stroking his daughter's silky hair, said, "Fenix saved my life." He turned to look at Jaymie and his stiffness faltered. "My dad has heart troubles. Mom and Dad were taking care of Fenix while Gabriela was gone because I had to work. But Dad had some problems. Mom brought Fenix back to our place so I could look after her while she took Dad to the hospital. She found me still sleeping and smelled gas. She called 911 and got me out."

"But nothing happened, Lo!" Gabriela said. *"Nothing!"*

"But it could have. The whole damn house could have blown to smithereens. They were lucky," Tiffany said, her voice harsh, her gaze full of loathing.

"What are you two saying?" Jaymie asked, frowning, looking back and forth between the siblings. "That Gabriela did something deliberate to the house? To the *gas?*"

"You tell *me* how *every* pilot light in the whole house — gas stove, furnace, water heater — were all out. *Every single one of them,*" Tiffany said, tapping the table with a sharp fingernail, making a clicking noise. "They had to call the fire department. It could have been tragic."

Jaymie didn't know what to think or what to believe. Of the three, Gabriela was the only one she knew, and the friend she had known for more than fifteen years would never have done that. And something was wrong with what they were saying. "But . . ." She squinted and shook her head. "Okay, I know a thing or two about gas appliances and furnaces. Gabriela, modern appliances have a device that shuts off the gas if the pilot light goes out."

There was silence for a long moment, and a shifty glance between Tiffany and Logan.

"Wait, *what?* Is that true?" Gabriela asked, her eyes wide.

Jaymie nodded. "There shouldn't have been any gas in the house, at least not enough to smell. As soon as a pilot light goes out, in thirty seconds a valve shuts off the gas." It was like a revelation to her friend, Jaymie could tell; her face cleared, and then she got angry. Jaymie remembered what Brandi's friend had said when texted, that there was no commotion in the neighborhood or at the Offerman home. "And I happen to *know* that there were no fire engines at your house, no emergency vehicles of any kind."

"Liars!" Gabriela set her food aside and said, her chin up. "You were blaming me for doing something I didn't do, and even if I did, wouldn't have hurt you!"

Logan, his expression stony, said, "Are you saying you'd prefer if I had died? Did you, or did you *not*, blow out the pilot lights?"

Gabriela's face twisted and tears began streaming down her face. "You're so mean, Lo! Tiffany has gotten to you. You *know* she hates me, she hates that I took you away from her, her precious baby brother. It's sick, what she's doing, and I can't believe you're letting her!"

Tiffany and Logan exchanged a look. Gabriela hadn't exactly answered, Jaymie realized, but that could have been emotion, not evasion.

"Sit down, Gabriela, you're making a scene," her husband said, his voice tense.

It was true; people seated nearby were staring.

"Is that what you care about? Making a scene?" She stopped, though, as more people entered and stared at her with curiosity.

"Gabriela, I care about you," Logan said, his voice filled with tension. "I want what's best for us."

Jaymie, watching him, heard the agony in his voice. He was deeply troubled, and gripped Fenix's spoon in his hand so tight his knuckles were white. The little girl was alarmed, ready to cry any moment.

"Why should I believe you when you follow me here and accuse me of something so awful? Hey, maybe *Tiffany* did it," she hissed. "*If* it happened at all! Maybe darling Tiffany blew all the goldarned pilot lights out!" She took a deep shuddering breath, her eyes flooded with tears. "I need some fresh air," she sobbed. She stormed out.

"What *actually* happened?" Jaymie asked, looking from one sibling to the other.

"What we said. You don't have to believe us," Tiffany said coolly. "We know you'll side with your friend. But it's true."

"But it *can't* have been dangerous," Jaymie insisted. "Modern technology wouldn't have allowed it." Again, she looked at each of them. She waited, then said, "There was no gas in your home. Come on, admit it."

"Does it matter? Would you have preferred it if the house had blown up or if Logan had suffocated?" Tiffany asked. "It's enough that she *tried* to kill him."

Jaymie shook her head. "It doesn't make sense. She was *genuinely* worried when she couldn't get ahold of her husband." Gabriela was her friend, and friends stick by each other. "And I know for a fact that you're lying about calling the fire department. There were no emergency crews at your house."

The two exchanged looks. Tiffany shook her head as Logan was about to say something. He closed his mouth and stonily looked off into the distance.

Their behavior made her uneasy and she was getting angry. "Tiffany, I think you should come out to the island and get all your stuff," she said, her tone stiff. "You're not welcome back in the cottage."

She walked away to find Gabriela but her friend was gone. Jaymie was left wondering, what was that about? Had she actually tried to kill her husband? It seemed unlikely, and those two siblings were lying about at least some parts of their story. It was confusing. She did suspect that Gabriela was cheating on her husband, but even so, why would she kill Mario, if he was her lover? It seemed more likely that Logan and/or Tiffany killed Mario.

Maybe. Possibly. Or maybe it was Terry, who she now knew had been around at the right time and had a boat, thus giving him the ability to kill Mario in the middle of the night and get back to his motel room with no one the wiser. Jaymie sighed and returned to the inn and headed for Mrs. Stubbs's room.

Her friend was throwing a doggie toy for Hoppy to retrieve, which he did only after shaking the stuffing out of it. "Where did you get that?" Jaymie asked.

"Dee knows that you often bring Hoppy here to visit, so she bought me a doggie toy to play with him," Mrs. Stubbs said.

"Aw, that's sweet." She made a cup of tea for them both and sat down in one of the chairs by the open sliding glass door. She told her friend what she had heard among Gabriela, Logan and Tiffany, and all that she conjectured, including Brandi, Terry, and her suspicions regarding that toxic relationship.

The woman nodded. "That makes sense of something I heard among them yesterday evening. DeeDee took me for a walk last evening. We went past the playground in the park, and I saw your friend with her husband and sister-in-law watching their little girl play. I told Dee to wheel me close by and turn up my hearing aids. I don't do it often, but sometimes I can turn them up and hear better than people with normal hearing. Then I sent her to get me an ice cream." She smiled, a sly look. "Dee can always be distracted by ice cream. And children. The two together . . . I'm lucky she remembered I was there at all. The adults sat together, but looked tense. Your friend complained that she was being trapped."

"*Trapped.* That's worrisome," Jaymie said. "I want to believe Gabriela, that she didn't do anything, and that Logan and Tiffany are lying about her blowing out the pilot lights in their house."

"You want to believe her, but you're not sure if you should?"

Jaymie nodded. "Did you hear anything else?"

"No, unfortunately, just bickering and sniping. You know, I had a thought: if you want to find anything out about this Terry fellow and his boat, perhaps check with the marina staff. Maybe they saw or heard something."

"Good idea. I'd better get going," Jaymie said. She leaned down and kissed Mrs. Stubbs's check. "Thanks for looking after my doggo for me."

She left through the sliding doors. Gabriela sat on the curb by the parking lot, her head in her hands. Jaymie sat down next to her, and Hoppy pushed his nose up against her hand.

She looked up, wiping away her tears, leaving a smear of mascara along her cheek. "I don't know what to do, Jaymie." She sounded frightened, as anyone would who was being trapped by loved ones.

"What happened at the house? I thought everything was good between you and Logan."

"It was . . . once." She scuffed her sandals in the grit gathered by a curbstone on the parking lot pavement. "You don't know what it's like, having your husband's family hate you. Tiffany has been trying from day one to undermine me. And now she's concocted this weird conspiracy theory that I tried to kill Logan by blowing out the pilot lights. I mean, how dumb do they think I am?"

"You did once believe that a water heater was something in the tap," Jaymie said, smiling.

Gabriela managed a weak smile and sniffed. "This is all Tiffany. It's her trying to pit Logan against me and make me out to be the bad guy so they can get Fenix away from me."

"So Logan and Tiffany together are lying, or did Tiffany do something to the pilot lights and tell Logan it was you?"

She shrugged helplessly. "I wish I knew. I don't know where to turn."

Jaymie thought of an old movie her grandma loved, *Gaslight*. It was about a woman slowly being driven mad by her husband, who wanted to get rid of her. He made her think she was imagining things until she questioned her own sanity. Was that what Logan and Tiffany were doing, setting Gabriela up for some reason? The thought chilled Jaymie to the bone. She *had* to find the answers.

She put her arm over Gabriela's shoulders and hugged her friend. "I've told Tiffany she isn't welcome out at the cottage, and to come and retrieve her stuff." She watched her friend, wishing she could climb into her brain and find the truth. It wasn't that she doubted Gabriela, it was just . . . she sighed. She doubted her, she admitted to herself. It was dumb, maybe, because the most likely solution to the murder mystery was that Kory had killed Mario in a fit of drunken anger. The second most likely solution was that Terry, jealous of his wife's involvement with Mario, had killed the guy and tried to pin the blame on his ex. "Come back with me now. You can't stay with Logan. Is Fenix okay with him?"

Gabriela nodded through tears. "He's such a great dad. He loves her. He'd do *anything* for her."

Anything? What did that mean, and how far would he go to keep his daughter, if he and his wife were headed toward a split?

Jaymie had a lot to do first. She left Gabriela with Val, at the Emporium. Charlie was coming back to retrieve Maxie, so Val had to wait for him before she could lock up, and then she would take Gabriela back to her place, where Jaymie could meet them. Val took Hoppy, too.

Jaymie picked up bread, milk, butter and eggs at the Emporium and walked it over to the Queensville house. Along the way she got a text from Jocie that made her smile. They were having a good time, but she missed Mama. She sent photos.

After gathering and sorting the mail, putting away the food, and leaving a note for Becca, who would be returning with Kevin the next day, Jaymie flushed toilets, dusted surfaces, then locked up and walked to Val's place. She met her friends, and together they all headed down to the ferry and to the island.

She left Gabriela and Val sitting on a bench waiting for the ferry while she wandered along the slips, examining the boats bobbing in place. There were a few people around, tinkering with their boats, taking them out to fish, sitting on the dock talking. Which boat was Terry's? she wondered. She saw someone she knew, Johnny Stanko; his work history was varied, but he had, she knew, a part-time job at the marina for the summer.

"Johnny, how are you?" she asked of the tall, shambling fellow.

He whirled. "Hey, Jaymie. Good to see ya! I'm doing swell."

He was the perfect person to ask, observant, but not obtrusively so. She glanced back at her friends, but they were deep in conversation. "Say, Johnny, one of my friends' husband has a boat here at the slip, a new rental, on Wednesday. Do you know who I mean?"

He wrinkled his face up. Johnny was in his early forties, and life, for him, had not been easy. His abundant hair was graying, and he had lines and scars aplenty. She had once helped him get out of an unjust murder accusation, and so he held her in high regard. But he didn't think too quickly, and before he spoke he liked to be sure. His expression cleared. "Sure . . . Terry. Don't know his last name." Typically, he remembered the vehicle better than the man. "He's got a fourteen-foot tan Starcraft . . . nice little boat. Suzuki motor. He dropped it Wednesday."

"He was alone?"

"Yup. I gave him a hand getting it in the water, but once in, he had no problems mooring it in his slip. He seemed to know what he was doing. Good nautical knots. What's up?"

"Johnny, I have a question, but can it stay between us?"

"You know me," he said, and mimicked a lock on his lips and tossing away the key.

She smiled. It reminded her of childhood secrets. "Are you around at night much?"

"Uh-huh. Sure. Me an' a buddy go out fishing lots of nights. Looking for channel cats."

Channel cats: catfish most often caught at night. "Okay, good. You may know this then. Here's his picture; did he take his Starcraft out Thursday night, late?" She had her phone out and had found a picture of Terry from her wedding, which he had attended with Brandi—they were still happy then—and Gabriela and Logan, holding Fenix. They were all in the photo.

He shook his head. "Nah."

"Okay."

She was about to turn off her phone when he said, "But the other guy . . . *he* took the boat out that night. I said something to him, but he told me his buddy Terry always let him use it."

"Wait . . . his buddy? Are you . . . who do you mean?"

He pointed at the pic. "*That* guy," he said, pointing at Logan. "He had a bunch of fishing poles and a tackle box, and he took the boat out."

✄ Eighteen ✄

As Gabriela and Val chatted on the ferry ride, Jaymie held Hoppy on her lap, closed her eyes and breathed in the cool air. As stunning as Johnny's news was, she didn't know what to make of it. Maybe it was nothing. Terry and Logan knew each other; maybe Terry knew Logan was visiting his wife and loaned him the boat to go night fishing. It could be that simple.

She sighed in exasperation and glanced over at Gabriela. She'd had such hopes for their holiday get-together, but it had gone bad from the start with the intrusion of Courtney — who had turned out to be a good addition — and the further intrusion of Tiffany, who had turned out to be a bad addition. She was going to pack up Tiffany's stuff and have it ready for her whenever the woman deigned to come out. At least it would regain some storage space for her actual friends. The woman was a menace as a vacation companion, hogging so much space there was little left for the four other women.

The ferry landed, and they walked back to the cottage. But as they approached they heard voices raised. As they topped the rise of the driveway and looked down to the grove where the trailer sat, they saw Melody, red-faced and angry, facing a man and arguing. As they got closer Jaymie recognized him. It was Andrew, Melody's husband, and he looked furious.

"Uh-oh, looks like trouble," Gabriela said. "I've had enough drama for the day. I'm going into the cottage and have a nap." She evaded the turmoil by going in the front door.

"You're being selfish, Mel. Totally self-absorbed, as always," Andrew yelled. "It's time for you to come home."

"Me? *I'm* self-absorbed? Says the king of the narcissists." Mel's face was pink with agitation, blotches breaking out on her neck as they did when she was extremely upset. "It's been what, three days? Go home, Andrew. You've been following us since the first day and I've *had* it."

"Bull crap! I went home and waited like a good little puppy dog, but you didn't phone or text me. What am I supposed to do, Mel? Huh? What am I supposed to think when you say you need time to think?"

"That I need time to think, you troll!"

Jaymie's eyes widened. She had no clue things were *so* bad between Mel, who downplayed her personal drama always, and Andrew, whose puffy face was marred by tear trails.

Melody took in a deep breath, looking for calm. "I need some breathing space to think. Let me have that."

"What does that mean, Mel? Breathing space to think? That doesn't freaking make sense."

Jaymie quickly trotted down the slope to her friend's side. She faced Andrew, whose soft curling hair and round face normally made him look like a baby. Right now he was red-faced and tear-stained, an angry baby having a tantrum.

"Jaymie, stay out of this." Detective Vestry stepped forward out of the shadows. "I was going to myself, but I don't want this to get any nastier. And Andrew Heath? You should leave your wife alone and go away."

"I'm not Andrew *Heath*! I'm her husband, but she's a *modern woman*," he said with a twisted grimace and the tone of someone saying something disgusting. "*Her* last name is Heath; I'm Andrew *Conners*."

Vestry, her tone calm, said, "My apologies, Mr. Conners, but you're not doing yourself or Melody any good here. I think it would be best for you both if you left."

"Who the hell are *you* to tell me to go away?"

She fished in her jacket pocket and pulled out her badge. "Detective Angela Vestry. You should leave." She clipped her badge to her slacks waistband, where it remained visible.

It was a delight to see Andrew's pink face pale. He stood for a long moment, the tableau frozen like a painting: Detective Vestry watchful, Melody, tears on her cheeks, stiff with anger, and Andrew, his expression now blank, his pale tufts of hair wafting in the breeze the only movement. It was evident that he was weighing his options.

"Fine. I'm going." He stared at Melody and his expression softened. "Mel, please come home. I love you. We have a great life together." He turned and glared at the detective. "Don't let *anyone* tear you away from it."

Melody didn't reply. Andrew whirled and walked away.

"I don't want to see you skulking around here," Melody called after him, her voice calmer. "I'll come back to Consolation when I'm ready, and not before."

Wordlessly, her husband, his body stiff with attempted dignity, strode away, brushing past Jaymie, then Gabriela and Valetta.

"Thanks, Angela," Melody said, putting her hand on the detective's shoulder. "I appreciate the support."

"De-escalation training comes in handy on occasion in my own life," the detective joked with a wry smile that Jaymie was astonished to see. "I have stopped a few fistfights at family reunions."

"He's not a violent sort," Melody said, dropping her hand to her side. Her expression was a mixture of relief and distress. "He's frustrated. And suspicious. And despite what he says, I think he's been hanging around since I got here. He must have been following us."

Vestry's eyes had narrowed and she nodded in a thoughtful way. It reminded Jaymie that she had stuff to tell the detective too.

"I'd better get going. I have to get back on the job. There's a murder to investigate, unless you've already solved it?" Vestry said to Jaymie with raised eyebrows.

Jaymie stifled her first reaction, which was anger and resentment at the woman's snarky tone, and tried to hold on to how charming and helpful she had been in this instance. "I'll walk you out."

"Thanks for lunch," she said to Melody, taking her hand and shaking. "I enjoyed talking to you."

"I enjoyed it too," the writer said. "I've got your deets; I'll email you. And I'll see you around here, of course."

"Let's catch lunch again before you go home. And if you have any more trouble with your husband, give me a call."

Jaymie led the way up the hill, leaving behind Mel, Val and Gabriela to talk. When they were out of earshot, she said, "Detective, I do have a few things to share, if you don't mind. Can we sit on the front step for a minute?"

"Sure. Let's."

They sat on the top step of the cottage front porch. Jaymie was uncomfortable talking to Vestry, but determined to share what she had learned, and even what she surmised. She looked off across the road for a moment, glimpsing the sparkling water of the St. Clair River through the line of pines. "I know you think I butt in,

Detective. I know you often think I'm in the wrong place at the wrong time, but to me . . . I care about this community." She looked over at the woman and saw the gathering storm clouds in her gray eyes.

She realized what it may sound like she was saying. "I'm not saying you don't, please don't think I mean that. We *both* care about this community. First, thanks for handling Andrew. I worry about Mel; where she lives she's cut off from family and friends, and I worry she doesn't have the support she ought to have."

"I like her. At first I was just a fan, but we talked about other stuff than her writing, and I like her. She's . . . difficult. Prickly, like me."

Jaymie's eyes widened. The detective glanced her way and snickered at her expression.

"I'll bet self-awareness is the last thing you expected from me. I *know* I'm not easy to get along with. I never have been. I can get on my high horse sometimes. That's what my grandmother called it . . . *Oh, Angela's getting up on her high horse again.*"

"I wouldn't say that, I—"

"Don't pretend we get along, Jaymie. I think you withhold information. Not always on purpose, but . . . And you think I'm not appreciative when you share, and you think I make it difficult to tell me things."

Jaymie was silent.

"I've talked to Chief Ledbetter," Vestry said. "Chief Connolly likes him and so do I; we always worked together when he was our chief. He remains a good resource who tells it like it is, and he likes you. He says you have a natural nose for news, and that locals confide in you naturally. Anyway . . . give me what you've got."

First, she told Vestry everything she had thought of and discovered about Mario and Hallie and Kory. She wouldn't feel right if she didn't give the woman everything. Then, trying not to add too many qualifications, she simply said that her friend Brandi had an adventurous love life, and had contacted, using a gaming or dating app, Mario Horvat. She had then met up with him at a cottage he was working on two nights before he died. Brandi wasn't there at the moment, but would confirm it when she got back.

"Interesting," the detective said.

Jaymie frowned and looked down at her feet. "Here's the thing: we all went to Grand Bend the day after they arrived—the day after she and Mario spent some time together—and Brandi's ex, Terry Xylander, followed us there and confronted Brandi. He said he knew she had slept with a guy already." She looked up and met the detective's gaze. "I found out today that he's staying locally at the motel between Queensville and Wolverhampton. Val can confirm. Or . . . I guess you can find that out for yourself. He has a boat, Detective . . . he has it *here*, a motorboat that he has in a slip in the marina."

"He could easily have gone around the island, spoken with Mario—"

"He *could* be the guy Hallie heard Mario fighting with." Jaymie was taking this one step at a time. It had occurred to her that just because Johnny said that Logan was the one who took the boat out, it didn't mean that Terry didn't have it later that night, or that Logan hadn't picked him up. "He could easily have pulled the boat up to the dock on the river side of Horvat's cottage—"

"—and argued with then attacked him—" the detective said, her brows raised.

"*With* the pie iron, which, if he was following us and lurking around our property, he could have seen me hang on the tree to dry."

"And he could have set fire to their home. The fire chief thinks an accelerant must have been used, and the fire started at the back of the cottage, on the river side."

Jaymie nodded. "I know it sounds like I've been snooping—"

"It does."

"But I'm worried about my friend. If Terry is violent I want him caught. He was angry that Brandi had been with another guy, though they are broken up."

"What does your friend say?"

"She doesn't think Terry would do anything like that."

Detective Vestry nodded. "Okay. What else? I know there's more."

Jaymie looked over her shoulder, wanting to make sure Gabriela wasn't nearby, especially since she had gone into the cottage earlier. In a soft voice Jaymie explained the situation with her friend as closely as possible without accusing Gabriela of trying to kill her husband in the first place with the blown-out pilot lights. Gabriela wouldn't do it, and the more she thought about it, the more it seemed likely that Logan and Tiffany were gaslighting her gullible friend.

"You think it is possible that your friend's husband is deliberately accusing her of trying to kill him? All to set up some . . . what? A better deal for custody of their daughter?"

Jaymie frowned down at her sandal-clad feet and wiggled her toes. "Sounds dumb, right?"

The detective sighed. "It's not the dumbest thing I've heard. Heck, it isn't even the dumbest thing that's happened in this town. I thought the pudding mould murder was weird last winter. Now a pie iron murder? Gaslighting? Cheating on your spouse using game apps?" She snorted. "Hasn't anyone in this town ever heard of murder with a gun?"

Jaymie sighed. "I know. Hey, remember, I was attacked with a wooden mallet a while back . . . you know, one of those meat pounding mallets. And my vintage bowl was stolen and used to whack a girl I was enemies with!"

The woman next to her was shaking, shuddering . . . was she having a fit? Jaymie looked over, and the detective was bent over, holding her stomach, laughing silently, so hard no sound was coming out of her mouth and she was turning red, her narrow face bright cherry. Jaymie snickered, then chuckled, then laughed too, until her stomach hurt.

Finally the detective wiped her wet eyes and regarded Jaymie with a friendlier look. "I appreciate you being open with me. That's all I want."

What she wanted was Jaymie handing over any information that came her way; Jaymie got it. "Uh . . . one more thing. I don't think this has anything to do with anything, but it's also possible that Gabriela's husband had access to Terry Xylander's boat the night Mario Horvat was murdered." She told the detective about her conversation with Johnny.

"We could propose the same scenario as the Terry and Brandi Xylander hypothesis."

"I don't think that makes a lot of sense. Why would Logan kill

Mario?" Jaymie sighed. "I can't believe I'm conjecturing all of this about my friends' husbands. It's ridiculous."

"We'll interview all of them, Terry Xylander, and Logan and Tiffany Offerman." The detective headed out, after telling Jaymie that they were expecting the cell phone records to come through any time now from Mario Horvat's cellular service provider. When it did, they'd be able to track down if there were other women he had been with, other women who might be angry at him enough to kill him, or boyfriends or husbands who might be similarly angry, as Terry was. They had not totally decided that Kory was the killer, even though he had been charged.

Jaymie headed back to the grove. Worry was tugging at the back of her brain, but she couldn't find the source for it, so she left it alone to simmer. Maybe it would come to her later. Melody, Val, and Gabriela were sitting in the shade with their feet up and lemonade in tall frosty glasses. She sat down with them for a while, but then got up and stretched.

"I'll be happier if I get done what I have to get done. I'm going to pack up all of Tiffany's stuff and have it waiting for her. I don't want her spending any more time out here than necessary. In fact, if she doesn't come for it today, I'll take it to her myself tomorrow morning."

"I should be the one to do that," Gabriela said.

"No, you stay," Jaymie said, one hand out. "You've been through enough with that woman. C'mon, Hoppy!"

Her little dog followed her inside and headed straight to his food bowl. In truth, Jaymie needed a few moments. She was accustomed to having alone time to read, reflect, sip tea and watch the world go by. Even when she was with Jakob and Jocie she could feel that tranquility, that sense of relaxation, steal through her. But this year with her friends she felt the need to be *on* all the time, to entertain, and make sure they were all having a good time. It hadn't been like that in the past, she realized, because they were on neutral ground, a campsite, where she was as free as they were to take time to herself.

She washed the few dishes and let them drip in the drainboard, then wiped down the surfaces in the bathroom. Rachel was immaculately tidy, thank heavens, and she never left the bathroom without it being spotless. Then Jaymie retreated to the bedroom where Tiffany had slept. How was she managing to style her hair without her product and devices? Maybe she had doubles of everything.

Where to start? There was a ton of product: mousse, serum, clay, cream, paste, pomade, wax . . . how did her hair look good weighed down by all of that, then sprayed with hairspray? Any time Jaymie tried adding product to her own hair it felt weighed down and sticky. And then there were the appliances: curling iron and straightener — that was a weird combo — a blow dryer, a volumizer hot brush and a set of steam curlers.

She found Tiffany's duffel bag stuffed under the other dresser and tackled the appliances first, wrapping the cords around each item and piling them into the bag. She then did the same for the products, trying to be careful, worried that a bottle would open and spill its contents.

She reflected back on the tangle among Gabriela, Logan and Tiffany. There were so many tensions and problems, not at all what she had thought their lives were like. Gabriela had painted a different portrait of her marriage when she first arrived. It was all happiness and fun, love and laughter, sunshine and rainbows. She had even mentioned trying for another baby. And yet she was the one who had masterminded coming to Heartbreak Island rather than camping at their normal campground. Why?

There was one answer, of course. Gabriela was there to meet someone. The question was, was it the same someone as Brandi had met? Was she, too, having a fling with Mario Horvat? As hard as it was to imagine, it must be so. If she accepted that, then it answered her question about Logan and gave him a strong motive. And Logan had taken Terry's boat out the night of the murder.

Jaymie knew she'd have to ask Gabriela, and she dreaded it. Her friend's feelings were easily hurt. She took offense, and then she'd cry and accuse the other person of picking on her. That was how many conversations ended between her and Brandi, and even her and Melody, with Jaymie and Rachel as the peacemakers.

She stared down at the duffel bag, which she had packed carefully, using dividers to keep the product bottles upright. She got down on the floor to look under the dresser, to make sure nothing of Tiffany's remained. Hoppy, who had trotted in to join her, snuffled around the bag she was packing. Then he shinnied under the dresser.

"Hoppy, what are you doing? Did you find something?"

A stray sock in his mouth, he tried to shimmy out from underneath, and whimpered, stuck. She carefully pulled him free, and with him, brushed by his hind leg, came a cell phone. Someone had dropped theirs. Weird, since typically they all had their phones on them 24/7. Maybe it was from a former guest, though she cleaned pretty thoroughly between renters.

A sock and a cell phone. The sock was Tiffany's; she remembered the woman wearing one like it with tennis shoes on the dinner cruise. So was the cell phone hers too? But no, she remembered Tiffany with her cell phone beside her on the table at the inn. Unless she had a second phone.

"Jaymie, are you coming back out?" Gabriela came to the door and stared down at her.

Jaymie concealed the cell phone. Until she had a chance to look at it and figure out whose it was, she didn't want anyone to know she had found it. Because there was one person who she knew had lost a phone, and that was Mario Horvat.

ɕ Nineteen ɕ

"I'M COMING OUT IN A MINUTE. Just give me a sec."

Gabriela disappeared, but Jaymie knew if she didn't go out, either Gabriela or someone else would be back to check on her. She spent the rest of the afternoon with her friends. They got out a game of lawn darts and played for a half hour, then chatted with an excited Rachel, who returned from the tart bakery with more treats and a couple of pints of the butter tart ice cream.

Gabriela looked tired, and Jaymie worried at the puzzle of her relationship with her husband, her sister-in-law, and possibly a lover. She wished she could come right out and say something to her friend, clear the air, but with so many tangles still knotted, she didn't know how or what to ask. It wasn't as easy with Gabriela as it would be with someone else, and if she was undecided, she needed to leave it alone until she had more clarity.

Val got her alone for a few minutes and told her what she had discovered through her nephew. Will told her that it would be dead easy, of course, to snoop on someone if you knew their passwords, or could figure them out. Even a tech newbie could do that. If a husband could gain access to his wife's account—or vice versa—he could snoop in whatever he wanted, private chats or messages meant to be secret. He could see where she had been, track her whereabouts in real time, maybe.

It was chilling to Jaymie how exposed their cell phone usage may have made them. If Brandi or Gabriela were secretly communicating with Mario and making plans, either husband could easily snoop using passwords they knew or had found out.

"What do you think this means?" Val asked.

"It doesn't seem as far-fetched as it did before, that either Brandi or Gabriela—or both of them, given what we know about Mario—cheated on her husband, who found out about it and took revenge."

"But which?"

Jaymie shrugged. "I wish I knew. Should I be warning my friends?"

"I don't know, kiddo. It's a police investigation at this point. You've told the police everything you know."

"Yeah, but Logan or Terry . . ." Jaymie sighed and shook her head. "I don't know what to do."

They returned to their group of friends and shortly after received a shouted invitation down the hill from Ruby; they were having a barbecue and party, and *everyone* was invited. The Redmonds were convivial, generous and wonderful hosts, and were having their annual end-of-summer blast. The food was bountiful, catered by the Ice House. Wine and beer flowed.

There were many neighbors Jaymie knew from the island, and quite a few she did not. Sammy Dobrinskie, Ashlee, and Sammy's mom were there, but Sammy was working for Garnet, keeping the tables of food supplied, the half barrels full of ice for the beer and wine, and making sure there were enough places to sit and be comfortable.

Melody, especially, made friends with the Redmonds. Jaymie was amused to overhear their conversation. Mel plied them with questions, especially when she learned their story, how Ruby had been the daughter of a Montreal mob boss, with Garnet, a former cop, hired to protect her. But the conversation soon headed off in other directions, finally leading to a long story about their sailing trip that summer, starting with the Bayview Mackinac race, which took them from Port Huron to Mackinac Island, after which they spent time sailing the Great Lakes.

Finally, Garnet offered Mel—and anyone else who wanted to go; he was tipsy by then and in a grand mood—a trip along the river on their sailboat.

The party lasted long into the night. But Jaymie couldn't stop thinking and wondering about the cell phone, which felt like it was burning a hole in her pocket. Whose was it? Should she be turning it over to Detective Vestry? But she hadn't had a chance to look at it yet; it could, possibly, be from a previous renter, or it could be one of the girls'. It could be Courtney's, or Brandi's; those two were still off on their "shopping" trip, which Jaymie knew was no shopping trip at all, but a break from the rest of them, a chance to cut loose and party.

Which was fine, except that Brandi's ex, Terry, might be a lunatic/stalker/murderer in a boat. Worried, Jaymie had Val check with the motel clerk she knew, and was relieved to discover that Terry was still there, at the motel, sitting by the pool all afternoon, and holed up in his room that evening, his car idle in the parking lot. Apparently, anyway. Jaymie fretted; what if he had rented a car and followed Brandi? But that wasn't possible, not if he had been by the motel pool all afternoon. And he wouldn't rent a car when he had his own with him. She shook her head, confused and upset. This was all taking a toll on her.

As the evening dwindled on, Rachel, especially, was getting along with *everyone*; she had met many of Garnet and Ruby's guests already serving at Tansy's Tarts, and was swiftly becoming an islander, as she jokingly referred to herself. Even Gabriela looked relaxed, sitting with Ruby and some of her friends, showing photos of Fenix on her phone.

Her phone . . . Jaymie was getting antsy, wondering if she could sneak away and perhaps discover whose phone she had found, and if she could break into it. Many people had them locked, though she never did.

Val ambled over and sat down next to her, where she sat in the shadows of the grove of trees that topped the hill. "You look like you're ready to jump out of your skin," she murmured, taking a sip of her wine and leaning close. "What is up with you?"

Jaymie told her, checking over her shoulder often, what she had found.

"Wow, a sock! What drama."

Jaymie smiled; it was good to have one friend in whom she could absolutely confide. "I'm dying to know what is on that phone, but I need time and privacy for that. I'm going to wait a bit, then sneak down to the cottage and check it out. Will you cover for me?"

"Sure. Just give me a sign."

"Done."

Val was called away to settle some point of contention among islanders; all knew her as impartial to a fault, and she also had the best memory of anyone local for past events through the years.

Gabriela slumped down in a chair by Jaymie and glanced at her. "I . . . I feel like maybe you believe those awful things Tiffany said about me."

Jaymie didn't know quite how to answer, so she stayed silent.

"I would *never* do anything to hurt Logan. He's Fenix's daddy!" she said, a sob catching at her voice.

Jaymie watched her for a long minute. As confused as she was, there was one thing she could ask. "Gabriela, why did you change the booking? I know all about it, how you used Brandi's email and canceled the campsite booking with a lie about a dead friend. Why did you change it and then lie to us all, that the campground was shut down because of a plumbing problem?"

Sighing, she slumped down in her chair. "I guess it's no secret now that Logan and I haven't been getting along," she said softly.

"I understand that," she replied, wondering what that had to do with canceling the booking.

"No, you *don't* understand. You have this perfect little life in your perfect town, with your perfect family and Jakob's perfect family." Her voice, filled with tension and anger, cracked. "You don't know what it's like to be criticized constantly. His mom is the worst, her and Tiffany. When Fenix was born that woman, Logan's mom, was always snatching Fenix out of my hands and saying I wasn't holding her right, I wasn't diapering her right, I wasn't feeding her right. *Nothing* I do is right." She wiped tears off her cheeks and took a long drink. She had been drinking all evening and was more than a little tipsy. Whenever that had happened in the past it had tended to loosen her inhibitions to the point of telling her deepest secrets. "After I had Fenix, Logan wouldn't touch me. We haven't had sex in three years. *Three years!*" she sobbed.

"I'm sorry, Gabriela," Jaymie said.

"I started playing this online game."

"LiveLoveLife?"

"You've heard of it?"

"I hadn't before Brandi told me about playing it. You assume a character and live life virtually. And you meet people." She slid a glance over to her friend. "You meet men."

"I needed something to make me feel better about myself. Can you understand that? I gained all this weight," she said, slapping her belly.

"Aw, honey, be nicer to yourself," Jaymie exclaimed, hurting for her friend.

"I can't take it off, and Logan doesn't want me. *Nobody* wanted me!"

"Except . . . ?" Jaymie felt there was an exception coming.

"Except one guy." She flicked a glance sideways, then stared straight ahead. "We flirted online, and it was so *fun*." She sighed. "I had a spring in my step."

This was her old friend, and she was in pain, Jaymie thought. No judgment, as Mel would say. She took a deep breath. "You cheated on Logan?" Jaymie said, keeping her tone neutral.

"No, I did *not!*"

"But . . . you planned to?"

Gabriela heaved a sigh. "I planned to. *That's* why I canceled the campsite booking and convinced Brandi to ask you if we could stay in your cottage. I had seen on your booking site that you had a renter cancel for the end of August."

"The night we got home from Grand Bend you took off to meet him."

Gabriela, eyes wide, stared at Jaymie through the gloom. "I was *going* to meet him." She paused, hung her head and said, her tone low, "But I didn't."

Jaymie wanted to believe her. "I think I heard you leave that night, out the front door," she said, not wanting to say that Rachel saw her go. "Where did you go then, if you didn't meet your . . . your fling?"

"I went for a walk," Gabriela said, turning away. "To think. I needed to sort things out. I went down to the Ice House patio and sat there for a while. It was good to be alone with my thoughts, in the dark, no noise, nothing."

"Who was the guy, the one you were going to meet?"

"I never knew his real name, because we never met, you see." Her gaze, dusky in the dim shadows, was pleading. She sniffed. "When it came down to it, I didn't want to cheat on my husband. I still love Logan." Her voice softened and broke on his name.

Jaymie was silent. If it was just a misstep, just a guy she chatted with and never met, then it was none of her business. But what if she was lying? What if she had met up with Mario? Jaymie shook her head, confused. The one sure thing was that Gabriela was most definitely not the hot redhead he was enamored with. She could be another of his online flings, whether they had ever gotten together or not. And either way, steady cheat or slightest fling, there was not a single reason on earth why Gabriela would want him dead.

There were others with strong motives: Kory; Hallie; Logan;

Terry; Brandi, even, or . . . she stilled. There was one person she hadn't considered as Mario's killer. Someone who had a nasty temperament. Someone who appeared to be trying to railroad an innocent person with a devastating accusation.

Tiffany. Her heart beat quicker. Who had shown up at the precise moment when everything went bad. Who, with her brother, had access to a boat and therefore access to Mario. Maybe Tiffany and her brother were in on it together, with Tiffany dispatched to keep track of Gabriela and report her movements back to Logan.

"Gabriela, come over here for a minute," Rachel said, beckoning to their friend, her face glowing with good humor and a few glasses of wine. She was the hit of the party, the new cute girl in town, and already had a date for the fall festival in two months. Gabriela got up and joined her, and she put her arm around her shoulders. "I want you to tell these guys about that time in college when Brandi had those two Colombian exchange students hidden in her room! You tell it funnier than I do. *¿Donde esta Brandi?*" She giggled woozily and tugged Gabriela toward a group of partiers.

Jaymie was left in the semi darkness of the edge of the patio, listening to the peeper frogs and chirp of crickets. Hoppy was sleepy; it was time to take him back to the trailer. She gave the signal to Val, who nodded. If anyone noticed her gone, Val would cover for her.

She scaled down the hill in the dark, the play of the narrow beam from her flashlight showing the way from step to step. Away from the party, their chatter and laughter was muffled by the trees and brush, just a hushed babble in the night. Soothing, in a way, like waves on a shore. She was not alone.

Back at the cottage she let Hoppy have one last piddle and some snacks, while she sat at the kitchen table in the cottage and turned the phone on, examining it in the glow of the table lamp that lit the kitchen. The phone had plenty of power, and it wasn't locked. She explored a bit, getting familiar with a different device. How could she tell whose it was? She wished she were more technically minded, but she wasn't. There were several apps on the main page, all dating apps. She found hundreds of text messages. The contact list was like a virtual little black book, with dozens of contacts with no real names, just screen names: 1HawtMama, BigNBootyful,

NastyGurl. And the reply contact name was always the same . . . HawtMarineBoy.

That, then, was her answer. This was most definitely a man's phone, and it *had* to be Mario's; Brandi had said he posed online in the game app as a hot young Marine stud, to her disappointment. Who else could the owner of the phone be? Could Brandi have ended up with it after their night together? Why would she keep it? It was a puzzler.

One constant messenger, a woman who the phone owner had apparently met repeatedly, was called BigRed. There were steamy texts back and forth, ones that made Jaymie blush. And the pictures! Maybe that was his redheaded lover, the one he was thinking of dumping Hallie for.

She was about to turn the phone off, knowing that now she'd discovered who it belonged to she'd have to turn it over to Detective Vestry in the morning, when one last picture caught her eye on the string of text messages from the phone owner's most ardent correspondent. It was the top curve of a pale breast, with a tattoo of a bird, or . . . no, that wasn't just any bird. She squinted and brought the phone up closer to her face.

It was a phoenix.

A phoenix . . . Gabriela saying she had her baby tattooed over her heart. Her baby, Fenix. So, she knew already what Gabriela had told her, that she had corresponded with a guy but had not met him. She could have sent the photo, and yet still be telling the truth. She heard voices; the others were coming back. Confused and worried, she shoved the phone in her hoodie pouch and stood, wiping a tear out of her eyes. Her mind stumbled, her thoughts chaotic. But she pushed them aside and pasted a smile on her face, rushing to the sink to be busy, putting away the last of the dishes in the drainboard.

"The party's over," Val said, with an apologetic and questioning look, as she kinda blocked the door from Gabriela and Rachel behind her. "One of Garnet's sailing buddies is ailing, so they're taking him to the mainland to the hospital in Wolverhampton."

"Oh, no!" Jaymie said, turning away from the counter, immediately concerned. "Do you think he's going to be okay?"

"I hope so. Among Ruby and Garnet's sailing buddies there were two cardiologists and a surgeon at the party," she said with a smile. "One of the cardiologists thinks it's probably angina. I advised a nitro pill and an eighty milligram aspirin, which they've given him, but the doctors advised taking him to the hospital. I agree. It's better to be safe than sorry."

"Hey, can we get through?" Melody said with a good-natured tone. She ducked under Val's arm. "I gotta use the head, as your sailing friend calls the washroom."

"I'd still like to have a campfire," Jaymie said.

"Let's do it," Val said. "I haven't toasted a marshmallow yet, and it isn't summer until I've thoroughly burnt a piece of fluffy sugar until it's a flaming torch."

"Good. I have a bag of the giant ones that Jocie loves. Change into your PJs and join me at the campfire. I'll make hot chocolate, too."

Jaymie got out the toasting forks and they gathered at the fire. The ring of familiar faces lit with golden light, giving a ruddy glow to each. Gabriela was quiet as the others chatted softly, her glance darting among them, frowning. They ate marshmallows and drank hot chocolate.

"I think I'll set one of the Jade Torrence books in an idyllic place like this," Melody mused, rubbing her fingers together, trying to rid them of the remnants of the sticky marshmallow she had consumed. "Seeming so peaceful, but with this undercurrent of drama."

"What do you mean?" Val said, rubbing a bit of blackened marshmallow off her cheek.

Melody cocked her head to one side. "It's serene — tiny cottage-filled island, sunny summer days, friendly islanders, peaceful on the surface — but underneath it all it's like the silty, greasy sand at the bottom of the river, dank and weedy, the lives of the islanders intertwined in dangerous ways."

Val barked a sharp laugh. "Evocative! Melody, you need to see the river at night. I get what you're saying and you're right; it can feel menacing in the dark. The sound of it sliding past and the current and the waves lapping on the shore; it's like whispers in the night, like it's telling secrets."

Mel sat up straight. "I *need* to see that! But I don't want to go alone."

"Come on; we're decent enough in our PJs," Val said, launching herself out of her lawn chair. She was wearing a PJ shorts set, and Mel wore shorts and a T-shirt. "The river is kinda cool and spooky at night. When I was a teenager we used to sneak over here for parties and steal a boat to get back to Queensville."

"You *what?*" Jaymie said.

"Shhh," Val said, her eyes sparkling behind her glasses. "Don't tell Becca I told. It's supposed to be a secret from you."

"Can I come?" Rachel said. "If I'm going to live here, I want to know all about the island."

The three set off. Jaymie was left with Gabriela.

"I keep thinking about what has happened," her friend said. "I have a confession to make."

Jaymie felt her stomach drop. "A confession?"

"Not a confession. More like a fear. Or . . . a confession and a fear."

"About what?"

"Logan. And Tiffany. You saw how they treat me, like a pile of doodoo."

That was so Gabriela. She was never one for swearing; every expletive she thought of she shifted to another word, something innocuous and childish. Not that Jaymie minded.

"And that story about something going wrong with the gas at the house? That's a lie."

Jaymie watched her eyes in the flickering fire. Knowing what she knew about the messages on the phone, she was torn. "Tell me more."

Gabriela teared up. "I'm scared, Jaymie. I think Logan may have done something . . . may have k-killed Mario."

Bingo. As much as she suspected Gabriela was holding something back, there *were* things that her friend didn't know, like that Logan had actually been away from the inn and had borrowed Terry's boat. That gave him the perfect ability to be on the island, or even to pull up to Mario's river-access dock. Maybe Gabriela was right. Maybe Logan killed Mario, or . . . Logan and Tiffany together killed Mario? Had Tiffany lifted Mario's cell phone somehow and planted it under the drawers to implicate Gabriela? She shook her head. When would Tiffany have had a chance to lift Mario's phone?

"So you admit you were here to meet Mario?"

"I swear I didn't know his real name until I found out about Brandi. We never hooked up. Honest!"

Troubled, Jaymie stared at her friend. It could be true. Brandi was the one who *had* hooked up with him. How much more likely was it, knowing what she knew now, that Terry had somehow gotten his phone and planted it in the cottage? It would have taken nerves of steel to do it, but there were many times when the cottage was unlocked and they were all down in the grove, oblivious. With access to the island whenever he wanted, it could be him. Perhaps he even set up Logan to use his boat that night, knowing what it would look like. Terry could have gotten it back and still come out to the island. Everything she suspected Logan of, Terry could have done. And he had shown himself to be jealous and combative already. He *could* have confronted and killed Mario. He *could* have intended Brandi to take the fall, if he was especially vindictive.

Rachel, Val and Melody returned, chatting and laughing. Jaymie was happy that her two old friends and Val got along. It could have been a bad mix, given Val was fifteen years older than them, but no, Val was her saving grace, as always. She sent her a grateful look and a shrug.

As Gabriela slunk away to the cottage and Rachel followed, Melody said, "Val suggested that if I wanted to write about a place like this, I should maybe spend a night in the trailer. Would it crowd you too much? I wouldn't want to put you out." As always when it came to asking for what she deemed a favor, Melody was diffident and uncertain.

"Hey, I said whoever wanted to sleep in the trailer could. The more the merrier."

"Exactly what Val said."

"That's settled, then."

๕ Twenty ๕

THEY ALL PREPARED FOR BED. Without Brandi and Courtney there, and with Val, Mel and Jaymie sharing the trailer, it left Gabriela and Rachel with the luxury of separate rooms. Jaymie decided to bank the fire, since she wanted to make breakfast over it in the morning.

Gabriela wandered back out and down the slope to the fireside. "What are you doing?"

"I want to use the fire in the morning, so I'm banking it."

"You're what?"

"Banking the fire; watch." Jaymie separated the coals and raked the ash off to the side. She had hot embers left, and she corralled them in the middle of the stone-rimmed firepit, piled the coals over the top and one piece of hardwood, a little damp. She then retrieved her shovel and scooped up the ash, piling it over the rest in the center. Finally, she got the old banged-up galvanized metal washtub they used to smother their fires and propped it over the whole affair, using a stone to create a gap at the bottom so the embers wouldn't die. She straightened, put the shovel aside and dusted off her hands. "You'd think it would kill the fire, but if you cover it with ash, the embers stay hot. In the morning I'll take the washtub off, stir the embers, add some kindling, and the fire will blaze right up again, and I can cook breakfast over it. My dad taught me how to do it."

"That's amazing how the fire doesn't die, it's just . . . hidden." Gabriela yawned and stretched. "I'm going to bed now. Thanks, Jaymie, for talking to me tonight. I appreciate it."

In the trailer Jaymie, Val and Melody chatted for a while. Jaymie had to identify each of the familiar—to her—night noises for Melody, and they chatted for a while about the week so far. Jaymie didn't say anything about her conversation with Gabriela. She didn't know what to make of it, was confused about what it all meant.

As the others fell quiet, snores erupting from Val and soft whiffles of breath from Mel, Jaymie turned on her side and hugged Hoppy to her. He curled up in the crook of her body and wuffled a soft appreciation for her companionship. She kissed his head, inhaling the doggie scent, made up of smoke, fresh air and ineffable Hoppy. Outside the island was as quiet as it ever got. An occasional shout of a partier would be heard, a dog barking, someone chopping wood to add a last log to a campfire. But that silenced eventually. Jaymie tossed and turned for a couple of hours. Worries about Hallie, Kory, sorrow for Mario . . . it all coursed through her brain, mingling with a deep concern that someone she knew was involved. Finally, though, she fell into a fitful sleep.

When she awoke she was disoriented. She sat up in her bed and looked at her light-up watch; three thirty. Why was she waking up at three thirty again? She had always slept like a log, but not since this holiday began. And she was alone. Mel and Val were gone, and Hoppy was scratching at the door to get out. "What is *wrong* with everyone?" she grumbled. The two new besties had probably gone for another walk for atmosphere, Jaymie thought sourly. That was Val, ever helpful.

Jaymie scrubbed her eyes and pushed her feet into flip-flops. A tiny dog's tiny bladder would wait for no woman. "Why couldn't they take you on their walk?" she grumbled. She stepped out of the trailer and Hoppy bounced off, barking. "Shush, Hoppy, what . . . ?" Someone was at the fire, a dark figure. "Who's there?" she said, approaching.

It was Gabriela, and she had the washtub off the firepit and was poking at something furiously, black smoke coming from the pit.

"What are you burning, Gabriela?" Jaymie asked, grabbing the poker from her hand. There was something curling and hissing in the firepit, and the smell was acrid, stinging the eyes and nose. She separated what was left of the item from the flames. It looked like a fake fur. Or . . . a sweater, or rug? No . . . it was . . . she lifted part of it up with the poker. It looked like the remnants of a cheap nylon Halloween wig. "What *is* this?"

"Just . . . it's an old toy of Fenix's, a . . . a d-doll."

"What are you burning it for?"

Gabriela's face, haunting in the fire glow, was curiously blank. She had on a long T-shirt nightgown that said *Mama Bear* in scroll and wore cheap flip-flops on her feet. "I feel so alone, Jaymie," she whispered. "This trouble with Logan and Tiffany . . ." She picked up a long stick from the kindling pile and tried to push the nylon hair from the edge back into the flames, now dying.

"Leave it, Gabriela!" Jaymie pushed it off to one side and stood guard. "What's going on? What are you doing out here in the middle of the night? Talk to me. You know you can tell me anything." She examined her friend's face in the faint light of the dying fire.

"I'm useless," the woman said, a pout on her round face, crossing her arms over her stomach.

"Honey, you're not useless, you have a good life. Even if you and Logan are having problems you still have Fenix, and your friends and family."

"I want something more . . . something *other* than just being a wife and mommy."

Taken aback, Jaymie frowned. "I thought you said that being Fenix's mom was fulfilling? And you have a job, too. You're doing *great*, Gabriela, truly!"

"You don't understand," Gabriela said bitterly, glaring at Jaymie. "You'll *never* understand. I haven't had a moment's peace since I started working. Logan called me lazy when I stayed at home to look after Fenix. And now he complains because I'm always working. It's not fun. If you *dare* tell anyone else that you want more than to be a mommy, you're made to feel guilty, like you can't love your kid and still want more."

"Come on, let's sit down and talk," Jaymie said, waving to the lawn chairs that circled the firepit. "I'm here for you; you know that."

"I don't *want* to sit," Gabriela said, her voice rising in tone and volume. "I need to walk. Or *something*. I don't know what I need."

Jaymie watched her, trying to figure out how best to help her friend. Edging toward her, she said, "What more do you want?"

Pacing away, Gabriela said, "Just . . . *more*." She turned and gestured to Jaymie. "Like what you have. A husband like Jakob who loves you, and . . ." She stared at Jaymie. "I want fame."

"*Fame?*" Whatever Jaymie had thought was coming next, it wasn't that.

"People fawn all over Mel," she said, throwing her hands in the air. "It's sickening. She's a total nutcase, you know. Mel is *disturbed*. Have you *read* her latest books, the Jade Torrence ones? They're all about murder and violence." Gabriela shot Jaymie an unfriendly look. "And *you* . . . I've seen you on TV. All the murders around here and you're right smack square in the middle of them."

"I don't understand what you're saying, Gabriela." Jaymie was perplexed, her mind going a mile a minute trying to figure out what her old college friend was saying. "Are you saying you want to investigate murders?"

"Of *course* not. You've got no right to get mixed up in that crap, Jaymie. It's none of your business. You're putting yourself in danger, and now you've got a kid! Hah! Me going back to work is a crime, but you investigating crime while you've got a kid is okay. They all think you're the be-all and end-all!" She was wide-eyed and becoming agitated. "And Melody!" she said, throwing her hands up in the air. "People fawning all over her books. Have you read the reviews for the Jade books? Like she's some Sue Grafton or something. It's revolting." She was quivering with anguish, tears welling in her eyes, sparkling in the faint light of the fire. "And then . . . and then look at me. I try to do everything I'm supposed to do. Try to say whatever people want me to say. I do *everything* right and I *still* can't catch a break! I still don't get the adulation you guys do. I don't understand." She sobbed and took in a long shuddering breath.

Jaymie was fed up with all the self-pitying moaning. It was a vivid reminder of all of Gabriela's worst character flaws, her loud and elaborately embellished self-pity. Sympathizing with her seemed to make it worse. "That's what you always do, isn't it?" she said, eyeing her friend. "You do and say whatever it is you think people want to hear."

"*Exactly!* I've always done and said everything I was supposed to do. And where did it get me? *Nowhere.* I'm still in the same miserable place I've always been. No one cares what I do. No one gives a darn if I live or die," she said with a sob.

"Gabriela, has it ever occurred to you that Mel and I do what we do because we *want* to, not so other people will look up to us, or give us accolades?"

The woman shook her head. "It doesn't matter anymore." She swiped tears from her eyes and focused on Jaymie, her eyes glittering in the firelight. "I have plans," she said, her voice softer. "I've been writing a book, you know."

The rapid change of subject was bewildering, and Jaymie was experiencing serious concerns about her friend's mental state. "You've been writing a book, like . . . a novel?"

Gabriela nodded. "It's going to blow little Melody's saccharine romances right out of the water. You know, some people *love* her books, but they're nothing but people getting together, falling in love and getting married."

"I *like* Melody's romances," Jaymie sputtered. "They're a nice escape."

"It's crap. Not real life."

"But you were complaining about the subject matter of her new Jade Torrence books. Those are harder edged. Is that what you want to write? What are you saying, Gabriela?"

"Look, real life is, you get married and you get bored. Fat. Sad. Depressed. And finally . . . ditched." She shook her head. "Do you have any clue how many times I've been ditched in my life? Dozens! And Logan was going to do it too. All he ever wanted was a child. Not a *wife*. Not *me*."

This was a different woman . . . finally the real Gabriela? Had she spent her whole life hiding until now? "I feel for you . . . I do," Jaymie said softly. She swallowed back a hard lump in her throat and moved toward her, ready to take her arm. "I want to help. Let's go and get you somebody to talk to."

Her friend blinked and emotions flickered over her face as she shook her head and backed away. She seemed, in turns, uncertain, angry, sad, and anxious. This was *not* Jaymie's old friend after all; this was who her friend had become after years of inner turmoil. Maybe she had to stop assuming she knew what her friend would and would not do. She took a deep breath and squared her shoulders. "Gabriela, tell me the truth once and for all about what happened at your house in Ohio. Did you try to kill your husband?"

Gabriela stared at her. "Jaymie, don't be ridiculous. A devoted wife and mom would *never* do that. Would she?"

"No, a devoted wife and mom would never do that," Jaymie said carefully.

"And as far as anyone else knows . . ." Gabriela paused and smiled, an eerily disconnected expression. "I mean, except for Tiffany and Logan, but they can't prove anything," she said, her tone becoming dreamy.

Confused and uncertain, Jaymie watched, wary, her stomach roiling with acid. There was something most definitely *wrong* with

Gabriela. What was she saying? What did she mean? Jaymie was afraid she already knew.

The woman brightened. "As far as anyone is concerned, I *am* a devoted wife and mom." Gabriela circled the fire, and from the other side of it tried to poke the thing in the pit back into the flames.

Jaymie smacked her stick away and used her own to once again remove the smoldering item from the firepit. "Stop it, Gabriela. Just *stop.*"

"What is *wrong* with you, Jaymie?" her friend asked. "You're so cranky tonight."

"What's wrong with *you?*" Jaymie said, watching Gabriela, who sighed in exasperation and rolled her glittering eyes. "About the problem with the gas pilot lights, what Tiffany and Logan spoke of," Jaymie said slowly. "You never did know anything about a house, not even what a water heater was." Her voice sounded ghostly, as she worked out what she was thinking. "And you haven't learned anything since, have you? I've always had to deal with the house in Queensville, so I know how to change a washer, fix a toilet . . . and I know about pilot lights, how if you blow them out, there is a valve that turns off the gas. But you didn't know that, did you?"

She stared at Gabriela, waiting. When the woman didn't respond she goaded her. "You did it, didn't you?" she said, her nerves shivering through her body, fear a slow trickle that would become a flood any minute. Her voice had a hysterical edge to it that sounded foreign. "You blew out all the pilot lights and left your husband in the house, hoping he'd die. Or that the house would blow up and . . . and he'd *die.* You didn't care about him, you didn't care about Fenix, you didn't care about how it might kill an innocent bystander, you just cared about *you.*"

"Do you *hear* yourself right now? You're talking crazy, Jaymie," Gabriela said, her eyes narrow.

Hoppy, who had been taking advantage of his unusual middle-of-the-night freedom to explore the bushes, yipped softly. "Hush, Hoppy," Jaymie said, putting out one hand. "I'm right, aren't I, Gabriela? And then, here . . ." She stopped dead, her eyes widening. She looked down beside the firepit and prodded the burnt object, what she now recognized as a cheap red wig. "*You're* the hot redhead who came here to meet up with Mario several times. You said you had to travel sometimes for work, even overnight. You have to check in with different stores around Ohio and Michigan. This is the wig you wore to meet up with Mario, or HawtMarineBoy, as he was known to you."

Gabriela's eyes flickered, widening, then narrowing. She glared at Jaymie. It looked like she was trying to figure something out.

Jaymie had never before been in this exact position. Had one of her friends committed murder? *Why?* It didn't make a bit of sense.

The wig. The slipping out at night. "You said you sat in the dark by the Ice House, but if you'd done that, if you were actually on the Ice House patio in the middle of the night, you'd know, it is *ablaze* with lights to discourage vandalism. There *is* no dark spot on that patio or anywhere around the Ice House." And the phone. The *phone!*

Horror was growing as she moved from uncertainty to growing conviction. "You knew Brandi was seeing Mario too!" Jaymie said, her voice choked with fear and sorrow. "You *knew* it. You stole Mario's phone and planted it behind Tiffany's stuff, to be found later. You were hoping to implicate Brandi with Mario's phone. But then when Tiffany showed up . . . wow." Her mind gathered all the little details together. "You picked up his phone the first night we were at the Ice House, didn't you? Oh!" A stray thought solidified her suspicion. "You went back in to retrieve your own cell phone, you said, but I remember you putting it in your purse before we left the table! You went back in and somehow slipped past them and stole Mario's phone."

"Now you're being idiotic," Gabriela said angrily.

"I know I'm right."

"You should write books, like Melody," Gabriela said dismissively. "If anyone had a plan, it must have been Tiffany and Logan, you know? First they say I tried to kill Logan, then they came here and killed Mario while blaming me! It's a conspiracy." She was going for an expression of wounded sorrow, but she looked evasive. And growing in her behavior was an agitation, an uneasiness that sharpened. "It's outrageous that my own friend wouldn't *get* that! You're all about being supportive to women until you get to me, is that it? I don't get the benefit of the doubt? I don't get any sympathy?"

Jaymie fidgeted with the stick in her hand, wondering what to do next. This was her old friend. What she was thinking, conjecturing, was outrageous, but . . . it pieced together tidily. Gabriela must have shifted the plan a couple of times. Facts, events, the timeline: it all lined up to confirm what she already knew. Gabriela thought Logan would die of gas inhalation, or at least she was hoping it. Jaymie's eyes watered up. Gabriela would have *murdered* her baby's father. It was a shocking blow.

Jaymie watched her friend, who appeared elaborately unconcerned. And yet . . . seeing her darting gaze, her curled fingers, her jerky movement . . . *knowing* she was trying to figure out what to do next, what move would get her out of a fix, Jaymie's heart pounded, a sickening thud in her chest. Now she understood. *That's* what Gabriela's fretfulness the first night was about. At first she was pretending to expect a text or call from Logan that didn't come . . . that she *knew* would not come, if her plan worked. She must have been on edge, waiting, expecting to get a "devastating" call from home that there had been a tragic accident and that Logan was dead. That was the real reason behind her growing agitation: the call that never came that night, and didn't come the next day either, as she got more and more worried.

But when all her plans went south, why kill Mario? It made no sense.

Hoppy yipped again. "Not now, Hoppy," Jaymie said, but caught movement out of the corner of her eye. Val was at the top of the rise above them, as was Melody, whose eyes glittered with tears. Gabriela had said enough that it was plain she had some involvement. But how much? Jaymie swiveled her gaze back to Gabriela, who was fortunately still facing her, her back turned to their friends on the rise. There was comfort in her friends—her *true* friends—being so close. It gave her courage and confidence. Jaymie used two fingers in a subtle movement to try to stay her friends until she heard what Gabriela had to say. "Tell me the truth," Jaymie said loudly. "You've been seeing Mario for some time."

Gabriela was silent.

"I'm confused, Gabriela," Jaymie said, shooting for a casual tone that didn't sound casual even to herself, especially as loud as she was now talking, her words echoing back to her. "Let's go back to the book you're writing. What is it about?"

"You'll see," Gabriela said.

"The book is about murder, Gabriela, isn't it? About killing someone?"

Gabriela's eyes widened again. "Why would you think that?"

Jaymie's mouth dried out. She licked her lips. She needed Gabriela to tell the truth, now, while Mel and Val were there to hear it. "I've figured a few things out," she said. "But I don't know some other things. Like . . . did you always intend to kill Mario, or was it a spur-of-the-moment idea? A plan you came up with on the fly?" The idea solidified into knowledge. "That's it, isn't it? Logan didn't die like he was supposed to. You wanted out of your marriage, but you wanted Fenix to stay with you, and you were afraid Logan would get custody, is that it? But then, because of your stupidity about household appliances," she goaded, "Logan didn't die. He and Tiffany showed up instead.

"I remember that night; you went sheet-white with shock when you saw her. You had been play-acting for two days, worried about Logan. You must have been sweating when no one from home called to tell you the awful news that your *dear* hubby had died in a gas leak, or house explosion, or whatever. And then Tiffany showed up, and being the cruel witch that she is, instead of accusing you, she decided to torment you. And . . . blackmail you." She remembered the words Mrs. Stubbs had overheard, Tiffany saying to Gabriela to *give up and let go* . . . "I suppose her motive was to get you to divorce Logan and give him custody of Fenix, but I'm not sure if Logan was totally on board."

Gabriela shook her head. Her expression was changing from fear to loathing. Jaymie could see Mel's shocked face in a slice of light from the cottage kitchen window, but she shook her head to keep the two from moving.

"So, was your second plan to kill Mario and put the blame on Logan and Tiffany?" She couldn't believe the things she was saying about her friend. Surely Gabriela would have *some* explanation, some alternate theory that was true.

But vague hope was destined to die.

"You should keep your mouth shut, Jaymie," Gabriela said, a huffy tone of self-righteousness creeping into her voice. "It's much simpler than that." She paused, her eyes flicking back and forth as she thought. "My husband and his sister found out about me fooling around on him and plotted to kill Mario and make me look guilty," she said finally, with an earnest manner. "It's weird that the police haven't figured this out, right? I thought they would have by now."

"Come on, Gabriela, stop lying. Aren't you tired? I know I am. What you're burning is no toy of Fenix's," she said, prodding the smoldering blackened heap. "It's a wig, a cheap polyester red wig." A memory flickered into a visual. "Cheap red polyester . . . like the long red threads I pulled off your sweater and threw in the fire the first night. You must have worn that wig often, when you met up with Mario. You don't need it now. He's *dead*." Her last word caught on a sob. "Why? Why *kill* him, Gabriela? I don't understand. He was going to leave his pregnant girlfriend for you!"

She watched her friend, wishing she'd tell the truth, and yet wishing it wasn't the truth. But Gabriela was now stubbornly silent. "I found the phone, you know that. It was on the floor behind Tiffany's duffel of hair appliances. You could have put it there at any point; you were in the cottage many times alone. We were supposed to find it after she was gone, right? Was that the plan? I was supposed to find it and turn it over to the cops and they were supposed to suspect Tiffany and Logan?"

Gabriela's face had darkened. "You *had* to figure it out, didn't you? You couldn't leave it alone."

"You *do* know that the police will be able to trace your phone calls and texts to Mario, right?"

"I used a fake name."

"That doesn't matter; that's not what they'll trace. They'll trace your actual phone!"

"But I used a burner!" she blurted out. Then her eyes widened and she clapped a hand over her mouth.

So *that* was how she planned to evade the police finding out she was one of Mario's conquests. "But you sent him a picture of your tattoo," Jaymie said wearily. "The tattoo on your breast of a phoenix."

She gasped. "He said he erased it! He promised—" She clapped a hand to her chest.

"What did you *expect*?" Jaymie said, anger and hurt and betrayal sending scalding pain shooting through her. There was no going back from this knowledge, no faint hope that she was wrong. "You believed a promise from a guy like that, an online lothario who kept prize tokens of his conquests? Of *course* he'd keep that picture!"

Gabriela shook her head, the first genuine fear Jaymie had seen in her eyes.

"Why did you come here, of all places, *knowing* I've figured these things out before?"

"I didn't think you'd figure *this* out," she said, her voice wobbling and teary. "I was going to have the last laugh." Gabriela paced, slashing the grass with the piece of wood as Hoppy backed away, yipping unhappily. "Or at least . . . *damn* you! Once I realized that Logan had lived, I went to plan B. You were *supposed* to figure out that I had tried to kill Logan and failed, and that he and his sister came here to kill Mario and incriminate me!"

She grimaced and stopped slashing, the piece of wood dropping at her feet. "Mario wasn't supposed to die. But he kept bugging me!" She smiled, an eerie mocking smile. "He said I was the love of his *life*. I wish I could have told Logan that. I would have liked to see his face . . . hah!" Her smile died. "Mario wanted me to come live in his craphole of a cottage with him." She threw up her hands. "He was being a freaking nuisance. The guy was dumb as a stump. He actually thought if I divorced Logan and moved here with him, my illicit lover, a thieving handyman, I'd get custody of Fenix! I was *never* going to move here with him. I wanted some fun. This vacation was supposed to be goodbye to both my problems, Logan and Mario. Once Logan was dead I could move on with my life, take Fenix and move to Ann Arbor. I have a job offer; my little girl and I could have a new life away from Logan's interfering horrible family. But Logan didn't die when he was supposed to, so I killed Mario instead. Logan is going to take the blame."

"But . . . how . . . how did you kill Mario? I don't understand?"

"Ohmigawd, it was *easy*!" she said with disdain. "He was so trusting, the idiot. He *was* an idiot, you know," she said with earnest emphasis, conversational and relaxed now that she had admitted the worst. "He was one of those dudes who think they're smarter than everyone else. He deserved whatever he got. He was fooling around with other women while telling me he loved me so freaking much!" She shook her head. "I hate to say it, but Brandi's right. Men are pond scum. We were supposed to meet up. If Logan was dead it all would have gone as expected. I would have broke it off that night."

"I don't buy that."

"Think what you will, it's true. I would have dumped him. He was tiresome. And that night he was worse than before. I went to see him and told him I couldn't stick around because my husband had showed up. I thought he'd back off but *nooo*," she said. "Instead he said he was going to go to the inn and confront my husband, tell him I was leaving Logan to move in with him."

"But Gabriela, you took the pie iron with you." Gabriela, as usual, was all over the place, admitting guilt but trying to backtrack from it at the same time.

Blinking, Gabriela stared. "Yeah. Okay. So maybe I did plan it out beforehand. I told you . . . plan B kicked in when Tiffany showed up."

Jaymie stared at her. "How could you *kill* a man? Bash him over the head and leave him for dead." Her eyes widened. "And you set fire to the cottage knowing there was a pregnant girl inside!"

Gabriela's eyes glittered. There were tears . . . actual tears that welled and spilled over. "You have to believe me, Jaymie," she said, hands out, palms up, a pleading gesture. "I didn't know she was there. When we set up the meeting he said he was going to send her to stay with her mom for the night! I *knew* that girl would be better off without Mario in her life. All he'd do her whole life would be to make her feel bad about herself. I know how guys like that operate. He'd cheat on her, bring home diseases, and finally dump her. Honest, if I had known she was there—"

"But you set it on *fire*. Why? If you were going to kill him, why set the cottage on fire too?"

She shrugged. "I knew Logan was borrowing Terry's boat to go fishing that night, so—"

"Wait . . . how did you know that? No one else knew Terry was here. How did *you* know?"

Her gaze was secretive, and sly. "I saw his boat in the marina. I'd recognize that thing from a mile away, the number of times I had to go out with Terry, Brandi, and Logan." She grimaced. "When I found out Tiffany and Logan were here I texted Logan, asking him what was going on. He is such a coward. He never once said anything about the gas in the house then. He was real casual at first. He told me he was going night fishing, borrowing Terry's boat." She smiled and tapped her head. "I told you, I'm way smarter than anyone realizes. I adjusted my plan accordingly. I figured . . . Mario would die, the cottage would go up in blazes, and I could play the wounded wife for a few days, then reluctantly admit that Mario was my lover and horrors . . . Logan found out! What had he done?" she cried, hamming it up. "Logan, you despicable *monster*, killing that man!"

Jaymie was thunderstruck, but the million times Gabriela had been sly and sneaky came back to her. "Borrowing" clothes and getting them ripped or stained and returning them to someone's closet without acknowledging it until caught. "Borrowing" money from the petty cash they were all supposed to contribute to. Jaymie remembered blaming Brandi for that. Brandi had, at first, said Gabriela did it, but when no one believed her she took the blame and apologized. Gabriela's cunning in *this* instance should not come as a surprise. What had started as a simple plan at first—kill Logan from a distance and get Fenix and her freedom all at the same time—had become complex when Logan lived and followed Gabriela to Queensville. But she had rolled with it, adapting. It just may have worked.

"You know . . . there's always an extra can of gas in Terry's boat," Gabriela said. "Logan *will* be blamed as long as you keep your mouth shut, Jaymie."

Thunderstruck, Jaymie said, "Or Terry will be blamed; the police will find out Brandi's been with Mario and blame her jealous ex. We'll all attest to his confrontation in Grand Bend. You covered all bases, didn't you?"

"It pays to be prepared."

"And all along it was you. Where did you get the fuel?"

"Oh, for heaven's sake, Jaymie. People are always thinking I'm dumb, or that I lack common sense. Don't be a putz. Mario had a boat dock. He had a boat. He had to have fuel right there in the shed." She looked rather pleased with herself. "I can't believe you didn't figure that part out. It's so *easy*!"

It all made a terrible and warped sense. And now what? Jaymie didn't have any more questions, though she was sure she would later. The future was not bright for her friend. Whether she paid the full price for her grave crime or got a lesser sentence on diminished responsibility, her life as she knew it was over. And yet . . . she seemed to assume Jaymie would stay quiet for her. "Gabriela, you have to know we can't walk away from this," Jaymie said gently.

Tears gleamed in her eyes. "Don't take me away from my baby girl," she whimpered. "I had no choice, you have to see that. Logan was going to take Fenix away from me!"

"Because you tried to kill him!" All her life Gabriela had been getting people to let her off the hook, pleading her sad life, her lack of knowledge, or whatever excuse she could concoct. But this was the end. "We're going to have to talk to Vestry. Gabriela, you know this is it; you have to turn yourself in."

"No."

"What?"

"I said *no.*" She was circling the fire. "I can't do that. I *won't* do that."

"I'm not giving you a choice, I'm . . . *oof!*"

Gabriela rushed her and tackled her, flailing with the piece of wood she had retrieved, sending Jaymie flying as Hoppy yipped, then howled as loud as any Yorkie-Poo could, an *a-roo-roo-roo* yodel. Jaymie hit her shoulder on the rock firepit and howled in pain. Her hand flung out, and the glowing coals burned her flesh. She screamed and struggled, the wind knocked out of her as she rolled around on the grass and dirt with Gabriela, who was swearing and flailing and shouting.

"*Jaymie!*" Val shrieked. "Help! Someone, *help!*"

The next moments were a confusion of grunts and shouts and screams as Melody yelled, "Gabriela, *stop!*" The writer had raced down the slope, grabbing Gabriela by the shoulders, and pulled her off Jaymie as she rolled away, her shoulder throbbing in pain.

Lights flicked on in neighboring cottages. Garnet Redmond's voice floated down the hill, "Is everything okay there?"

"No!" Jaymie shouted, clambering to her feet.

"Garnet, get Ng on the phone!" Valetta shouted as she sat down on Gabriela's feet. "And call nine one one. *Murder!*"

Hoppy yelped and barked, racing at the three women on the ground, then returning to Jaymie, who held her burned hand, crying in pain.

Gabriela wailed, kicked Val away, and struggled to get out from under Melody, who surprisingly enough managed to thrust her arm through her friend's arms and hold them behind her back as she thrashed about. "I thought you were my *friends*," she grunted, her voice breathless.

"Shut up, Gabby, dearest," Melody said, lying across her, weighing her down. "Your reign of brainless terror is over."

Rachel stumbled from the house onto the back deck, rubbing her eyes and blinking, with a puzzled frown. Light from the kitchen flooded the slope, reaching down to the firepit. "What's going on?"

"It's a long story," Jaymie said wearily, struggling to her feet, then bending over at the waist, resting her hands on her knees and trying to catch her breath as the pain began to numb. "A long and sad story."

✄ Twenty-one ✄

SHE TOLD THAT LONG SAD STORY in detail to Detective Vestry, corroborated by Mel and Val, both of whose word the detective seemed more inclined to take than Jaymie's, despite their recent rapprochement. Or maybe that was Jaymie's insecurity speaking; she was a mess of nerves, the attack by her (former) friend leaving her shaken and frightened.

It was early. Garnet and Ruby had come down to help Jaymie and her friends in the wake of the violent encounter, then invited them up to their cottage to let the police do a thorough search of her cottage and property. Hoppy was curled up on Ruby's bed sleeping, and Val and Rachel were sharing the Redmonds' pullout couch, napping. But Jaymie, weary to the bone, had not been able to sleep, her nerves frayed, her insides still quivering like a vintage-recipe Jell-O mould. Melody, sitting with her, fueled by a bottomless pot of coffee, tried to calm her with the weirdly practical gambit of filling her in on a few things she had puzzled out in her private conversations with their friends.

"One thing I figured out that you probably don't know was what was wrong between Brandi and Gabriela," Mel said.

"What do you mean, *what was wrong?*" Jaymie said. She sat in an Adirondack chair by the Redmonds' firepit, far enough away from the cottage so the others could catch a little more sleep. She had eschewed going to the hospital and had taken some pain pills, but her shoulder still throbbed, as did her burnt hand, neatly bandaged by paramedics. "They were always fighting, since the first day we met. It never took much to get them fighting."

"But it was always over something stupid, and then they'd make up. This was deeper. And longer lasting. And it felt like it was Brandi that was holding a grudge. Gabriela could hold a grudge, but *Brandi?* Nuh-uh. I wondered, what had Terry done that broke up him and Brandi?"

"Again, it never took much," Jaymie said. "Brandi was always breaking up with guys."

"But this went deeper. Remember she said he cheated on her? She loved Terry. When he cheated on her with *Gabriela* it broke her heart."

"Cheated on Brandi with . . . *oh*. Okay, I get it now," Jaymie said, thinking of comments Brandi had made that now made sense. She had made pointed comments about Gabriela's pretended chaste behavior outside of marriage. "I'm surprised beyond a few pointed hints she didn't think we'd overhear that Brandi didn't tell us. You remember what we overheard on the cruise, the argument between Brandi and Gabriela?"

"She was never like that," Melody said. "Remember? She'd do crazy crap, but she never snitched on anything crazy anyone else did."

Looking back, Jaymie could see the wounded expression on Brandi's face, the knowledge that one of her best friends would cheat with Terry writ there, if you knew what to look for. Which she hadn't, at the time. "You're right. I figured out a lot, but I missed a lot, too, it seems. I don't suppose Brandi knew about Gabriela's affair with Mario."

"But I have a feeling that Gabriela did know Brandi was flirting with Mario online in that gaming app. You know how tech-savvy she was, though she could barely change a lightbulb. I'd bet she purposely targeted Mario once she found out Brandi was having an online fling with him."

Jaymie nodded. "That makes sense. She always wanted whatever Brandi had."

"Ever since Brandi stole a boyfriend of Gabriela's in college," Mel said.

Jaymie sighed. "That's where it started, I guess, the incessant competition between them." She squinted into the rising sun peeking through the trees along the cottage lane. "You know, even after what Gabriela said, I still can't figure out why Logan took Terry's boat out the night Mario died. I mean . . . that was one thing that kept tripping me up."

"Lord, Jaymie, you need to follow social media better," Rachel said, joining them, yawning and still sleepy. "Logan goes fishing all the *time*."

"Huh . . . Gabriela said they all went fishing together, but I thought it was just . . . I don't know. Logan seems like such a button-down kind of guy, not outdoorsy in the slightest."

"Not everyone who is outdoorsy wears flannel and looks like a lumberjack," Mel said. "He's the kind of guy who buys the best creel—only wicker will do—a Tilley Endurable hat, and one of those fisherman flotation life vests that holds all his lures and bobs."

Jaymie eyed her. "You know about fishing gear?"

"I did have a childhood," Mel said dryly. "I may not see my family much, but I still have a grandpa who lives to fish."

"Those two are pretty good friends, Terry and Logan," Rachel said, throwing herself down in an Adirondack chair and grabbing Mel's coffee cup, draining it, then making a face. "Yuck, no sugar. It was exactly what it seemed; Logan wanted to do some night fishing."

"Despite Terry sleeping with Gabriela?" Jaymie said doubtfully.

"I don't imagine Brandi shared that with anyone, much less Logan," Mel said.

"And knowing that, Gabriela took advantage, hoping to throw the blame on her husband for Mario's death. If I had shared my thoughts with you guys, you could have told me and I may have figured that all out earlier," Jaymie reflected.

"You know, Detective Vestry was real close to figuring it out, now that I look back on our conversation," Melody said, picking at a ragged nail. She had a bruise on her hand from Gabriela's fighting her, but otherwise was unscathed. "She was pretty sure it wasn't Kory. In fact, Kory was only in jail because Ng arrested him at the scene on probable cause. They quietly released him to his mom yesterday . . . I guess day before yesterday now. She didn't buy it from the beginning, and I think she knew it was one of us, though she's smart enough not to broadcast that. She didn't know which one. She would have got there eventually. She was even going to check out *your* cell phone records to see if you were cheating on Jakob with Mario!"

Jaymie gasped. "No, you have to be . . ." She sighed in exasperation when she saw Melody snickering and then breaking out into a full-throated laugh, joined by Rachel. "You're kidding. *Dang* it, Mel, you have to stop reeling me in like that." Her friend was trying to make her laugh after an awful morning, and Jaymie appreciated it, but the overwhelming sting and pain of betrayal lingered. Gabriela had killed someone. And she had used a vacation at Jaymie's home to further her plan.

Rachel showered at the Redmonds' and happily headed off to her new job, figuring that since she couldn't get into the cottage at the moment she could likely use a uniform that Tansy had on hand for her staff. It was going to be nice having her around. Jaymie decided to consult with her family to see if they'd agree to let Rachel live in the cottage for the off-season, if she wanted to stay there, until she figured out what she was doing. They usually closed it up in September, but there was no real reason to.

Ruby and Garnet made them breakfast and took Hoppy for a walk. The police should soon be done with the cottage, Jaymie hoped. She heard a commotion down in the grove and went to the top of the hill. It was midday; Brandi and Courtney had returned. "Bran, up here," she yelled. "Come up here. We have to talk."

"What the heck is going on? What are the police cars doing at your place?" Brandi said, traipsing through the grove and looking back over her shoulder as she scaled the hill, Courtney following closely.

When she got to the top, Jaymie hugged her, and then explained what had happened. Brandi fainted. A handsome paramedic was, fortunately, close by and revived her. They had a date set for Wingding Wednesday at the Ice House.

℘ Twenty-two ℘

THEY ALL—EXCEPT FOR RACHEL, who stayed with Tansy and Sherm, though she visited with them at the cabin—retreated to Jaymie's home in the country to stay for a few days while the police finished up their investigation at the cottage. Kory had indeed been released from jail, of course, and all charges dropped. He had been able to give the police some missing details of that night, information that Detective Vestry had initially held back, of course, but now relayed to Mel when they had lunch again, with the proviso that she keep it to herself.

Of course Mel divulged everything to Jaymie. "She was showing off, trying to impress me. She should know better than to trust a writer," Melody said, justifying herself. "We're blabbermouths by nature. In fact, everyone should be told at birth: never tell a novelist anything you'd mind seeing in print."

Kory had been sleeping in a hammock down by the cottage's dock, in the deep shadows by a hedge. He was drunk, but he had a foggy memory of a conversation he overheard between Mario and someone else, a conversation that included words like *husband*, *child* and something about *telling the truth*. That, Jaymie realized, was of course Gabriela telling Mario about Logan being at the inn, and objecting when he said he was going to storm up there and tell her husband what was going on. Then there was a yell, and a scream, and a confused jumble . . . Kory roused himself enough finally to stumble down to the water as the cottage behind him blazed, and found Mario; he had tried to pull his friend away from the scene. But there was no hard evidence against him, only circumstantial.

But Gabriela's fingerprints were on the pie iron, and Mario's blood was imbedded in the gallery of her diamond wedding ring, so she was having a difficult time denying what she had done. There was no other way the blood could have got there but that she had been the one doing the killing and the blood splashed onto her hands. That was one way they knew Kory *hadn't* done it.

It all correlated with what Jaymie had been able to tell the detective, everything Gabriela had confessed to her, even the obvious lies. Despite what she told Jaymie, that she had gone to talk to him and cancel their rendezvous, Gabriela had gone to meet Mario with the pie iron and a clear intention of killing him. Once she discovered Logan was alive and plan A had not worked, she coolly moved on to plan B. She had already set up a late date with Mario for that night before she stole his phone, so he knew to expect her, which was in part why he caused such a scene at the Ice House. He wanted to leave and get back home, though he had not gotten Hallie to go to her mother's. He had tried, but she was tired and stubborn and had gone to bed. He hadn't counted on losing his phone and making Hallie look everywhere for it, and he had not expected Kory to be sleeping in the hammock nearby when he met his "date" down by the water.

Had he recognized his hot redheaded lover that first night at the Ice House? Jaymie didn't know, and now no one would, with Mario gone. It was possible that he had recognized Gabriela, and that was who he was moving toward when Courtney headed him off.

It was odd to realize, for Jaymie, that Gabriela knew Mario's cottage better than anyone. She had been there before, so she knew exactly how to approach it from the water side without being seen. One other random detail Jaymie learned: Hallie's baby was, indeed, Kory's. He was planning to stick around, even if Hallie didn't want him as a boyfriend anymore. She needed time to figure it all out, her mother said, when Jaymie ran into her in Tansy's Tarts as the mom picked up some back pay Hallie was owed.

It was devastating and confusing to think of the friend she had known for a decade and a half as a murderer, but she had her friends to talk it over with. They cried and drank wine and cried some more. They ate chocolate, and had another bonfire, this time in the yard of the home Jakob had built with his bare hands. They video-chatted with Jocie and Jakob, whose trip was also winding down. The father and daughter would be leaving Poland in two days, scheduled to arrive home shortly after the group left.

Becca, who had been delayed in London by a medical appointment, finally did arrive in Queensville in time to see Jaymie's friends, who she knew slightly. On their last evening together she insisted on treating them all to dinner at the Queensville Inn. Mrs. Stubbs presided. They would, she said, all come to a tea party in her room the next time any of them came back to Queensville or Heartbreak Island.

But the last day they were all back out on the island again. Jaymie and Mel wandered along the road for one last walk. There was a truck parked a couple of doors down the road from the Ice House restaurant. Workers were tearing down the burned-out remnants of the A-line cottage.

"Chief Ledbetter!" Jaymie said. The retired police chief was standing on the road by the burned-out hulk looking at some plans with a young woman in a hard hat.

"Jaymie! Good to see you. Ms. Heath, good to see you again."

"What are you doing here?"

"It's all in the works and nothing is final yet, but I got that brother of Valetta's to make some inquiries. I guess Mario had a will and left the whole shebang to little Hallie. Least he could do, all the trouble he caused her. Anyhoo, if it all goes according to plan—depends on insurance companies and lawyers and such—it looks like me and the missus are buying this plot of land. That young lady there," he said, pointing to the hard-hatted woman, "is a contractor, giving me a quote. If it all works out I'm gonna order an A-line cottage same size as that one, and they're going to build it right there, on the footprint of the burned-down place. Brand spanking new."

"You'll be our neighbor," Jaymie said with a sigh of satisfaction. "Good thing to know. Is your wife happy?"

"She's already planning the décor. It's cheap enough we can go hog wild. I can keep my eye on things around here," he said with a wink.

Jaymie smiled. "Chief, one thing I am still puzzled about: Hallie told me that Mario had a grown-up son who was on the island making inquiries about Mario. I don't get it. Who is he, and why haven't I heard anything in the press or anywhere else about him?"

"Because he doesn't exist. That feller was a private investigator. Mario was suspected of insurance fraud on a property he owned before this one, back in Ohio. Feller was trying to gather intel."

"I'm surprised Hallie didn't tell Mario about it."

"She did, I imagine, but he knew there was no 'Terry,' so he shrugged it off. Or she didn't remember to tell him. M'wife always claimed women get pregnancy brain and don't remember much. That poor little gal did have a few others things on her mind."

"True. Why the name Terry?"

"Maybe it was his real name. How many Terrys do you know?"

"Too many," Jaymie said.

• • •

THEY WERE ALL GATHERED in the parking lot above the river, where their packed cars were waiting. The friends had finally been able to clear every last thing of theirs out of the cottage and had spent a few hours cleaning up. Rachel was taking a few days off to take Melody home to sort out her own life.

Jaymie took Mel aside. They stood by the parking barrier away from the others. "Are you sure you're going to be okay?" she asked the writer. "I'm worried. Andrew was acting weird."

"I'll be all right," Melody said, hugging Jaymie. She actually clung to her for a few minutes, then took a deep breath and pulled away. "I'll call you."

"Promise? *Promise* me you'll stay in touch?"

"I'll stay in touch," Melody said, cupping Jaymie's cheek. "I love you, kid. I hope you know that."

"I do." They hugged again, then returned to the others.

Tiffany and Logan had, of course, headed home already, taking Fenix with them, refusing Gabriela's jailhouse request to see her daughter. Jaymie was deeply saddened by the little girl's plight, with her mom in such deep trouble, but if Gabriela had cared so much about her daughter's well-being she wouldn't have tried to kill Logan. Jaymie didn't know what Logan was truly like, but he appeared to love his little girl. Jaymie had apologized in her mind for suspecting the two, but given how poisonous a person Tiffany was, it had seemed logical.

Brandi, of them all, was probably the most deeply hurt. Despite their problems, she and Gabriela had spent a lot of time together in recent years. The betrayal stung. Fortunately, Courtney was always there to be the supportive second fiddle to Brandi's flamboyant first chair. Brandi told the others she would be checking in on Fenix. She still, despite their problems, had a good parental relationship with Terry, and Terry was good friends with Logan. There were inevitably many points of connection.

The five women clung to each other, warm bodies close, breath mingling, a sisterhood of shared remembrance. "I'm going to miss you all!" Jaymie said, releasing them finally and wiping the tears from her cheeks.

There was more weeping, more clinging, more hugging and more mutterings of getting together sooner this time. "So, Brandi, what are we going to do next summer?" Jaymie said with a teary smile.

"I am going to book us a week at Poplar Bluffs Campground, and we are going to go *camping!*"

"Exactly," Jaymie said, pointing and laughing. "No more procrastination." She thought for a long moment. "Maybe a long weekend is enough, given how busy we all are. Four days. Nothing but us." She paused, then met Courtney's sad gaze. "And our new friend, Courtney," she added, and the woman smiled broadly, ducking her head to hide a happy tear in her eye.

"Agreed." Brandi sighed, her eyes welling and mascara running. She teetered to Jaymie for one last tight hug. "We *have* to get going. I can't *wait* to see my babies."

They all got into the two cars, doors slamming, last shouts of farewell hollered. Then they drove away and Jaymie stood, alone, listening to the seagulls shriek and cry on the breeze. Hoppy, leashed to a nearby post so he wouldn't get in the way of the cars, whined impatiently.

"Yes, sweetie. Let's go to Valetta's so you can play with Denver."

• • •

VALETTA HAD A COUPLE of bronzed shirtless young fellows working in her laneway when Jaymie walked up.

"Aha, you found someone to do the catio?" she said to her friend.

Val stood, arms crossed, watching them work. They shoveled mixed concrete into wheelbarrows and trundled them around the back. "No, I *told* you what I'm going to do and I'm sticking with it. I've hired them to do the cement pad, but I'm hiring *myself* to do the work. I downloaded some plans, I've ordered the materials, and I am going to build it myself!"

"You know, I'm kind of handy too," Jaymie said. "Jakob taught me how to install a new subfloor in my vintage trailer, but I did the work all on my own. And I'd love to know how to build a catio . . . or we could call it a catpoochio? We need one for Lilibet and Hoppy in the country. My poor little guy can't go outside on his own because of the lack of fencing and the coyotes."

"I'd love the help. I can't do it yet, though; I have to let the concrete cure. But into September . . . maybe the middle? I'll take a few days off and we'll tackle it. You help me, and I'll help you."

"Sounds like a plan. That'll give me time to get Jocie back into school and settled." The breeze tossed the tops of the trees. Jaymie looked up, and the leaves turned over, showing silvery undersides. "Fall is coming." She changed her mind about visiting, given how busy Val was at the moment. "I think we'll go home now and get ready for the family's return. Helmut offered to drive to the airport and pick them up. He came and got Jakob's pickup this morning to leave at his mom and dad's, so Jakob can drive home from the family farm. They're due back this evening sometime."

Val smiled. "You go then; be with your family."

• • •

IT WAS EVENING. She stood in the window of the cabin finishing up the last of the dishes from her lonely dinner. She set them to drain and walked out into the dark, the air crystalline and the white moon rising over the deep forest of dark pines and maples across the country road. A V formation of Canada geese flew, honking, overhead. Whenever Jocie saw them, in fall, she laughed and called it "flight training" for their migration south. Though they never really seemed to leave, gathering in stripped fields nearby to eat leftover corn and grain.

A breeze stirred the treetops and riffled over her bare arms. Nighttime temperatures were now dipping into the fifties . . . too chilly for bare arms. She dashed back in, grabbed a soft pashmina Becca had bought her on one of her trips, and wrapped it around her, sweeping her long hair up and over the wrap. She was dressed especially nicely, in a long skirt and pretty coral sweater with a V-neck, and the long silver necklace Jocie had given her.

She returned outside, making Hoppy stay in, despite his whining. She sat down on the chair by the door and waited.

There was a rumble down the road. She looked one way, then the other, and then . . . a white pickup in a cloud of gravel dust. It pulled off into their wide drive and the door flung open. Jocie, weeping, raced to her and flung her arms around Jaymie's body and Jakob wrapped his strong arms around her too. She wept, her tears mingling with his and hers, all together, as the car door "open" signal binged, Lilibet meowed inside impatiently, and Hoppy yipped at the door, yodeling his greeting to his family.

"I missed you so *much*," Jakob whispered in her ear, kissing it, his beard tickling in a familiar way. "I love you, liebchen; I love you to the heart of my heart."

"I missed you too, Mama. I have so *much* to tell you!"

"I can't wait," Jaymie said, her voice smothered, as Jakob would not let go of her. She inhaled him, his smell, his beard balm, his mustache wax, and his pepperminty breath mingling with the scent of Jocie's bubblegum-scented shampoo. Her beloved people were home . . . home and all together, finally. *I'm the luckiest woman on earth,* she thought, but could not say with Jakob's lips over hers.

⚘ Vintage Eats ⚘

Hobo Packets: Kid-Friendly Camp Meal
By Jaymie Leighton

Some of my fondest childhood memories are from our annual camping trip to Lake Huron. Mom declared it her vacation too, so for many meals we would do something simple, like sandwiches or canned beans. But my dad, memorably, took a page from his own childhood one year and told me (I was seven or eight) about Hobo Packets. When *he* was a kid (in the Dark Ages, he informed me, which qualifies this as a vintage recipe!), he was a Boy Scout, and they did campouts. His own favorite foodie memory was making Hobo Packets with his troop. Something about pairing food with a memorable event made it important to him, and he passed that on to me. The next year I begged to repeat the experience, and it became a family tradition, whether we were camping or just out on Heartbreak Island at the cottage after a long day cleaning it up for the next renters!

Hobo Packets are simply a protein of some sort, paired with vegetables and potatoes in a foil package, cooked on an open camp-fire. However, there is no reason in the world why you couldn't do this over your backyard fire, in the barbecue, in your fireplace, or even in the oven!

The very first thing is to start your fire. Get it going with some good chunks of hardwood that will burn slowly, and add in some charcoal briquettes, if you like, then let it burn down to embers. You want heat, hot red coals that will last for a while, not flames. While the fire is burning down, make your Hobo Packets.

The beauty of foil pouches is that you can customize one for each diner's taste. Here is a list of ingredients to start you off and some simple tips that will make the experience more enjoyable.

Assemble the ingredients:

Protein

There's no law that says you need to use meat. You could do

vegetarian packets for the vegans in the family. For those who eat meat, consider boneless chicken (thigh or breast), boneless steak (a thin cut), or best of all, to me, a thin ground beef patty seasoned with onion soup mix or just garlic and onion. You could even make your packets with chunks of sausage, if you prefer!

Vegetables

I always start out with thinly sliced potatoes—you could use sweet potatoes, if you like—but other than that, the ingredients vary according to what I have. So you could include any combination of carrots, onions, mushrooms, broccoli, cauliflower, zucchini, or bell pepper rings. Hard veggies like the carrots and potatoes should be sliced thinly if they are included raw, and the others should be in smallish pieces. I always put in some whole garlic cloves; the flavor permeates everything deliciously.

Seasonings

You could go crazy, but don't add *too* much! A little sea salt and freshly ground pepper is all you need, but my friend Rachel put together Hobo Packets for me and a group of our friends, and she, a newly inspired cook, used fresh herbs to wonderful effect. So if you're doing this at home and are close to your herb garden, consider sprigs of thyme, sage to go with chicken, rosemary to go with beef, or even some variations, like lemon thyme, or tarragon if you want to be fancy! And don't be afraid to add a pop of citrus with wedges or slices of lemon, or even orange slices! If you make your packets with sausage, add some apple slices!

These would be super fun to do with kids. I've been told that picky eaters are more likely to eat what they have a hand in cooking. My Jocie is not at all picky, but we're going to do a girls night, just her and me, and we'll definitely do these together!

To make the packets, start with a double layer of heavy-duty foil;

this is all-important, because you don't want the precious juices from your meat and veggies to drain away! Lay the foil out and coat the cooking area with olive oil or butter, then, starting with the potatoes, layer your veggies and seasonings, then layer in your meat and herbs. Some say the meat should go on the bottom, but I'm not sure it matters. Top with dollops of herbed butter if you want a real taste treat. Take a second layer of doubled heavy-duty tin foil and put it over the top, then bring up the bottom edges and crimp the bottom and top foil layers together, making a nice tight seal all the way around so none of the juices escape.

These should be nestled gently in among the coals and allowed to cook for at *least* thirty minutes, but better, forty. Some people say you should cook them on a grate, rather than in the coals; truth be told, if they're on the coals there will be some charring on the bottom, but I love that part. If you don't like the char, put them on a grate close to the heat and turn them occasionally, with tongs, being careful not to pierce the foil. When you take these out/off of the fire, let them rest for ten minutes and *carefully* open! There *will* be steam, so watch your fingers.

And . . . *enjoy!* Throw more wood on the fire and eat right there, in the great outdoors. Or . . . indoors by the fireside. Half the fun of this method of cooking is in sharing the experience!

℘ About the Author ℘

Victoria Hamilton is the pseudonym of nationally bestselling romance author Donna Lea Simpson. She is the bestselling author of the Lady Anne Addison Mysteries, the Vintage Kitchen Mysteries, and the Merry Muffin Mysteries. Her latest adventure in writing is a Regency-set historical mystery series, starting with *A Gentlewoman's Guide to Murder*.

Victoria loves to read, especially mystery novels, and enjoys good tea and cheap wine, the company of friends, and has a newfound appreciation for opera. She enjoys crocheting and beading, but a good book can tempt her away from almost anything . . . except writing!

Visit Victoria at www.victoriahamiltonmysteries.com.

CPSIA information can be obtained
at www.ICGtesting.com
Printed in the USA
LVHW090916080320
649314LV00002B/63